THE VISCOUNT'S UNWANTED BRIDE

JAYNE RIVERS

To all those who've loved and lost,
It's okay to love again.

CHAPTER 1

London
November 1822

"I AM DETERMINED TO MARRY THIS SEASON," LADY KATHERINE Drake declared, then continued too quietly for her sister-in-law to hear, "whether I truly want to or not."

She'd been thinking on the matter for weeks now and decided that it had been inconsiderate of her not to wed last year. Her brother, the Earl of Longley, and his wife, Amelia, had sacrificed so much to give her the opportunity to find a suitable husband, and yet she'd dithered and dallied until the season had ended with her still unmarried.

Yes, they'd told her not to accept the first offer that came her way and to be selective in her choice, but they'd still expected her to choose *someone.*

She owed it to them to do better.

Amelia glanced up from her small writing desk in the corner of the room and arched one of her dark eyebrows. "You should only marry if you meet a man that you want to spend the rest of your life with."

Kate huffed and looked past Amelia to the window. The

sun shone through, warming the space and brightening the gilt frames of the portraits on one wall. It wasn't that she didn't agree with Amelia. She knew she was in a privileged position—her brother had married a fortune so she wouldn't have to—but guilt ate away at her because she hadn't done right by him in return.

Andrew had risked it all to finance a season for her, and she'd wasted it. She wouldn't do so again.

Kate returned her attention to the sketchbook on her lap and frowned at the dress design she'd been working on. Something was missing. The design was pretty, but it had no individuality. Perhaps it needed more beading? No, that wasn't it. Ah, detailing at the bottom of the bust. Smiling, Kate added a small but intricate design that she hoped the modiste would be able to mimic. Perfect.

"Kate."

She turned to Amelia, who'd risen from her chair and was padding across the drawing room toward her. "Yes, Amelia?"

Amelia sank onto the striped chaise beside her and started to reach for her hand before looking at her own and realizing they were ink stained. She grimaced and laced them together instead. "I'm serious. Andrew and I just want you to be happy. If you don't find the right man this season, then don't marry. You're important to us, and we'd hate for you to be miserable."

Kate's heart squeezed. Her sister-in-law wasn't exactly the best at talking about her feelings, so the fact that she was trying to do so for Kate's sake meant a lot. That said, Amelia and Andrew were also important to Kate, and she didn't intend to bankrupt them in her search for a suitable husband.

"You married someone you were uncertain about," she pointed out. "It ended well for you."

Amelia rolled her eyes. "I also negotiated for something I really wanted, so I knew that however my marriage turned out, I would at least have one thing that could bring me joy."

Kate dropped her head in acknowledgement. There was no denying Amelia's point. While she was sure she didn't know all of the details of their courtship, she'd heard about the deal Amelia had struck with her brother. One that had ended with them blissfully in love and with an adorable son who was just now napping in the nursery.

Was it too much to hope that a man Kate could genuinely care for might materialize from the ether this season?

Perhaps the gentleman she'd been waiting for had been traveling abroad on the continent or exploring the Indian subcontinent. Surely there were plenty of dashing second sons or perhaps highly ranked military personnel whom she hadn't already met.

"Kate?" Amelia prompted.

Kate shook herself. "My apologies. I was woolgathering."

"No apology necessary." Amelia's piercing blue gaze searched hers. "Promise me that you will only wed if you really wish to."

Kate murmured something that wasn't really an agreement but wasn't a denial either. Eager to change the subject, she showed Amelia her sketchbook. "What do you think of these?"

Amelia took the book from her and flipped through the pages, studying each design with care. Kate smiled to herself. She knew that her sister-in-law had no interest in fashion, but she'd always encouraged Kate to pursue her interest in art, however it manifested, so she was never dismissive even when she didn't share Kate's enthusiasm.

Amelia paused on the most recent design. "What colors did you have in mind for this?"

"Perhaps a pale shade of green paired with yellow accents." With her light auburn hair and fair skin, green generally suited her well, and this season, she could get away with wearing slightly more daring color combinations than she had previously. A debutante in her first season was often restricted to insipid colors—ones that did nothing for Kate's complexion.

"My ladies."

They glanced up to find the housekeeper, Mrs. Smythe, hovering in the doorway.

"Luncheon is served in the family room."

Amelia smiled. "Thank you, Mrs. Smythe. Has George stirred?"

"Not yet, my lady. His nanny is with him if he does." Mrs. Smythe bobbed her head respectfully and backed away.

Amelia closed the book and rose. "Shall we join Andrew and your mother?"

"I suppose we ought to." Kate wasn't particularly hungry, but their cook often only provided light sustenance for luncheon, so she was sure there would be something she'd enjoy.

She and Amelia wandered along the hall and down the stairs, Kate's skirt swishing around her legs. They entered the smaller family dining room that adjoined the formal dining room. Kate's mother, Dowager Countess Brigid Drake, was sitting on the far side of the moderately-sized, square table, and Andrew sat on the left. Amelia went straight to the chair closest to Andrew, and he stood to kiss her cheek as she reached him.

Kate's face heated. No matter how many times she saw them display such casual affection for each other, it still made her blush. Her gut tightened as the desire for a similarly devoted relationship flashed through her, but she tamped it down and took her seat. She didn't need a husband who adored her as Andrew did Amelia. Any gentle, kind man of means would do.

"How has everyone been this morning?" Andrew asked

Amelia as he reached for a plate of cold meat and helped himself to a piece, signaling the beginning of the meal.

Kate filled her plate with cold meat and fruit along with a thick slice of bread slathered with butter. Her mother poured tea for each of them. Kate tested the temperature and waited until it cooled further to take a sip.

"I've decided to marry this season," Kate said, repeating what she'd told Amelia earlier. "It's time."

Andrew's reddish eyebrows drew together. "Very well, Kate, but please remember that there's no rush. You may take your time to ensure you secure the best match for yourself."

Kate speared meat with a fork, stuffed it into her mouth, and chewed, trying to ignore a flare of irritation. They were all acting as if she could dillydally to her heart's content and it wouldn't impact them, but that wasn't the case. The longer she took, the more strain it would put on the rest of the household. Seasons were not inexpensive.

"I've already told her as much," Amelia said, saving Kate from responding.

"Good," Andrew replied, sitting back and watching Kate for a long moment before returning his attention to his meal.

The remainder of luncheon passed uneventfully. When everyone had finished, Kate returned to her room and summoned her maid, Margaret, who helped her dress in a pelisse to stay warm. She and Margaret took the stairs back down, exited through the front door, and took the family's carriage to visit her friend, Lady Sophie Carlisle.

While this was Kate's second season, it was Sophie's first. She was a year younger than Kate, but they'd met when Sophie's sister had married Andrew's best friend.

Kate knocked on the door.

The butler opened it and gave her a tiny smile. "Shall I see if Lady Sophie is available?"

"Yes, please."

A moment later, he returned and escorted Kate and Margaret to the drawing room. Sophie had been sitting on a padded chair near the fireplace. She bounced to her feet, her ginger hair flying, and hugged Kate.

"I'm so glad you're here," Sophie exclaimed. "I'm excited for our ball tomorrow."

Both Kate and Sophie had been invited to attend the Earl of Wembley's annual ball, usually the first significant event of the season. They'd come together as soon as they started receiving invitations to coordinate which events they most wanted to attend.

"Do you know what you'll be wearing?" Kate asked as she followed Sophie to a pair of chairs. She glanced at her maid. "Margaret, you may visit with your friends if you wish."

There really was no point in her lingering when Kate wouldn't need her for anything, and she knew that Margaret was close with some of the maids in the Carlisle household.

Margaret curtsied. "Thank you, my lady," she said and excused herself.

A maid entered with a tray of tea and delicate little cakes. She set it on the table and withdrew. Sophie poured them each a cup of tea and added sugar to her own. Like one of her older sisters, she had a sweet tooth.

"My mother has had a dress made for me with the most abominable ruffles," Sophie said, helping herself to a piece of cake and popping it into her mouth. "If not for the green trim, it would be completely intolerable. I don't know why she thinks I need so many ruffles but there was no dissuading her."

Kate grimaced. She was lucky that her mother, while interested in fashion herself, wasn't overbearing in her opinions. She guided Kate, letting her know what criteria to work within, such as the pastel shades she had been stuck with last season, but she still let Kate choose what she preferred within those parameters.

Sophie, it seemed, was not so lucky.

"It's nice that she cares," Kate offered, unsure what else to say.

Sophie snorted. "She still feels guilty for treating Emma like an afterthought, especially after she ended up being one who secured a duke, so she's determined not to do the same with me. You're right, it's nice that she's invested in my season, but I do wish she'd allow me a little more say in some matters."

"Perhaps she'll release her grip on you as we get further into the season." Kate chose a bite-sized piece of cake and tasted it. "Mm." Lemon. Tart but sweet. Very nice.

"What about you?" Sophie asked. "What will you wear?"

Kate hesitated, not wanting to come across as a braggart for being granted more leeway in her choice of attire. "Do you recall that ice-blue design I showed you?"

Sophie's lips formed an O. "That will look so pretty with your eyes."

"I hope so." Kate knew that the color of her dress could determine whether her eyes looked like a smoky shade of gray or just dull like pieces of rock.

Sophie sipped her tea and then set the cup down. "So, now that the time is almost upon us, which men ought I stay far away from?"

Kate considered this for a moment. "The Earl of Winn is a drunkard and a lecher. The Duke of Wight is terrifying. He's lost three wives. *Three.* All younger than him. That doesn't seem… coincidental."

"Mm." Sophie nodded. "I've heard about him. I'll be keeping my distance. Mother certainly won't push the matter. Not after… you know, Emma. Who else?"

"As far as I'm aware, most of the other titled peers have nothing particularly wrong with them. At least, not that I know about. Some of them are dreadful bores but not nefarious. Then there are the younger sons. Among their number are a handful of rakes and fortune hunters. Not all of them. Some are pleasant. I'll point out which groups to avoid."

Sophie grabbed a second cake. "Thank you, Kate. I'm so fortunate to have your help."

Kate waved her hand dismissively. As far as she was concerned, she was the lucky one to have Sophie with her this season. She had made some friends among the other debutantes, but no one she was so close with and none so genuine. Everyone had an agenda, and although Kate had the social acumen to operate within the *ton* effectively, it was nice to spend time with someone she didn't have to be on guard with.

"Are there any gentlemen you have a particular interest in?" Sophie asked before eating the cake in only a couple of bites.

Kate shook her head. "If there were anyone I cared to get to know better last season, I might well be married by now. I'm hoping there will be some different men seeking brides this year. How do you feel about your presentation at court?"

Sophie had been presented earlier in the week.

She pursed her lips. "I think it went well."

"Good. I'm glad to hear it. I, um, have a favor to ask if you're willing."

"Of course." Sophie grinned. "Anything for you."

Kate laughed. "Wait until you find out what it is first."

"Ooh, is it something scandalous?"

"No," Kate protested, her cheeks heating. "Well, not really. It's just that... I want to marry this season. If I find a gentleman of interest, will you help me make his acquaintance as best I can?"

Sophie's eyebrows rose. "What exactly are you asking of me?"

Kate glanced around, making sure no one was nearby to overhear her, before whispering, "You know how protective my mother can be. Perhaps you could just distract her a little so she doesn't run men off before I have the chance to get to know them?"

Sophie narrowed her eyes. "Only if you promise to be careful. Lady Drake worries about you for a reason."

"I know, but it isn't as if I want to sneak around, having secret liaisons. I simply want more than two minutes of conversation with a man."

Her mother was an excellent society mama and meant well, but she could be a little bit overly concerned with propriety at times. Spending an extra handful of minutes with a gentleman inside a room where half of the *ton* could see them would hardly render Kate unmarriageable.

"I will do what I can." Mischief glittered in Sophie's blue eyes. "On another note, did you bring any of your sketches with you?"

"I did, but the sketchbook is in the carriage."

"Excellent. I wonder if Mother will accompany us to the modiste if I ask to go there now. She is always more open to different styles when you're around."

"There's no harm in asking." Perhaps Kate could show Madam Baptiste her latest sketches and see if she had a suitable fabric to create the dresses with.

"Wait here," Sophie said. "I'll be back in just a while."

When her friend left, Kate mindlessly ate another piece of cake. She didn't care for sweets the same way Sophie did, but nobody disliked cake, right?

When Sophie returned, it was with pelisse on and Lady Carlisle and Margaret in tow.

"Good afternoon, Kate," Lady Carlisle said with a nod of acknowledgement. "You have excellent timing. We were advised earlier today that Sophie's latest order is ready to be collected."

Sophie gave Kate a meaningful look, obviously hoping she'd be allowed to choose something more to her taste to wear to her first ball. The four women made their way out the front door to where Kate's carriage waited.

"Would it be convenient for us to ride with you?" Lady Carlisle asked. "Or would you prefer for us to take a separate carriage?"

"You can ride with us," Kate assured her. The two households weren't particularly far apart, so it wouldn't be an inconvenience to drop the Carlisles back home before returning to her own.

"Thank you, Kate."

A footman opened the door and assisted each of the ladies inside. He closed the door, and the carriage started to move, bumping over the cobblestones as it made its way along the street.

Madam Baptiste's shop occupied a stone building on the corner of a busy road in a popular shopping area. The premises had large windows with dresses and swathes of fabric displayed in them. The carriage stopped outside for the ladies to disembark, and the footman hovered outside as they entered the shop, ready to carry whatever items they emerged with.

"Ah, Lady Carlisle, Lady Sophie, Lady Katherine," Madam Baptiste exclaimed, her dark eyes glittering as she greeted them.

She was a striking woman, with sharp cheekbones and an angled jaw that were at odds with her curvaceous figure. Kate had always thought she'd like to draw her—not that she was forward enough to ask.

"Are you here to collect Lady Sophie's gowns?"

"That's correct," Lady Carlisle said. "May we see them?"

"Of course, my lady. Please come this way." She led them through a door into the back of the shop and then into a room where a small pedestal was positioned in front of a full-length mirror.

A girl emerged from even deeper within the shop with a

dress draped over her shoulder. Kate grimaced at the sight of ruffles and creamy fabric. This definitely wasn't the best look for Sophie.

"This is the one you requested I focus on first." Madam Baptiste took it from the girl and held it up. "Would you like to try it on before taking it home?"

Lady Carlisle nodded.

The shop girl helped Sophie undress and don the ruffled gown. Despite it not particularly suiting her, it did fit well.

The girl disappeared into the back and brought out another two dresses, one of which was similar to the first, but the other was sleeker and in a pale shade of blue. It hugged Sophie's body more closely and made her complexion look like strawberries and cream rather than washed-out porcelain.

"I like that one," Kate said, doing her best to help her friend.

"As do I." Madam Baptiste met Kate's gaze and waggled her eyebrows. "The delicate shade of blue is perfect for her eyes."

Lady Carlisle made a sound of agreement.

"May I wear it tomorrow, Mother?" Sophie asked, obviously doing her best to keep hopefulness out of her voice.

"Very well."

Madam Baptiste's assistant helped Sophie out of her clothes and back into her original day dress.

Meanwhile, Kate opened the sketchbook she'd brought in with her to the page with her most recent designs. "Would something like this be possible?" she asked Madam Baptiste.

The modiste leaned over to get a better look. "I believe so. Lovely design. Very elegant without being bland. It's a shame you were born into nobility. You have such an eye for fashion. You'd have been a talented modiste."

Kate's chest warmed. Perhaps some women would be insulted by a modiste implying that she had a practical working skill, but Kate liked that someone who actually knew what she was talking about thought Kate had potential, even if nothing ever came of it except for feeding her ego.

"What colors were you thinking?" Madam Baptiste asked.

Kate explained her vision, and the modiste collected a number of fabrics and displayed them for Kate to peruse. She chose the ones that most fitted the design as she'd envisioned it and asked Madam Baptiste to bill the cost to her brother. Lady Carlisle went outside to fetch the footman and then loaded him up with the dresses.

As she and Sophie climbed into the carriage, Kate glanced across the road, then stopped short. A man she'd never seen before but who was undoubtedly either wealthy or a member of the aristocracy stepped down from the carriage opposite them and walked toward the entrance into the tailor's shop across the street.

He wasn't classically handsome—his features were too harsh for that—but there was something captivating about his dark hair and eyes and the way he carried himself. Perhaps it was fanciful of Kate to think so, but it seemed as if he had the weight of the world on his shoulders and she wanted to know why.

"Kate, are you coming?" Sophie called from within the carriage.

Broken from the trance, Kate took the footman's free hand and stepped up. "Do either of you know who that man across the road is?"

Both women looked out the window.

"What man?" Sophie asked.

"The tall gentleman wearing all black."

Lady Carlisle was confused. "There's no one there."

Kate peeked out the window and slumped. He must have entered the tailor's. She was tempted to suggest they sit there until he re-emerged, but that certainly wouldn't be considered appropriate behavior for an unmarried lady, so she resigned herself to waiting until later to learn her mystery man's identity.

As the carriage trundled back toward Carlisle house, she couldn't get the view of his profile out of her mind. Why did the set of his strong shoulders seem so sad? Who was he, and what secrets was he keeping?

CHAPTER 2

Lord Theodore Blackwell, Viscount Blackwell, ignored the urgent knocking on his office door as he continued reviewing the most recent ledgers for the Blackwell estate's country house and tenant farms.

The door opened, and his brother, Nicholas, stuck his head through. "Come to dinner before you start gathering dust."

Theo glanced up from the ledger. "I'm not finished yet."

Nicholas waved dismissively. "It can wait. You can afford to stop working for half an hour. The estate won't crumble if you pause for sustenance."

Theo narrowed his eyes, tempted to make a snappish reply and resume ignoring him.

"Besides," Nicholas continued, "your chair needs a respite. At this point, the poor thing must be on the verge of fusing to your backside, and lord knows I'll never get you out of your office once it does."

With a sigh, Theo rose and stretched. Nicholas did have a point. He'd been sitting for so long that his back and legs were beginning to feel chair shaped. The muscles between his shoulder blades were knotted, and his neck was stiff as he shifted his head from side to side.

"Fine, I'm coming."

"Thank God." Nicholas darted a look around as if worried their mother might hear him taking the lord's name in vain. Not that he needed to worry. She was safely ensconced in their home in Oxfordshire.

Theo strode out of the room and found a maid hovering near Nicholas. As they walked down the corridor toward the dining room, she hurried into the office, presumably to pull the curtains to block out the rapidly descending darkness.

The corridor was lit by flickering candles, but despite the clusters of small flames, it was cold enough that he was glad to be wearing a coat. The fires must have been lit only recently so the house hadn't warmed yet. In the dining room, only two placings had been laid out at the head of the table— one at the end and the other at the right-hand side.

Theo sat at the head of the table and Nicholas to his right. They'd been born only two minutes apart, but those crucial minutes had dictated who would become Viscount Black-well. There were times when Theo wished that Nicholas had been born first. Not that his reckless brother cared much for responsibility.

Footmen lifted the covers on their plates, and he breathed in the aroma of chicken and vegetables. He thanked the servants, picked up his cutlery, and started on the chicken. It was tender and juicy, just as he liked it. He internally patted himself on the back at hiring such an excellent cook.

"I'm worried about you."

Theo was so startled that he almost dropped his knife. "I beg your pardon?"

Nicholas grimaced but held his gaze, dark brown eyes locked on dark brown eyes. Staring at his brother was as good as looking into a mirror. "It's not healthy for you to hide yourself away as you do and avoid anything fun."

Theo's jaw clenched, and he had to let out a long exhale before it relaxed enough to continue chewing. "I'm not hiding. Between parliament and managing the estate, I'm simply busy."

Nicholas arched an eyebrow. "So busy that you don't have enough spare time to attend the opera or flirt with any of the young, pretty women who'd love to keep you company?"

"Yes, I'm that busy." Theo looked away under the guise of focusing on his meal. "I honestly have no time for whatever things you might consider to be fun."

Perhaps that was a little overdramatic, but the idea of going out in society made his gut churn unpleasantly and a nervous sweat form on his upper lip. Society had not been kind to him after his wife died. Gossips had whispered that he'd had something to do with her untimely demise.

Of course, he had—but not in the way they thought.

Still, he couldn't handle the assessing looks and the way they would smile to his face but exchange nervous glances as soon as his back was turned.

"See, I don't think being busy is the problem," Nicholas said, spearing a piece of carrot with his fork and popping it into his mouth. "I think you're afraid. You remember how they were after Elizabeth passed away, and you'd rather molder in your office than venture out and see if it's really as bad as you fear."

"That's not it at all," Theo insisted, then intentionally filled his mouth so he'd have a reprieve before replying. "I'm behind on my reading for the next parliamentary meeting, and then there's some kind of discrepancy in spending at Blackwell Estate that I need to get to the bottom of."

Honestly, he suspected that the discrepancy was nothing more than his mother spending more than she ought to, but Nicholas didn't need to know that.

Nicholas reached for a glass of wine and gave him a look that said he wasn't fooling anyone. "How's this? I'll give you the entirety of the next two days to get your affairs in order, but Saturday night, you're coming with me to the opera. You can spare a few hours. You're a viscount, not a king."

Theo pursed his lips. "You know that Mother would have a conniption if you and I were seen together somewhere so public."

Their parents, in their infinite wisdom, had decided to lie and claim that Theo was born a year ahead of Nicholas, the better to ensure that Nicholas never challenged Theo's role as the heir apparent. It was meant to be a simple, harmless deception to prevent in-fighting, but the problem was that anyone who saw them standing side-by-side would know beyond a shadow of a doubt that they were twins.

They were identical.

It was a shame that their parents hadn't realized that before it was too late to do anything about it.

At first, their parents tried to maintain the ruse, sending the boys to separate schools and limiting their circle of acquaintances so that no one would notice their similarities, but eventually their father had decided it simply wasn't worth the effort—especially since Nicholas showed no signs of wanting the title and the viscount and viscountess wouldn't get more than a public scolding should the truth come to light.

After that, they'd been allowed to interact more freely—to their mother's dismay—but their personalities were so different that their lives outside the house rarely overlapped. Lady Blackwell had wanted to keep up the charade because she feared being the subject of gossip if their lie became public knowledge, but their father had the final word.

Alas, she still became vexed if she heard they'd been out and about together. Theo found the entire thing wearisome, but he cared for her, so he tried to humor her.

"What about a masquerade ball?" Nicholas asked, refusing to drop the subject. "She won't care who sees us at one of those. Provided we have different costumes, no one will look at us twice."

Theo felt like banging his head against the table. "No, thank you. I have no desire to rejoin society."

Nicholas smashed his cutlery down hard enough that they both flinched. "You're too young to waste away like this. Elizabeth's death was tragic, but it wasn't your fault, and you shouldn't let it stop you from living."

"It *was* my fault," Theo said quietly.

Nicholas could insist otherwise until he was blue in the face, but it wouldn't change the reality. Theo had failed Elizabeth, and it had cost her life.

"There's no reasoning with you." Nicholas shook his head, disgusted. He grabbed his wine glass and emptied it far too quickly to be healthy. "I won't watch you wither up and follow her into an early grave."

Theo's heart clenched. He closed his eyes, and an image of Elizabeth's face appeared on the inside of his eyelids. She had been so pretty, so bright and full of life, until all of the vivacity had drained out of her and she'd been left a shell of her former self.

"They are right to whisper about me as they do." Perhaps if he'd been a better husband, Elizabeth would still be with him.

"Ridiculous," Nicholas grumbled but didn't argue more, instead finishing his meal in silence.

There was a tension between them that Theo didn't like, but he wasn't sure how to get rid of it either. He wasn't willing to give Nicholas what he wanted, and his brother wasn't the type to accept anything less. As the younger child —even by only two minutes—he was used to getting his way.

As the silence dragged on, consuming painful moments, Theo considered starting a conversation about the latest bill he'd been asked to vote on, but he knew Nicholas wouldn't really be interested and that he'd only get angry about Theo trying to distract him. Instead, he allowed the awkwardness to continue.

They finished the meal, and Nicholas rose to his feet.

"You ought to consider remarrying," he said as he straightened his cravat and smoothed down the front of his waistcoat. "It's been long enough, and you need an heir."

"I have you," Theo pointed out.

"Yes, well, I have no desire for a wife or a title. I quite like my life the way it is."

Theo shrugged. "Think how many young ladies you could impress with the title 'viscount.'"

Nicholas raised an eyebrow. "That does not tempt me."

Theo sighed, and his shoulders sank. Servants cleared the dishes from the table, and Theo pulled himself together enough to prevent any of them from asking questions. Most would be too intimidated by him to dare, but some had been with the family since he was a boy and tended to take more liberties with formality.

He considered returning to work. Lord knew there was enough of it waiting for him. But he didn't have the heart to delve back into financial records and political essays tonight. A sense of unease itched beneath his skin, and he felt like if he didn't release some energy, he'd be awake all night.

He ran a hand through his short dark hair before striding out of the dining room and taking the stairs to the second floor, then walking along the corridor to his bedchamber. He summoned his valet, stripped out of his clothes, and redressed in a pair of riding pants and a loose-fitting shirt.

"I'll be in the boxing room for a while," he told his valet, Barlow, and the man retrieved a small box and passed it to him. That done, the valet excused himself.

Theo opened the box and withdrew the soft lengths of fabric within. He wrapped them around his knuckles, palms, and wrists in a way he'd done so many times before, making sure that they were well padded before tucking the loose ends into the bands around his wrists.

He stood, stretched his arms above his head, and wandered down the corridor to the small room at the end. He closed the door behind himself and bounced up and down on the balls of his feet to warm them up. He jogged the length of the room a few times to loosen his muscles and then circled around to the heavy bag strung up from a chain in the center of the room.

The bag had been filled with sand and made a satisfying thud as he drew back his fist and slammed it into the fabric. He punched the bag again and again, first only hitting it at head height as if aiming for an opponent's face but eventually shifting further down and practicing uppercuts and hooks too.

He feinted left and went right, dodged and weaved, keeping light on his feet throughout it all. He used to enjoy sparring with his friends at a gentleman's boxing club, but few people were willing to get in the ring with someone who was rumored to be a killer, and of those who were, most of them weren't doing it to be sporting. They wanted to say they had gone a round with him and survived.

He was tired of that, and he didn't want to give anyone any more reason to talk than they already had.

When his fists ached, he switched pushing the bag with the balls of his feet or pivoting and slamming the bony part of his shin against it. His shins throbbed, but it hurt far less to kick like this than it had when he'd first started out. His body seemed to be adapting to take the punishment.

When he was exhausted and everything hurt, he summoned a maid and asked her to fill a tub with hot water for him. He waited until she was done before returning to his bedchamber. He didn't need his valet's assistance to undress, so he shed his clothes and lowered himself into the tub, his muscles twinging in protest.

He washed himself thoroughly, toweled dry, and dressed in a pair of trousers and a shirt intended to be comfortable rather than tidy. He ought to go to sleep, but after expending so much energy, he wasn't tired yet. Unfortunately, he didn't feel like cozying up with a book, either, so the only viable option was to return to his office and the stack of work that awaited him there.

He poured himself a finger of brandy and took it to his desk, where he settled on the chair and took a sip, savoring the burn as it tracked down the inside of his throat. He lit the candles that stood in a large brass candleholder on the corner of his desk, and they cast light and shadows across the desktop.

The light glinted off the miniature of Elizabeth that sat in a frame less than a foot from the candles. Theo picked the miniature up and studied it. The likeness was remarkable. The portrait had been painted in the first year of their marriage. Her cheeks were plump and pink with youth, and her brown eyes sparkled with joy.

Things had been so good then. In fact, their marriage had been wonderful up until the storm that killed his father. Then it had all gone to hell.

Several unopened letters were piled on the opposite corner of the desk. He set the miniature down, grabbed the letters, and flipped through, noting the return addresses. He froze on the last one. It was a letter from Elizabeth's parents. With a sinking heart, he opened the paper and read the familiar flowing letters.

His stomach flipped over, and with each word he read, he fought the urge to use one of the candles to light the paper on fire and watch it go up in flames.

Why did they have to keep doing this to him? Why couldn't they just let him be?

CHAPTER 3

"I'M GLAD YOU'RE THE ONE COMING WITH ME TO THE Wembley ball rather than Amelia," Kate said as she and Lady Drake made their way up the stairs and down the corridor to the family wing of the London townhouse to choose her dress for the night.

Lady Drake laughed. "Amelia has many strengths, but most of them exist outside of the ballroom. Since she doesn't enjoy such affairs and I do, and she has George at home to fuss over, it only makes sense for me to be the one to accompany you."

Kate muffled a giggle. She loved her sister-in-law, she really did, but Amelia had no patience for dancing or socializing, which meant that nearly every invitation she received was given a polite rejection.

The doorway to Kate's bedroom was already ajar. Margaret hovered near the wardrobe. She'd let the drapes down so they couldn't see outside, but Kate knew it must be almost completely dark by now. Her mother perched on the red striped ottoman and patted the cushion beside her, signaling for Kate to join her.

"The blue dress, please, Margaret," Kate said as she claimed the spot beside Lady Drake.

Margaret searched through the dresses until she found the one Kate had referred to and lifted it out. "This one, my lady?"

"Yes, thank you."

"Are you sure that's the one you want?" Lady Drake asked, examining it with a keen eye. "It's beautiful, but it's not the most eye-catching gown in your collection."

"That's true, but there will be opportunities to push the boundaries of convention later in the season. Tonight, I simply want to make a good impression." She knew the pretty shade of blue flattered her complexion and that the dress was different enough from others to attract notice without being provocative or particularly daring. She thought it would do nicely.

"In that case, I have the jewelry you requested." Lady Drake gestured to Margaret, who picked up a small box that had been resting on the dressing table and handed it to Kate.

Kate opened the box, and a smile stole across her lips. The sapphire necklace and earrings would perfectly complement her dress. While the Drakes hadn't been able to buy her much new jewelry for the season, she had some already, and Lady Drake and Amelia had both promised her access to whichever jewelry of theirs she'd like to borrow.

"Thank you, Mother. This is exactly what I wanted."

"I'm glad to hear it. While you dress, I'll go and ready myself. I'll be back soon."

Lady Drake left. Margaret laid the dress on the bed and helped Kate out of her day dress. She stripped down to her undergarments. The layered petticoats allowed Margaret to move her limbs around until the gown slipped into place over top.

She stood still while Margaret laced the back. Once that was done, she sat at the dressing table so Margaret could brush and style her hair. The maid arranged curls artfully around Kate's face and pinned the rest into an elegant knot on the back of her head.

"Is that all right, my lady?"

"Yes, thank you, Margaret."

She stood and stepped into a pair of blue satin slippers, then checked her reflection. She was a little pale, so she pinched her cheeks to get some color in them before donning her gloves.

"You look lovely, my lady," Margaret said as she moved into place beside her, a small smile lighting her face.

"She does, doesn't she?" Lady Drake asked from the doorway. "A true diamond of the first water."

Kate laughed. "I don't think you can be considered a diamond if you don't marry within your first season."

Lady Drake tsked. "That seems like a silly rule. We'll just have to make our own." She offered Kate her arm. "Shall we?"

Kate looked her mother up and down. Lady Drake looked very nice in a dark purple dress that emphasized her slender figure. Her gray-streaked hair—a similar shade to Kate's— was twisted into a sleek chignon, and her hazel eyes were bright with anticipation.

"That dress suits you nicely," Kate said, accepting her mother's arm.

They made their way down the corridor, then downstairs, and were passing through the foyer when Amelia and Andrew emerged from the drawing room. Amelia carried baby George on her hip, and he was dozing, his jaw slack and lips parted.

Andrew put his hand on Kate's shoulder and kissed her cheek. "Stunning, as always. The gentleman of London will never be able to resist."

Kate rolled her eyes. "You silver-tongued devil."

"What?" He grinned. "It's true."

"You make being the perfect society miss seem so effortless," Amelia said ruefully.

Kate shrugged, self-conscious. "You know the meaning of words I've never even heard before. We're each skilled at different things."

"I know. Good luck." Amelia hugged her with her free arm and backed away.

"Are you sure you don't need me to attend with you?" Andrew asked, a furrow forming between his eyebrows. "It would only take me a short while to change into something appropriate for a ball."

"That's not necessary," Lady Drake said before Kate could. "Last season, it was good to have you with us for at least the first few balls, but Kate is a recognized member of society now, and I'm capable of making any introductions necessary."

Andrew inclined his head in acknowledgement. "If there are any events you would ever like me to attend with you, all you need to do is let me know. I want to support you in every way I can."

Kate pressed her lips together so she wouldn't blurt out that he'd already done more than enough. He married Amelia, an heiress with a substantial dowry, partly to ensure that Kate was provided for. The whole thing had worked out well, but he'd had no way of knowing that at the beginning and he'd done it anyway. She couldn't expect any more from him than that.

They bid their farewells, and Kate and Lady Drake made their way out to the carriage. Their driver had prepared the most extravagant carriage for the occasion. It was black with red velvet cushioning and red drapes that could be drawn to cover the windows.

Kate accepted a footman's hand and stepped inside, glad that the curtains had been left open so she could watch the streets pass by. The occasional lamp lit the road, lighting the way for them, and they arrived outside the Earl of Wembley's house at the same time, it seemed, that every other guest did, joining the end of a long line of carriages waiting for their passengers to disembark.

When they finally reached the front and a footman opened the door, Kate stepped out and realized that Sophie and Lady Carlisle had been in the carriage ahead of them. She met Sophie's eyes and grinned. Sophie looked like she was practically bouncing on the balls of her feet, only stopping when her mother nudged her with her elbow.

"It isn't ladylike to bounce," Lady Carlisle murmured.

Sophie clasped hands together in front of her. "Sorry, Mother. It's just that I'm excited, and Kate looks so stunning, wouldn't you agree?"

Kate stepped down, paused to wait for her mother, and then took Lady Drake's arm. "You look very nice, too, Sophie."

It was true, she did. Sophie would always be the kind of girl to attract attention—not because she was outstandingly beautiful, but because she was always moving, always expressing herself so freely. Kate was a little bit jealous of that. She tended to let her art speak for her and was more careful with her expressions and words.

They climbed the stairs together and greeted their hosts. The earl smiled at each of them and welcomed them to his home. Lady Wembley had a few more words to say, oohing and aahing over the cut of Kate's dress and the flounciness of Sophie's.

"Always lovely to see you, Lady Drake, Lady Carlisle," she said with an openness that spoke of sincerity. "Lady Katherine, such a shame you did not find a husband last season. Hopefully you will find someone more promising among this season's crop of bachelors."

Kate forced herself to smile rather than grimace and bobbed a curtsy. "I'm sure I will, Lady Wembley."

Sophie narrowed her eyes, apparently taking this as an affront to her friend even though Kate knew it hadn't been intended as such. Lady Wembley was a straightforward sort. She hadn't meant to insult Kate. She'd simply been stating matters as she saw them.

They moved farther into the ballroom, and Kate took stock of who was present. As well as many of the women she met last season, there were a smattering of new debutantes along with their matchmaking mamas.

As usual, the earl and countess had spared no expense. Lush greenery that looked like something Kate had seen in Amelia's books about tropical island countries was placed strategically around the room, creating small alcoves where more private conversations might occur. Musicians played on the elevated stage, and rich crimson-and-gold curtains fell from the ceiling to the floor behind them.

Ornate chandeliers hung above couples who swirled on the dance floor, and dozens of candles illuminated the space, reflecting off the gold of the gilded trimmings and decorative designs on the walls. Each corner had a pillar in the Roman style that Kate suspected were more for appearances' sake than practicality. They did, indeed, make the room seem quite grand.

Opposite the entrance, a wide double door opened onto a smaller space, through which she could see a table laden with finger foods. Last year, Kate would have been eager to sample the delicacies, but after a season, she'd realized that almost every ball had a variation of the same offerings. That wasn't to say the food wasn't nice, but she had other priorities.

Namely, finding a husband.

Sophie nudged her arm. "Are those cakes?"

Kate sighed. Sophie, it seemed, was still swayed by the food.

"Would you like to have a look?" she asked, supposing

that she could as easily study the ballroom floor from beside the food table as she could from the entrance.

"Yes, please," Sophie said.

Kate and Sophie crossed the room together. Kate looked around for her mother and saw her speaking with the Duchess of Arundel. Pleased that she was otherwise occupied, Kate wound around the edge of the dance floor and took up a position near the open doorway while Sophie helped herself to one of the cakes from the table and offered another to Kate.

"No, thank you," Kate said, surveying the male partner of each dancing couple. "Tonight is all business for me."

What she most wanted was to identify the man she had seen outside the tailor's, but she also wanted to get an idea of any other eligible gentleman who might be available for her to meet. She instantly dismissed the married couples and focused on the others.

She recognized many of the same men she had met last year. She'd already decided not to pursue anything further with them unless there was absolutely no one new to interest her. There was a reason she hadn't set her cap for them last year, after all.

"This is good." Sophie licked her lips, and Kate noticed a couple of gentlemen looking their way. She couldn't tell if Sophie's enjoyment of the cake had attracted their attention or if they'd already been looking before that.

As soon as she caught the taller man's eye, the pair started toward them.

"Do you know who they are?" Sophie asked quietly.

From behind her, Kate sensed Lady Carlisle—who'd followed them over—perk up and pay attention.

"No, I don't think I've met either of those gentlemen before," Kate said.

"They're new to Town this season," Lady Carlisle said. "I

am acquainted with both of their mothers, so I can make introductions."

The two men stopped in front of them, both smiling broadly. They were a genial-looking pair with well-fitting suits and the same kind of pent-up energy that Sophie always exuded.

Lady Carlisle stepped forward between Sophie and Kate. "Good evening, Mr. Bromley, Mr. Garfield. Have you met my daughter, Lady Sophie Carlisle, or her friend, Lady Katherine Drake?"

Both men bowed.

"I, for one, have not," Mr. Bromley said. He was relatively short and stocky but still taller than Kate. His hair was even redder than hers, and his face was liberally splashed with freckles. "Charmed, my ladies."

Kate glanced from Mr. Bromley to Sophie and had to stifle a giggle at the thought of what flamingly redhead children they might produce together.

"We've recently come from Oxford," Mr. Garfield said. "We completed our studies only a few months ago."

Kate nodded, unsurprised by this. The men must still be older than she but they had a sense of immaturity about them that made them seem younger than their years. So far as she could tell, they were sweet, but she'd prefer a more mature, refined man as her husband.

"Are you enjoying London?" she asked.

"We are." Mr. Garfield extended his hand toward her. "I would enjoy it more if you would grace me with the next dance."

Kate looked to Lady Carlisle, seeking silent approval. Lady Carlisle gave a subtle nod.

Kate took his hand. "I would enjoy that very much."

Mr. Garfield led her onto the dance floor. She wondered idly if Sophie would dance with Mr. Bromley but didn't look around to find out because she didn't wish to appear rude.

They danced a cotillion, and she quickly realized that Mr. Garfield may be a studious type, but he wasn't much of a dancer. It was only thanks to her quick footwork that she emerged from their dance with her toes intact. His hand was sweaty where it rested on her dress, and she couldn't help but feel a pang of sympathy for him. He was clearly nervous.

She tried to guide him as best she could without making it clear she was taking the lead, but she was relieved that he didn't try to make conversation and was especially glad to find another gentleman standing with Lady Drake and Lady Carlisle as they approached. She thanked Mr. Garfield for the dance, and he shuffled off, red cheeked, to find his friend.

"Kate," Lady Drake said, reaching for her daughter. "This is Mr. Marcus Adair, the youngest son of Baron Marwick."

Mr. Adair smiled, displaying nice teeth. "It's a pleasure to meet you, Lady Katherine. It's unfortunate that I wasn't able to make your acquaintance last year. I was staying with my mother in Essex. She was unwell but has since recovered."

Kate curtsied. "I'm pleased to hear that she's better now."

"Mr. Adair rather enjoys the country." Lady Drake looked thrilled to impart this bit of information. "Apparently his family owns a rather large number of hounds."

Mr. Adair ducked his head bashfully. "I'm afraid I'm not much for the city. I prefer a vigorous walk through the country-side with canine companionship."

Interesting. Kate enjoyed both the country and the city. They each held their own appeal. In the country, there were so many beautiful things she could sketch and paint, but in the city, she was able to spend more time with friends and had a wider selection of fabrics and threads available for her needlework and designs.

What did impress her about Mr. Adair was that he obviously had gotten past the impulse to gad about around Town. If he'd ever had a wild streak, it would seem that he left it long behind him. That appealed to Kate. She didn't need a great philosopher for a husband, but she would like someone sensible.

"I quite like dogs myself," she said, offering him a friendly smile. "While I'm not a particularly adventurous sort, I do enjoy painting the landscape."

"Lady Katherine is a very talented artist," her mother said, practically beaming.

Kate felt her cheeks heat. "I'm passable, but I do not think anyone would consider me to be exceptional."

"Perhaps you don't do yourself justice," Mr. Adair said with a twinkle in his eye. "Would you like to dance, Lady Katherine?"

Kate graciously accepted his hand and returned to the dance floor. The opening strains of a waltz began, and Mr. Adair guided her into position with the ease of a man accustomed to dancing. A smile tugged at the corner of her lips as he settled a warm hand on the small of her back. The fabric of her skirt swished around her calves, tickling the sensitive skin there.

It took less than ten seconds to confirm her initial theory. Mr. Adair was an exquisite dancer. She barely had to think as she let him steer her around the dance floor, moving effortlessly between other dancing couples without coming anywhere near to treading on her feet.

"What do you like to do other than paint?" he asked before spinning her out and then in again.

"I enjoy sketching." She searched his gaze for any hint of disapproval. The last thing she wanted was to be stuck with a man who looked down on her hobbies. When she found none there, she continued, "I also do needlework and design some of my own dresses." That last part came out in a rush as she was anxious to learn how he'd react.

He grinned. "What a useful skill for a young lady to have."

That was all. No comment on the appropriateness of an earl's sister doing work usually left to commoners. Excellent.

"Other than walking in the country, what activities do you like to participate in?" she asked, keen to know more about him.

A man stumbled somewhere behind her, bumping into her, and Mr. Adair's arm curled protectively around her.

"We breed horses," he said. "I have been known to race a time or two."

"How exciting." He was definitely someone who would prefer to have a primary residence in the country. It was just as well he was the third son and not required to attend parliament.

The waltz ended, and Mr. Adair returned her to her mother with the promise to call on her tomorrow. Kate watched him disappear back into the throng of guests, feeling hopeful that she had found a candidate. Someone she could potentially like and respect enough to marry.

But then she spotted something beyond Mr. Adair that quickly erased all thoughts of him from her mind. A familiar tall figure with dark hair had just entered the ballroom and was looking around, getting his bearings.

It was the man she'd been searching for.

CHAPTER 4

F ORTUNATELY, AT THAT MOMENT, L ADY C ARLISLE AND S OPHIE joined them.

Kate leaned close to Sophie. "There's a man over there I want to talk to," she whispered, keeping an eye on both of their mothers to make sure neither of them was listening in. "Very stylish. A little flamboyant." Definitely different from how he had been dressed the other times she'd seen him. "Keep them distracted for me."

Perhaps she should have just asked for an introduction, but she couldn't help feeling that if she took her eyes off the man for even a minute, he'd disappear.

"Who?" Sophie asked, looking around in a way that wasn't at all subtle.

"Over there." She gestured discreetly toward the man. "He's wearing the sky-blue waistcoat with a fuchsia cravat."

Sophie giggled as she spotted him. "I should have realized that a man who would pair those colors would be your type. Of course you would prefer a fashionable gentleman to one who dresses in conventional black."

Kate shrugged one shoulder. In truth, he had been wearing dark colors when she'd seen him last, but she also couldn't deny that she liked his bravery and committing to a pink-and-blue ensemble, especially considering that it contrasted with the harsh lines and angles of his face.

"Oh my." Sophie made a show of fanning herself. "I feel a little faint. Is it warm in here?"

As their mothers began to fuss over her, Kate slunk away and wove between groups of people deep in conversation, edging closer to the man. She didn't know exactly what to do or say, but she wasn't going to let that stop her from meeting him and making an impression.

As she drew near, inspiration struck. She feigned tripping and tumbled forward as gracefully as she could, praying he'd catch her.

Fortunately, the universe was listening, and the gentleman turned just in time to see her fall. He caught her in a pair of lean, strong arms, and she got her first proper look at his eyes. They were very wide. Wide and brown. For some reason, she'd fancied that they might be black. Her gaze dipped, and she noticed there was a sweet little freckle on his chin.

"Are you all right, miss?" he asked in a warm, rumbling voice.

"You saved me." She blinked up at him, fluttering her eyelashes and hoping he wouldn't question what, exactly, she'd tripped over. "Thank you, good sir."

His touch scalded her, and she drew back before anyone could comment on her making a scene. Honestly, she was lucky her mother hadn't noticed. Hopefully Sophie had well and truly diverted her attention.

The man chuckled. "I was just in the right place at the right time. I'm glad to be of service. Are you well? Did you injure yourself?"

"No." Her cheeks burned even hotter. "I just need a moment to myself. Perhaps some fresh air."

He cocked his head, studying her face as if making sure

she was telling the truth. "Would you like me to escort you to the balcony?"

Her heart thudded. In some circumstances, that might be quite a scandalous request, but she'd already noticed that the balcony here opened onto the room containing the refreshments and that it didn't look to have any hidden nooks and crannies. Groups of people had been coming and going from it as they enjoyed glasses of lemonade and pieces of cake.

"That would be much appreciated. Thank you..." She waited, giving him the opportunity to introduce himself, but he didn't do so. Perhaps he was a very literal sort and hadn't noticed the opening she'd left for him.

He took her arm and escorted her around the dancers and through the doorway, skirting the revelers who'd chosen to pause for something to eat and heading straight to the balcony. She watched him out of the corner of her eye. There was something slightly different about him. He didn't hold himself in quite the same way he had when she had seen him getting out of his carriage.

Or perhaps she'd simply read too much into it and was being fanciful. It wouldn't be the first time.

There were a pair of women on the balcony. Kate recognized one of them but couldn't put a name to the face. She just knew that the woman was an exceptional cellist. Her savior led her to the edge of the balcony and rested his forearms on the railing.

"Is this your first season?" he asked, and it didn't escape her notice that he had yet to inquire after her name or reveal his own.

"My second," she corrected him.

One of his eyebrows rose at that. "A pretty girl like you didn't get scooped up last season? What's wrong with the gentlemen of the *ton*?"

She laughed. "You say that as if the idea that I might have turned them down never occurred to you."

His other eyebrow rose. "Touché, my lady."

"I'm certain I didn't see you last season," she said, hoping he might provide a clue as to his identity or what he'd been doing with his life.

He paused before he spoke, and his eyes darted to the left. "I was occupied by my duties to the House of Lords last season."

She frowned. Was that a lie? Something about his words didn't ring true.

Was this man some kind of scoundrel?

"You are a lord, then?" she asked.

His lips twisted in a roguish smile. "Do you not recognize me, my lady?" But then, as quickly as the question had come, he cleared his throat and straightened. "Forgive me for being bold. May I get you any refreshments?"

She tilted her head to the side, curious. He was behaving most strangely. "No, but thank you for offering." She heard movement behind them but didn't turn to look around. "You are welcome to get something for yourself, though. I'll be fine here."

"Perhaps I should...." He trailed off, his eyes widening, lips parting.

She spun to follow his gaze. Standing in the open doorway behind them were Lady Talbot and Lady Bethel, two of the worst gossips in the *ton*. They were staring askance at Kate and her companion.

And that was when Kate realized. The sounds she'd heard earlier had been the other women from the balcony retreating back inside the ballroom, leaving her alone in a dimly lit space with a gentleman she didn't know.

She was in trouble.

"This isn't how it looks," she protested, backing away to ensure that there were at least several paces between her and the mystery gentleman. "We haven't been alone out here. There were other women...."

She stopped talking when she realized they clearly didn't believe her. Panic constricted her chest and she struggled to draw in a deep breath. She met the man's eyes and he looked as disturbed as she felt. They had to clear up this misunderstanding. Urgently.

"This gentleman was just helping me," she hastened to add. "I was overwrought and needed fresh air." A breeze mussed her hair as if to lend credence to her story. She turned toward the man and added, "Is that not right?"

The man's lips moved in what might have been a silent apology and then he brushed past her, picking up speed until he was running, and within two seconds he'd disappeared inside the ballroom and was gone from view.

Kate's heart dropped. Oh *no*. This was even worse than she thought. The fact that he'd run made them look guilty. Perhaps if he'd stayed, they could have talked their way out of this, but how was she supposed to do that on her own?

Lady Talbot tutted disapprovingly but her eyes—those of a vulture—gleamed with excitement. No doubt she was already composing the rumors she would spread throughout the *ton*.

"I expected better of you, Lady Katherine." Lady Talbot addressed her friend. "Won't you go and get Lady Drake? She needs to know what her daughter has been up to."

Lady Bethel snuck a look at Kate and another at Lady Talbot and then obediently trotted away like a puppy eager to please its master.

"Nothing is amiss, Lady Talbot," Kate assured her.

Lady Talbot looked down her nose at Kate. "Save the protestations for when your mother arrives."

Kate looked toward the refreshments room. Earlier, she'd been so reassured by the presence of others, but there were currently none in sight. A situation that had seemed slightly daring but harmless enough was now far more damaging.

She couldn't help but wonder what would happen if she simply ran away like the gentleman had.

Could she leave all of this behind, or would her name be dragged through the mud, her dreams of marriage destroyed?

The silence between Kate and Lady Talbot was excruciating. Kate didn't meet her companion's eyes, but she could feel the woman's gaze raking over her, searching for anything amiss, any button that might have been opened or fabric that might have been torn.

Never mind that all Kate and the gentleman had done was converse. By the time Lady Talbot was done with her, everyone would believe she'd been discovered half dressed and in a scandalous clinch.

Her stomach rolled, nausea sweeping through her. This was bad. Really bad.

"What on earth is going on?"

Relief swamped Kate as Lady Drake appeared. Her mother would fix this. She'd know that Kate hadn't been up to anything nefarious.

"Your daughter has been caught in a compromising situation with a gentleman," Lady Talbot declared.

Lady Drake looked at Kate. "What is she talking about?"

"It was nothing. There has been a misunderstanding. We weren't alone for more than a few seconds. I'm sure someone from within the room could see us most of the time we were out here. There is no need for all of this fuss."

"She was alone out here with that—"

"Lady Talbot," Lady Drake said sharply. "Please allow me to speak with my daughter in private."

Lady Talbot's expression soured, but she stepped aside as Lady Drake put her arm around Kate's shoulders and walked with her back through the double doors, around the refreshments table, and into the ballroom.

Kate was beyond relieved to find that the dancing was still in mid swing. Lady Bethel must have already begun spreading word of what had happened, though, because she could feel eyes on her as she passed clusters of chattering women. She felt like a scolded child but knew that the consequences of her misstep could be much, much worse than anything a child would do.

Beside her, Lady Drake kept her chin high until they'd bustled out through the exit and sent for their carriage. Kate did her best to do the same. All of this had been blown wildly out of proportion, but if her mother didn't wish to speak until they were alone, then she'd honor that.

The carriage pulled up in front of them, and Lady Drake ushered Kate inside first, then followed her. They remained silent until the carriage had pulled away from Wembley House.

"What have you done?" Lady Drake asked softly.

"I tripped," Kate lied, keeping her gaze down so that her mother wouldn't see the guilt in her eyes. "I needed some air, and a gentleman assisted me. When we went out to the balcony, there were two other women there, so we weren't alone. They left at some point, and I didn't notice, and then when Lady Talbot and Lady Bethel came out..."

Lady Drake sighed. "It looked as if you were having a private assignation."

"We were nowhere near each other," Kate protested. "We weren't doing anything scandalous."

"Sometimes, my dear, it doesn't matter what the truth is— it only matters how the situation *looks*."

Kate knew this, but had it really looked so terrible?

"Who was the gentleman in question?" Lady Drake asked. "Was he elderly? Infirm? Anything that would render him harmless?"

Kate's teeth sank into her lower lip, and she squirmed. "I'm afraid he didn't tell me his name."

Lady Drake's eyebrows flew up. "You weren't previously acquainted with him?"

"No," Kate admitted, slumping into the seat, wishing it would swallow her up so she would no longer have to deal with her mother's disappointment.

Lady Drake pinched the bridge of her nose. "Then we are in even more trouble than I'd feared."

"Mother, I'm—"

"Shush. Let me think."

The quiet pressed in on Kate as she closed her eyes and mentally replayed the evening, wishing she'd never spotted the gentleman and asked Sophie to distract their mothers. She'd considered the ball a relative success until that point. She'd met at least one gentleman she'd been interested in getting to know better. But now…. Had she ruined it all?

The carriage slowed to a stop outside Longley House, and Lady Drake shepherded her inside. Kate held her tongue, certain that anything she might say would only make things worse.

Boden opened the door, his expression impassive. "Lady Drake, Lady Katherine. I trust you enjoyed your evening."

"It was a shambles," Lady Drake declared. "Please bring the earl and countess to the drawing room. There is something I must discuss with them at once."

Worry gnawed at Kate's gut, and she skulked behind her mother into the drawing room. The housekeeper hurried in and lit several candles, clearly having not expected this turn of events.

Kate perched on the edge of a chair and buried her hands in her skirt, twisting them in the fabric the same way anxiety was twisting up her insides. The clock ticked, painfully loud with no conversation to drown it out.

Lady Drake sat on a chaise and folded her hands on her lap. Minutes crawled by.

When Andrew and Amelia joined them, Andrew wore

sleep clothes and was disheveled, while Amelia's nightdress was covered by a robe.

"What's going on?" Andrew asked, walking deeper into the room.

Amelia paused in the doorway and said something to the housekeeper.

"Your sister's reputation is under dire threat," Lady Drake said.

Her words made both Amelia and Andrew turn to Kate.

Falteringly, she explained what had happened, leaving out the fact that her trip had been intentional.

"By now, Lady Talbot has no doubt twisted events to fit her narrative, and rumors will be spreading through the *ton*," Lady Drake added, still not looking at Kate.

Never in her life had she felt so small. "I'm sorry." She could apologize a thousand times, and it wouldn't be enough to erase the disappointment on Andrew's face. "I didn't mean for any of this to happen."

She'd let everyone down. They'd all done so much for her, and she'd ruined everything.

Mrs. Smythe bustled in with a tray of tea and biscuits. She set it on the table, and Amelia immediately went over and poured a cup of tea with a little sugar, then picked it up, along with a biscuit, and offered them to Kate.

"Oh, I don't think I can—"

"It will help," Amelia insisted. "You've had a shock. The sweetness will clear your mind."

Kate wasn't entirely sure she believed that, but she intended to do exactly what everyone asked of her because she'd made a mistake and had to make up for it however she could.

Her hand trembled as she took the tea, and she was lucky it didn't slosh over the brim of the cup as she raised it to her mouth and forced herself to take a sip. She placed the teacup down, afraid that if she held onto it for too long, she'd spill it, and took a bite of the biscuit instead. It was like ash in her mouth, and when she swallowed, the lump strained almost painfully on its way down her throat.

She looked around, noting the stress brackets at the corners of Amelia's mouth and the way her mother rubbed at her temples as if they throbbed. This was all her fault. Her family had done so much for her, and she'd repaid them by causing a scene and perhaps even rendering herself unmarriageable.

The biscuit dropped onto her lap, and tears began to spill from her eyes. Her lower lip wobbled, and she bit it, determined not to make a sound.

"There, there." Amelia dragged a chair over beside her and patted her arm. "It's all right."

Kate sniffed and resisted the urge to point out the obvious: This was very much not all right.

"Oh, sweetheart." With a sigh, her mother got up and came across to crouch beside her in the most unladylike fashion. "We'll find a way through this."

"Can you describe the man to me?" Andrew asked gently.

With a deep breath, Kate gathered herself. She blinked rapidly to clear her vision. "He was perhaps your age or slightly younger. His hair was dark brown and short. His eyes were brown too."

Andrew grimaced. "Many men are my age with brown hair and brown eyes."

"Uh… he wore a blue waistcoat and a pink cravat." She wasn't going to mention that she'd found the combination quite dashing. "He wasn't what I'd call handsome, but there was something striking about him."

He turned to Lady Drake, clearly hoping she might recognize this description, since she'd also been at the ball. She shook her head, indicating that it didn't mean anything to her.

"I'll ask Wembley for a copy of the guest list," Andrew said after a long pause. "Perhaps we can narrow down the possibilities. The man must take responsibility for his actions."

A chill swept through Kate. *Take responsibility?* What, exactly, was Andrew considering doing? All the man in the pink cravat had done was escort a young lady who'd claimed to feel unwell to an occupied balcony for some air. He didn't deserve to be forced into marrying her or…

She gulped.

Amelia harrumphed. "I don't believe that challenging this man to a duel and getting yourself shot would be the most comforting course of action to Kate. I also doubt that she would wish to find herself tied to a man who, by all accounts, abandoned her in an attempt to save his own skin."

Kate agreed with her, but her normally easygoing brother's jaw was clenched and his eyes were sparking with temper, so she didn't utter a word.

"This calls for something stronger than tea." Andrew marched out of the room and returned with a bottle of golden-brown liquid and a stack of small glasses. He placed the glasses in a row and filled each of them. "Drink up."

"What is it?" Kate asked, picking up a glass and sniffing. Its scent reminded her of jam that had sat in the sun for too long but with a strange, chemical undertone.

"Sherry." Andrew downed his drink in a single mouthful, refilled his glass, and did it again.

To Kate's surprise, her mother shrugged one shoulder and swilled her own drink. Amelia pulled a face, took a tiny swallow, and placed it back on the table.

Kate sampled her own. It tasted sweet but burned the inside of her throat. As soon as the sherry hit her stomach, warmth began to fill her.

"I'm truly sorry to have caused so much inconvenience," she said, staring into the golden depths mournfully before trying it again.

"We'll get through this," Andrew assured her. "Finish your

sherry and go to bed. There's nothing more we can do before the morning anyway."

Half an hour later, as she lay staring at the ceiling, Kate couldn't sleep a wink. All she'd wanted was to meet a handsome man who'd made a remarkable first impression on her, and now she feared that she'd wake to discover she was ruined.

CHAPTER 5

THEO STARTLED AWAKE WHEN A LOUD CRASH ECHOED THROUGH his bedchamber. He bolted upright, his heart racing, and he raised his fists instinctively to protect himself.

"Damn." Another crash, this one smaller. "Fucking hell."

He peered through the darkness, his pulse beginning to calm. He recognized that voice. "Nicholas?"

A large body collapsed on the edge of the bed, and warm breath reeking of alcohol bathed his face.

Theo cringed away. "Dear God, man, did you empty a tavern of its stores last night?"

Or should that be "tonight?" He wasn't sure whether he'd slept long enough for a new day to have arrived.

"I gave it a damn good try," Nicholas slurred, scooching closer in an apparent effort not to fall off the edge of the bed.

"What the hell is going on?"

Nicholas rolled onto his back. "I fucked up."

"How?" Theo fought off frustration. Nicholas had always been reckless and irresponsible, but surely whatever he'd done could not be dire enough to warrant this display. "Couldn't this have waited until morning?"

"Morning," to Nicholas, usually meant around noon.

"No, no, no." Nicholas covered his face with his hands. "I've only just arrived home, and I've delayed for too long already. You need to know. Oh, it's such a fucking mess."

"What did you do?" Theo gritted out, his patience waning.

Nicholas groaned. "You're going to hate me."

For the first time, genuine fear curled in Theo's gut. Nicholas had made many mistakes before, but he'd never been this reluctant to own up to one. "For the love of God, man, what did you do?"

Nicholas was quiet for so long that Theo wasn't sure he was going to reply, but finally, he did. "I accepted an invitation to the Wembley ball on your behalf."

Theo shook his head, trying to make sense of that. "If I remember correctly, the Wembley ball was last night, so it's not as if I was forced into going because of you. I don't understand the problem."

"No, you don't comprehend what I'm telling you." Nicholas exhaled roughly, drowning them both in beer breath again. "You weren't interested in going, so I went in your place. I *pretended* to be you."

The squirming worry in Theo's stomach tangled tighter. Wherever this was going, he got the feeling he wasn't going to like it. "And what did you do while people thought you were me?"

"I was…"

"Yes?"

"Uh… I…"

"Spit it out."

"I was investigating potential wives for you!"

Deathly silence fell between them.

Theo didn't think he could possibly have heard Nicholas correctly. He'd told his brother that he had no interest in remarrying. Had insisted as much. And yet Nicholas had chosen to ignore him.

"You deserve not to be sad and lonely anymore." Nicholas flopped onto his side and slung his arm across Theo's abdomen. "I hate seeing you like this. Elizabeth wouldn't have wanted you to suffer."

Theo shoved Nicholas's arm off. "Don't tell me what Elizabeth would or wouldn't have wanted."

"I'm sorry. I'm sorry."

Fury simmered beneath Theo's skin. "None of us can possibly imagine what Elizabeth might think. She's gone, and I'm not marrying again."

"Um… about that."

Theo squeezed his eyes shut. "What did you do?"

"So… uh… I may have been caught alone with a marriageable chit on a balcony, and I'm pretty sure the ladies who saw us mistook me for you. In fact, I'm quite certain of it."

The air was punched out of Theo's lungs, and he sucked in a breath so sharp, it hurt. Now he understood why Nicholas was beside himself.

"Did you ruin her?" he demanded.

"No." Nicholas sounded aghast at the possibility. "I'd never do that. I misjudged. We weren't supposed to be alone, but in two seconds, it all went to hell."

Theo massaged his eyelids. "What happened after they caught you?"

Silence.

"Nicholas, speak."

"Erm, I may or may not have made a speedy exit."

Theo opened his eyes and narrowed them at his brother, trying to read his expressions in the dark. "Are you telling me that you left a debutante alone after she had been caught with you on a balcony with no chaperone in sight?"

"It could… possibly… be construed as that. I panicked, Theo. I never intended to cause any harm. I just wanted to see if there were any young women who might bring some life back to you and to Blackwell."

Fuck.

Fuck, fuck, fuck.

"And you believe that you were mistaken for me?"

Nicholas nodded. "As I said, I accepted the invitation in your name. I greeted the hosts as you. Considering how long it has been since you made an appearance in society, word of your presence likely spread through the assembly in minutes. No doubt that's why the gossips came looking for me on the balcony."

"And they weren't disappointed by what they found," Theo gritted out, pushing the blankets off. He struggled out of bed and went to the nearest candle to start a flame. The darkness was making it too difficult to think. He needed to be sharp so he could understand the full ramifications of what Nicholas was telling him.

Nicholas had pretended to be him.

Nicholas had been found alone on a balcony with a young lady of marriageable age, presumably from a good family, considering her presence at the ball.

Whoever had caught them thought they knew exactly who the man in question was and had every reason to make that assumption because of Nicholas's ruse and the fact that few people knew they were identical twins.

Ergo, someone believed that Viscount Blackwell had ruined an innocent. They would either expect him to marry the lady or to meet for pistols at dawn with her father, brother, or guardian.

Theo pulled on a pair of trousers and a loose shirt—one of the ones he typically used for boxing. He padded over to the desk on the opposite side of the room from his bed and sat on the chair behind it.

"Why would you do this to me?" he asked, still confused

as to why Nicholas would impersonate him in the first place, let alone get him into this shambles of a situation.

"I didn't mean to." Still on the bed, Nicholas made a visible effort to sit up.

Now that Theo could see more clearly, it was obvious his brother had not only drunk his own weight in alcohol but had also taken a walk through somewhere muddy and fallen flat on his face. The bedding would need to be washed.

"You're always sad," Nicholas said, looking as lost as a motherless puppy. "I wanted to help. You were so happy when you fell in love with Elizabeth. I thought if I could find someone else, then you'd be happy again. The timing on the balcony was… unfortunate. I didn't realize we were alone until it was too late. The young lady…. She seemed so promising."

Ah, so he had been too busy congratulating himself to pay attention to their surroundings. How typical of Nicholas. Theo hated to think what kind of debutante his brother might have found so impressive. Most likely she had either been the type to use her wiles—and enjoy doing so—or someone with no regard for society's strictures.

Theo crossed to the nightstand and picked up the tall glass of water he always kept there overnight. He passed it to Nicholas. "Drink. All of it."

As Nicholas gulped down the water like a man stranded in the desert, Theo rang for a maid. He requested a cup of tea and more water and then paced the length of the room until the maid returned with them. He refilled Nicholas's glass, gestured for him to drink it, and fixed himself a cup of tea.

Nicholas's glazed eyes had cleared slightly, and his pupils were more reactive as he focused on Theo.

He was sobering up. Good.

"So, tell me if I have this right." Theo wished he had a sweet treat to go along with his tea. He wasn't usually a fan of cake or biscuits, but a little sugar would definitely improve his current mood. "Somewhere out there in London is a young lady whose name you don't know who might be ruined unless I marry her. Does that sum it up?"

Nicholas's Adam's apple bobbed as he swallowed. "Yes. But I should be the one to marry her. I can tell everyone that I lied and that I was the one there last night. If we attend a large social event side-by-side so people can see how similar we look, they might believe it and then she can marry me, not you. I don't wish to marry but I'll do it because this was my mistake and you shouldn't have to pay for it."

"Or they might not," Theo pointed out. "They could think you're sacrificing yourself at the matrimonial altar to save me. And who do you think her parents are going to push for her to marry? A second son or a titled peer?"

Nicholas withered.

"That's not even taking into account how furious Mother would be." If they made a spectacle of themselves, she'd react as though the world was ending because so much of her existence hinged on having the admiration of her peers.

"Mother would get over it."

Theo snorted and buried his face in his hands. Perhaps she would, but she'd make them regret their actions first. "Christ, Nicholas. You knew I never wanted to remarry."

"It was an accident." Nicholas's misery was evident in the slump of his shoulders and the redness of his eyes, but the fact that he felt guilty didn't make this all better.

"It's always an accident with you." Perhaps that wasn't entirely fair, but Theo wasn't feeling charitable right now.

"I'm willing to marry her," Nicholas said earnestly. "I'll fix this."

Theo sighed. "Let's not rush into anything."

He needed to cool his thoughts. As angry as he was, he wouldn't be coming up with a solution to their predicament anytime soon. That in mind, he grabbed the box containing his wraps and stalked toward the door.

Nicholas scrambled off the bed and stumbled toward him, nearly tripping but catching himself before he hit the floor. "Don't leave. We can make this better, right? Just tell me what to do, and I'll do it."

Theo backed away. "I need time alone, or I might say or do something I regret."

Nicholas's face crumpled. "I'm sorry, brother. I'm here when you need me."

Theo nodded once, briskly, and shut the door behind himself, leaving Nicholas to sleep off his overindulgence while he went to the boxing room to work out his frustration.

He used one of the candles in the corridor to light the ones in the boxing room, then sat on a sturdy wooden stool in the corner while he opened the wrap box and went through the familiar, reassuring motions of securing the fabric in place across his knuckles and around his wrists.

Once the wraps were in place, he began by throwing punches that didn't hit the bag. His mind was still slightly dulled from sleep, and he didn't want to jar himself into the moment too roughly. Instead, he worked up to it, gradually adding more weight behind his strikes as his body started to awaken and his nerves came to life.

As soon as he was in the right mindset, he beat the bag until his fists throbbed and his breaths came in heaves.

Fuck this goddamn morning.

He didn't want to deal with his mother's out-of-control anxiety over society's opinion of her—which would be inevitable if Nicholas jumped headfirst into this scandal he'd inadvertently created—but he also didn't want a wife.

He didn't want to watch another woman he cared about wither away, growing more and more distant with every day that passed.

He didn't want to visit his wife's bedchamber only to find

her sobbing quietly because her monthly flow had arrived again.

More than anything, he didn't want to watch another strong, vivacious woman lose her spark and her will to live.

That's all he could offer to anyone who married him. He'd condemn any wife of his to a life of misery and despair. He didn't want that. Nor, unfortunately, did he want to condemn a young lady to being cast out of society just because his brother had acted foolishly, as usual.

His arms grew weary, but no matter how many punches he threw, it didn't calm the thoughts racing through his mind. It seemed like whatever he did, someone would be hurt as a result. His mother. Nicholas. This unknown woman. Sweat soaked his hair and trickled down the back of his neck. The sound of his breathing filled the space.

Eventually, he gave up on finding peace and padded back to his bedchamber to bathe.

Nicholas was unconscious on the bed in a slightly awkward position. Theo considered rearranging him but decided that he deserved to wake with a kink in his neck. His brother's intentions may have been good, but he'd still gone behind Theo's back and done something he had known he wouldn't approve of.

Sometimes, execution mattered more than intention, and his execution had gone very wrong.

Reluctant to disturb Nicholas despite his simmering anger, Theo used cold water to clean himself and sniffed his armpit to make sure he didn't smell intolerable before dressing in simple trousers and a shirt—so as not to need the assistance of his valet—and wandered downstairs.

The delicious, yeasty aroma of fresh-baked bread permeated the ground floor of the house, and he followed the scent to the dining room. The maid he'd woken must have roused Mrs. Browne, the cook, because breakfast was ready much earlier than usual.

He fixed himself a plate of eggs and sausage, slathered butter and jam on a thick slice of warm bread, and sat at the head of the table to eat. He wolfed down the bread, hungry from exercising, and only slowed once his gnawing hunger had dissipated.

As he lingered over the eggs and sausage, he found his gaze drawn to the empty chair opposite him. Once upon a time, that seat would have been filled by a young woman with dark hair that refused to do as it was told and a smile that had warmed his heart and made him believe he'd never be alone.

He'd been naive.

"My lord?"

He glanced up at the butler, Albert, who stood a few yards away with his palms folded neatly over his rounded abdomen, clutching a sheet of paper to his body.

"Yes, Albert?"

Albert cleared his throat. "Master Nicholas requested that we obtain copies of the scandal sheets as soon as they're available and provide them to you. This is the first."

Fucking Nicholas.

Theo wasn't sure whether to be grateful for his brother's foresight, even in an inebriated state, or furious at the reminder of how badly Nicholas had blundered.

"Thank you." He held his hand out, and Albert hesitantly passed him the paper. Theo could hardly take his frustration out on his loyal staff. It wasn't their fault his brother never thought anything through.

"Is there anything else, my lord?"

"Not right now, Albert."

Theo spread the sheet on the table and skimmed over the first few chunks of text, searching for his name. For a moment, he thought perhaps Nicholas had been overly cautious in thinking he'd been recognized, but at the bottom, in the corner, was a small piece about the discovery of the unwed Lady Katherine Drake, sister to the Earl of Longley, alone in a compromising position with the also unwed—and terribly infamous—Viscount Blackwell.

Damn.

He read the text again. What the hell had Nicholas done? He claimed that nothing had happened between him and the chit, but this article made it sound as if they'd been practically *in flagrante*.

With an earl's sister, no less.

And this godforsaken piece-of-trash paper had identified her by name.

And Theo.

Nicholas could tell people it had been him all he wanted, but Theo doubted anyone would believe it. Lady Katherine's guardian certainly wouldn't settle for Nicholas when they could turn their daughter into a viscountess.

The bottom dropped out of his stomach, and he thought he might be sick. He'd have to marry her now or the poor girl would be ruined.

CHAPTER 6

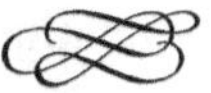

Kate shifted impatiently from one foot to the other as she waited for the footman to hand her the basket of scandal sheets he'd been sent out to collect. As soon as he extended it toward her, she snatched the handle, pausing briefly to apologize for her rudeness before rushing with the basket to the drawing room, where her family was gathered to find out how bad the situation was.

Andrew and Amelia sat on one chaise, cups of tea already poured, as if tea could solve any issue that plagued them. Her mother sat opposite, and Kate dropped onto the chaise beside her, grateful for the fire burning in the hearth because it warded off the chill in the air. Last night had been relatively mild, but the weather had turned overnight, and it was now raining lightly.

She looked at the paper on top of the others, reading quickly and immediately recognizing her name in an article near the bottom right corner. Without reading more, she passed the other papers around. Her nerves would get the better of her if she had to check them all herself.

"There's a brief mention of you in this one," Amelia said, reading faster than anyone else. "It follows a description of the Wembley ball and simply says that an unmarried miss was heard to have been caught on a balcony with an unidentified lord."

"A lord?" Andrew's eyebrow rose. "And he didn't stay and do his duty to ensure no harm befell you?"

Kate winced. Whoever the man was, he'd just lowered himself in her brother's estimation. She returned her attention to the article with her name in it, horrified to discover that the writer had taken liberties with the truth, alleging that her hair had been unpinned and her back unlaced when they were come upon.

"I am *not* a harlot," she breathed, incensed. "The man didn't lay a finger on me except to escort me to the balcony."

She kept reading but stopped when her mother gasped.

"I've identified our mystery gentleman." Lady Drake's voice was shaky. "It seems you made the acquaintance of Viscount Blackwell yesterday evening."

Viscount Blackwell.

Kate's stomach hardened, and her pulse thundered in her ears. "Surely not." She rubbed her chest, hoping to ease the sudden tightness there. "Lord Blackwell hasn't ventured into polite society for years. That's what you told me, isn't it, Mother?"

"That's certainly what I believed." Lady Drake's mouth pursed. "He married young and he and his wife rarely attended society events. He hasn't been at any since his wife… passed away."

Kate heard the pause before she finished the sentence and mentally filled the gap.

Before he'd *killed* her.

Because everyone knew that Viscount Blackwell was rumored to have murdered his wife when she failed to produce an heir. Just as, if gossip was to be believed, he may have done away with his father to shorten the wait to inherit his title.

"Look at this." Lady Drake thrust the scandal sheet toward Kate, who took it with trembling hands.

Kate read the headline: *Is Lady K to Be the Next Ill-Fated Viscountess Blackwell?*

Amelia tore it from her and scoffed. "No one will make you marry a murderer. I won't have it."

"But what if I'm ruined?" Based on these papers, everyone would assume she'd been engaging in an illicit liaison. No one would ever believe that the whole thing had been nothing more than unfortunate timing.

Amelia balled up the paper, tossed it aside, and took Kate's hand. "You will *not* marry a murderer. Will she, Andrew?"

"No, of course not." Andrew was frowning as he flipped through another paper. "Although I never bought the stories about Blackwell. I know the circumstances didn't look good, but as far as I could tell, he seemed a decent sort."

Decent?

Decent?

Was he prepared to base Kate's future safety on "decent"?

She really hoped not.

"Give me the paper," she said, reaching for the one propped on Andrew's knee. "I want to see all of them."

He let her take it. Amelia and Lady Drake stacked the rest in the basket and placed it next to her so she could read them at her own speed. She made her way through them one by one, her heart growing heavier and her head lighter with each new piece of information that burrowed into her brain.

Eventually she could no longer focus on anything, and spots were dancing in front of her eyes.

Before he'd fled, she'd liked the man she'd met last night. She'd never have thought him a murderer. But many members of the *ton* seemed to believe he was, although there must not be any evidence, or he'd have been locked away.

She didn't know what to do. Her name had been

mentioned enough times throughout the articles that if she did not wed, she knew she would bring shame to her family, and if any gentlemen would have her, they'd certainly be ones she wanted nothing to do with.

But her other option—finding a way to make Lord Blackwell marry her—didn't appeal either. First, she'd have to be brave enough to perform her marital duties, and then, if she failed to conceive, she might find herself in an "accident" like the one that had befallen his previous viscountess.

From what she could recall, the viscountess had supposedly died as the result of a carriage accident, but the couple had been seen arguing heatedly beforehand about her lack of ability to produce an heir. Add to that fact that no one had witnessed any such accident, and that several people had spotted the disheveled viscount carrying his wife's limp, bloody body a short time later, and it didn't look good for the viscount.

Yet perhaps she didn't need to worry about that particular fate. Lord Blackwell obviously wasn't inclined to marry her, or he wouldn't have fled at the first opportunity. Andrew could challenge him to a duel to force his hand, but she didn't want her brother to put himself in danger, and also… well, she'd prefer a husband who hadn't been marched to the altar at gunpoint.

The door opened, and Boden stepped inside, his iron-gray hair smoothed carefully into place and an inscrutable expression on his face.

"My lord." He addressed Andrew directly. "There's a caller here for Lady Katherine."

Kate inhaled sharply. Could it be Lord Blackwell?

Had he seen the papers and decided he ought to do the respectable thing? Her feelings were so mixed up, she didn't know whether she wanted that or not. Part of her was furious at being put in this situation when absolutely nothing untoward had happened, but a larger part of her feared that she was about to lose many of the things she held dear.

Andrew nodded. "Bring them in."

Kate swallowed. She supposed they were doing this, then.

But a few seconds later, it was Sophie who raced through the doorway, not the harsh-faced, well-dressed gentleman from the ball.

Sophie's eyes glittered with unshed tears, and she threw herself at Kate. "I'm so sorry!"

Kate opened her arms and wrapped them around her closest friend. "I'm all right."

"No, you're not." Sophie drew back, scowling. "You've been compromised. Oh, I should have protected you from that dastardly man."

Kate's lips twitched as, for the first time in hours, amusement flashed through her. "Alas, I didn't need protecting from Lord Blackwell, but rather from the vultures of society. He didn't lay a finger on me in any untoward manner, Sophie. It was simply unfortunate that we didn't realize our companions on the balcony had left before Ladies Talbot and Bethel came across us."

Sophie blinked rapidly, her eyelashes dark against her milky skin. "Are you sure you're unharmed?"

Kate grimaced. "Well, my reputation is very much muddied, but I myself am unharmed."

Sophie breathed a sigh of relief. "That's something, at least. What will you do now?"

"I don't know."

Andrew rose and indicated to the door. "I'll be in my office if you need me."

He grumbled something under his breath about needing to send a strongly worded note, but Kate couldn't make out his exact words.

"Please don't challenge anyone to a duel," she called after

him. He wasn't usually the hot-tempered type, but she couldn't be too careful.

He made a gesture she couldn't interpret and disappeared around the corner.

Perhaps sensing that some time alone with her friend would help Kate more than having them all hovering there, her mother nudged Amelia and nodded toward the exit. Kate sent her mother a smile of gratitude as she guided a confused Amelia out with a suggestion that they check on baby George.

"Must you marry him?" Sophie asked, angling herself toward Kate.

Kate drew in a deep breath. "I don't even know if that's an option. He ran like the devil was on his tail when he realized we'd been caught alone. I could be mistaken, but that doesn't seem like particularly gentlemanly behavior."

Sophie hesitated. "Do you *want* to marry him? I know you were interested in talking to him, but I wish I'd never agreed to help. This is all my fault."

"No, it's not," Kate assured her. "It was my poor judgement."

"But it wouldn't have happened if I hadn't distracted our mothers. Did you know who he was when you…?" She trailed off.

Kate shook her head. "I didn't have a clue."

Even if she had, she couldn't guarantee she wouldn't have wanted to meet him.

All right, so she'd probably have thought twice about venturing onto the balcony with him, but she'd always been a touch whimsical, and there was something intriguing about a man with a black reputation.

Provided he didn't want to kill *her*, of course.

Sophie looked uncharacteristically serious as she whispered, "If you don't marry him, you might be ruined."

"I know," Kate admitted.

"But even if you don't, I'll stand by you." She raised her chin, her blue eyes defiant. "It's just… it's *unfair.*"

Kate didn't argue. She agreed with Sophie. But some things wouldn't change overnight, and society's expectations of young unmarried ladies were one of them.

"Do you think he's truly a killer?" Sophie asked, glancing around as if afraid Lord Blackwell might be hiding behind the curtains, listening in. "Did he seem violent?"

Kate tilted her head back and forth. "I only spoke to him for a few minutes. He came across as being solicitous but perhaps not overly fond of society's rules." After all, he hadn't introduced himself, and he'd not thought twice about escorting her to the balcony.

Sophie's nose crinkled. "You must have gotten some kind of impression of the man beyond that."

"Not really." Kate wished she had more to offer. All she knew of him was that he had an air of mischief about him that contrasted with the weightiness she'd thought she'd noticed when she'd seen him prior to the ball.

Boden coughed discreetly into his handkerchief. Kate jumped in place, shocked by his presence. She hadn't noticed him enter.

"Lady Bowling is at the door, my lady."

"We're not at home, Boden," Lady Drake called as she swept into the room. "Good lord, that woman is a dreadful gossip."

"Understood, my lady."

"Wait." Lady Drake stopped him. "The only person we are at home to is Lord Blackwell."

Boden bowed. "Very well, my lady."

Lady Drake turned to Kate and Sophie. "I suggest you hide somewhere deeper in the house. No doubt Lady Bowling is only the first caller of many. Everyone will want to know what happened at the Wembley ball, and what better way than to come by under the guise of being concerned for your well-being?"

"We'll go upstairs," Kate agreed. "If Sophie wants to stay."

Sophie rolled her eyes. "Of course I do. You need me. We can sit in that window in the library with a view of the front door and keep watch."

That was as good an idea as any, so Kate went along with her, although she darted into her bedchamber to retrieve her sketchbook and a pencil before heading to the library.

"Would you like tea?" she asked Sophie, realizing she should have done so earlier.

"No. I wouldn't mind one of Mrs. Baker's cakes, but not quite yet. Let's get comfortable first. Something tells me you've had a long night."

"You're very perceptive."

They arranged their armchairs in front of the window, and it wasn't long before a pair of women similar in age to Lady Drake approached the front door and knocked. Boden turned them away.

Kate sank lower into the chair even though she knew they weren't visible from the street. The last thing she wanted was to feel like she was on display.

And yet, as one person after another traipsed up to the door and tried their luck at persuading Boden to let them in, she couldn't help feeling like she was the *ton's* chosen entertainment for the weekend. Very few of them actually cared about her. They just wanted to be the one to hear what actually happened between the previously faultless Lady Katherine Drake and the notorious Lord Blackwell.

When Kate couldn't stand watching for a moment longer, she began to sketch Sophie, from the slightly upturned slope of her friend's nose to the freckles she refused to hide beneath powder, to the faintest lift at the corner of her mouth that always hinted at trouble.

"Do you think Andrew will challenge the viscount?" Sophie asked, propping her chin on her hand.

"I hope not."

"That would be romantic, in a way."

Kate made a noise of disagreement. "Do you know what would have been romantic? Lord Blackwell telling those terrible gossips to mind their own business and then waxing poetic on the beauty of my eyes or some such thing."

Sophie's eyes narrowed. "You're feeling maudlin, aren't you? We need cake."

"I'm not—" she protested, but Sophie was already on her feet and walking away.

When she returned, it was with Mrs. Baker close behind, carrying a tea tray on which were two small pieces of cake.

"Here you go, dear." Mrs. Baker fussed with the tray, positioning it on a small table between them. She then poured tea before tailoring it to each of their preferences.

"Thank you, Mrs. Baker." Kate didn't think she could stomach any food, but she appreciated both Sophie's and the cook's efforts to improve her mood.

"You're very welcome, Lady Katherine."

Mrs. Baker retreated, and Sophie enthusiastically bit a chunk out of her cake.

"So good," she murmured after swallowing. "Mother is less concerned about me watching my figure than she was about Violet and Emma with theirs, but we still don't get cake often. You should have some."

Kate studied the cake reluctantly. It was nice that Sophie was trying to help, but she really didn't think that a piece of cake would solve anything.

"Go on," Sophie encouraged.

With a sigh, Kate picked up the cake and nibbled on the edge. Her mouth was dry, and it was difficult to swallow. As she'd expected, the tiny mouthful sat uncomfortably in her gut and didn't help at all.

A carriage pulled up outside, and she frowned. She didn't recognize the crest on its door.

"Who's that?" Sophie asked around a mouthful of cake.

"I've no idea."

They watched together as a tall gentleman in a hat got out of the carriage and marched straight up to the door. They waited for Boden to turn him away, but when he entered the house, Kate sat up straighter.

Oh, heavens. It was him.

Lord Blackwell was here.

CHAPTER 7

"The Drakes are not receiving callers this morning," the butler informed Theo crisply.

"I believe they'll be at home for me." Theo withdrew his card from his pocket and offered it to the man, who read the name and curled his lip as if he'd smelled something rotten.

"As you say." The butler stepped aside to let him in.

Theo entered before the butler could change his mind and waited while he closed the door. He was relieved to get out of the rain, which had eased in the past hour but showed no signs of stopping yet.

"I'll show you to the earl's office. I assume you wish to speak with him?"

"Yes, thank you."

Actually, he'd like to make the acquaintance of the chit he'd supposedly ruined, but he could understand why he wouldn't be allowed direct access to her considering the circumstances. Goddamn Nicholas.

He wasn't surprised that the Drakes weren't receiving callers today. He hated to think how many gossips and opportunists must have turned up on the doorstep in the hopes of finding out what the awful Viscount Blackwell had done to that sweet innocent girl.

Thanks, Nicholas.

If his brother never put another foot out of line, it would be too soon. Theo deserved an award for taking his frustration out on a bag of sand rather than his twin. Perhaps it would have been for the best if he had blackened one of Nicholas's eyes. At least then he wouldn't venture out into society and do any more damage until the eye had healed.

He followed the butler down a corridor to a closed door. The butler knocked.

"Come in," a male voice called.

Theo steeled himself. He hoped the earl was as amiable as he recalled. He'd rather not get a bloodied nose if the man punched him for tainting his sister.

"Viscount Blackwell is here to speak with you, my lord," the butler said.

"Is he?" Longley's voice was deceptively mild. "Please show him in."

"Yes, my lord."

The butler allowed Theo to enter, the faintest smirk appearing on his lips as if he would enjoy whatever punishment the earl saw fit to bestow upon this vile besmircher of maidenly virtue.

Theo raised his eyes to the earl's and immediately stopped walking, almost tripping over himself. Longley had always been an affable fellow—in appearance as well as manner—but right now, he looked murderous.

Theo clasped his hands in front of his groin, slightly concerned that the earl might threaten his ability to reproduce. "Thank you for agreeing to see me, my lord."

Longley jabbed a finger at the chair on the other side of the desk. "Sit."

Theo sat.

The smug butler retreated.

Longley stared at him for a long moment. "State your business."

Dread curled in his gut. He didn't want to do this. After he'd lost his wife, he'd sworn that he'd never marry again. He wasn't sure that he could survive a second marriage going so dreadfully wrong, and he didn't want to condemn a young lady to a life of misery with him either. He'd already proved himself incapable of keeping a wife happy.

Theo cleared his throat and forced himself to speak. "To begin with, I'd like to assure you that I did absolutely nothing untoward with your sister." Once Nicholas had sobered up, Theo made him swear to that on the family bible. "That said, I understand that that isn't how the situation came across, and now Lady Katherine's reputation is at risk."

Longley bent, withdrew a bottle of liquor from within his desk, and poured a portion into a small glass. He didn't offer any to Theo. "Go on."

Lord, the man was determined not to make this easy.

"I am prepared to marry Lady Katherine." The words were bitter on his tongue, and as Longley swilled his drink, Theo wished he had one of his own. It hadn't been easy to arrive at this decision, but offering himself as a sacrificial lamb would protect both his brother and mother, the two people he loved most in the world.

Longley drained the glass and set it down. "Considering the position you're in—and the fact that it's all of your own creation—you probably ought not to make the possibility of marrying my beloved sister sound comparable to walking to the noose. Unless, of course, you'd prefer to settle this via pistols at dawn."

Theo's stomach lurched, and he blinked at Longley, unable to form a response. He hadn't thought the earl had it in him to threaten a duel. He'd always been so friendly and nonconfrontational. Apparently, when it came to his sister, Longley was far from easygoing.

"That won't be necessary," he bit out. "My apologies, Lord Longley. I have nothing against Lady Katherine."

How could he? He'd never even met her.

"Your expression says otherwise," Longley said coldly.

Theo dragged his hand through his hair. He was getting this all wrong. "I truly don't. It's just that I never intended to remarry, so this is taking some adjustment."

Longley glanced at his bottle as if debating whether to pour himself another, but he must have decided against it, because he flattened his palms on the desk and leaned back in his chair. "Why would you be conversing with a young unmarried lady at the Wembley's ball if not to find a wife?"

"She tripped and required assistance." Another piece of information he'd gleaned from Nicholas. "I was there to catch up with an old friend, but when I came across her, it seemed the polite thing to offer to accompany her to the balcony for air."

In reality, it wasn't a decision Theo would ever have made, but Nicholas had always been more reckless than he was.

"Mm-hmm." Longley looked dubious. "You are fortunate that Kate has already told me the same thing and assured me that nothing happened between you other than a case of unlucky timing."

Thank God. Some women would have seen the opportunity to secure a match with a lord and lied to trap him into it. At least he now knew that Lady Katherine possessed a basic level of human decency.

"So, how do we proceed?" Theo asked.

Longley stared at him, his hazel eyes thoughtful but unrelenting. "I will never ask my sister to marry anyone she doesn't want to. You're welcome to make your offer to her, and whatever her decision is, I'll stand by it."

Theo cocked his head, caught off guard once again. He would assume that most guardians of young ladies entangled in a scandal would be only too happy to make decisions on their ward's behalf—especially if it were possible to extricate them from a situation with their reputation still mostly intact.

That Longley was giving control to Lady Katherine—Kate—spoke volumes about his affection and respect for her.

"May I speak with Lady Katherine, then?" He might as well get this over with as quickly as possible. Hopefully God would hear his prayers, and she would turn him down. Even better, perhaps she'd already won the affection of a higher-ranked peer, so no one would remark upon this unfortunate incident when she married him instead.

"Boden!" Andrew called.

The butler appeared behind them as if he'd been hovering there the whole time. He probably had. Servants were notoriously nosy.

"Yes, my lord?"

"Please ask Lady Katherine to come down to the drawing room. You may inform her that Lord Blackwell is here to call on her."

The butler bowed. "Very good, my lord."

He gave Theo a dirty look as he backed away.

Longley rose and gestured for Theo to precede him through the office door. He led Theo down the corridor and across to a drawing room decorated in shades of white and green. "You can wait here."

"You aren't staying with us?" Theo asked, surprised for a third time.

"No. Kate will bring a chaperone with her, and she'll be more comfortable discussing matters with you without me here to overhear them. That said, if you put a foot out of line, I'll know about it."

Theo didn't doubt that. There was something oddly unsettling about this serious, flinty-eyed version of the earl.

Longley nodded once and departed. Theo debated

whether to sit on one of the chaises or the many chairs but opted to remain standing in a show of respect for Lady Katherine, who would no doubt join him soon.

He paced across the room and back, wondering how he might phrase this so as to give her the genuine option of marriage should she want it while also encouraging her to refuse him.

He honestly didn't want the girl to be ruined. She didn't deserve that. But she also deserved better than a lifetime bound to a man who'd already driven one wife to her death.

Soft footfalls approached, and a moment later, the butler entered and held the door open. Two women came through, arm in arm.

Two.

Neither was a maid. They both wore dresses fit for aristocrats. To his consternation, both women had reddish hair and therefore could be Longley's sister—although the one on the left's hair was brighter than the other's. They both had light eyes and pretty smiles.

He looked from one to the other, and his gut sank to his shoes. Dear God, he had no idea which one was Lady Katherine Drake.

He bowed to them. "My ladies."

Both women curtsied to him in return. As they straightened, he studied their faces, desperate for any hint as to which woman he ought to be addressing. The one on the left had a hint of mischief in her eyes and an impish twist to her smile. She was definitely the sort of young lady his brother would be able to lure onto a balcony.

Deciding that the redheaded imp was most likely Lady Katherine, he angled himself toward her. "May we speak in private, my lady?"

She frowned, her cheeky smile twisting down in disapproval. "I suppose we could, but I'd have thought it was Lady Katherine you're most in need of talking to."

The air in the drawing room chilled by several degrees. Painfully slowly, Theo turned toward the other woman. The one with hair that was more a burnished shade of blonde than red and gray eyes that gleamed with intelligence and not even the faintest trace of mischief.

Oh, hell.

This was Lady Katherine.

He'd directed his question to the wrong woman, and judging from the imperious arch of her eyebrow and the thin line of her lips, she was unimpressed by his error. Of course she was. Anyone would be if they'd supposedly had a scandalous interlude with someone the night prior and he couldn't recognize her the following day.

But by God, she wasn't at all the type of woman he'd have expected his brother to pursue. Everything about her from her body language to her attire screamed that she was a proper, well-raised gentlewoman. He'd never have guessed this demure creature had the fortitude to venture onto a balcony alone with someone as rakish as his brother.

Drawing in a deep breath, he bowed so low, he felt like a pauper scraping before the king. "My apologies, Lady Katherine. Your companion is correct. It has been a long night and I'm out of sorts. I should have addressed myself to you immediately."

"It's all right, Lord Blackwell." Her voice was soft and melodious, but there was a coolness to it he'd no doubt deserve if he'd actually been the man she'd met last night. "We were never officially introduced. I'm Lady Katherine Drake, and this is my friend, Lady Sophie Carlisle. She's been good enough to keep me company on this trying day."

Great, he'd not only ruined this girl without even making her acquaintance, but he'd also wounded her pride.

He took her hand and bowed over it. "Lord Blackwell, at your service." Letting her go, he nodded to Lady Sophie. "A pleasure, my lady."

"Shall we sit over there?" Lady Katherine asked, gesturing toward a chaise in front of the empty fireplace.

"Yes, let's."

"One moment, please." Lady Katherine went to the door and spoke to someone through it. On her way back, she murmured something to Lady Sophie, who wandered down the other end of the room, where she could be present as a chaperone without interfering with their conversation.

He looped his arm through Lady Katherine's and walked her to the pair of chaises that faced each other. She lowered herself gracefully onto one, and he sat opposite.

He peeked at her out of the corner of his eye, once again surprised that his brother had chosen Lady Katherine to speak with over the many other debutantes who'd no doubt attended the ball.

Perhaps it had been as simple as what both claimed—she'd needed air and he had escorted her—but Nicholas had said that he thought Theo might genuinely like the chit. Maybe his brother was more astute than Theo had given him credit for.

With her casual elegance and carefully contained beauty, Lady Katherine was definitely the sort of person who would attract Theo's interest if he were actually looking for a wife. He'd married a vivacious woman before, and it had ended poorly. At first glance, Lady Katherine couldn't be more different from Elizabeth.

"Lady Katherine," he began awkwardly. "I'm sorrier for what happened yesterday evening than I can say. You have my most heartfelt apology for any distress this situation has caused you."

She interlocked her fingers and rested them on her lap. "I appreciate that, but as far as I can tell, only one action actually requires an apology. Most of this was due to bad timing, but it was incredibly poor form of you to disappear the way you did as soon as we were discovered. If you'd stayed, we might have been able to smooth the situation over, but when you fled, it made us look guilty."

His jaw clenched. She had an excellent point. Fucking Nicholas. "I understand that, and I apologize. I panicked, and it was wrong of me to leave."

Her eyes searched his, but based on the way they tightened at the corners, she didn't find what she was looking for. Probably because he was lying, and she could somehow sense it. If there weren't so much at stake, he'd be impressed by her perceptiveness.

A short, plump woman with red cheeks and a motherly air bustled into the room and set a tea tray on one of the side tables.

Lady Katherine thanked her and poured them each a cup of tea. "How do you like yours?"

"Black."

She placed the cup near him, positioned her own, and offered him a biscuit.

"No, thank you." He didn't think he was capable of eating anything when his entire future might depend on the outcome of this conversation. "Lady Katherine, I never intended to remarry, but considering the circumstances, I would like to offer my hand in marriage in order to rectify any damage to your reputation caused by my reckless actions."

CHAPTER 8

Fury burned in Kate's gut as she stirred her tea and inhaled slowly so as not to curse at the viscount. Ladies should never utter curses, but especially not when they were directed toward titled members of the aristocracy.

The sheer audacity of Lord Blackwell in offering to marry her when he didn't even have the decency to recognize her. He was clearly not the sort of man who would make an acceptable husband.

How dare he treat her so poorly?

Yes, he'd done the "proper" thing by coming here to offer for her, but he'd spent several minutes with her last night and had still somehow mistaken Sophie for her!

He'd clumsily tried to cover for himself, but he'd done a poor job of it and Kate saw through his act. He was lucky she'd not taken it upon herself to empty his teacup all over his nice black trousers.

"I will think on it," she said, knowing that she couldn't turn him down out of hand. She was upset right now and therefore not likely to make a rational decision. She needed time to weigh her options.

Lord Blackwell's eyes widened. "I beg your pardon?"

She glared at him. "I said that I shall consider your most generous offer. I don't currently feel able to make an informed decision. After all, I hardly know you."

"Many have married upon lesser acquaintances," he said, a furrow between his brows that implied she confused him.

He wasn't the only one confused.

A couple of days ago, she'd seen a handsome man with the weight of the world on his shoulders, and she'd wanted to get to know him. Yesterday, she'd met a flamboyantly dressed lord who'd deserted her the second something went wrong. Today, here he was, the weight back on his shoulders as he attempted to do the right thing.

What was happening with this man?

She set her spoon aside and curled her hands around her cup of tea, grateful for the warmth it provided. She glanced out the window. The rain had stopped, but gray clouds loomed overhead, and she wouldn't be surprised if the rain started again later.

"What would you be doing today if not for the situation we find ourselves in?" she asked, curious to learn more about him—in order to inform her decision if nothing else. Considering the rumors about the viscount, she needed to determine his character.

He drew back slightly, the furrow between his brows deepening. "Either managing my estate or reviewing documents for parliament."

"Do you always attend parliament?" She'd heard that some lords didn't care for the future of the country and chose to ignore their seat in the House of Lords.

He nodded stiffly. "I consider it my duty to England to attend. It's the only reason I come to London these days."

How fascinating. If he was only in London to sit in parliamentary sessions, then why had he been at the Wembley ball?

"Do you enjoy it?" she asked.

He pursed his lips. "I don't do it for the sake of enjoyment. I do it to serve my country in the best way I can."

So, no, then. She'd assume he didn't enjoy it.

"That's very honorable of you." She sipped her tea, searching for another avenue of conversation. She was angry with him and wary of him but also needed to work out whether she could salvage this situation.

"Is this your first season?" he asked, eyeing the biscuits but not making any move to grab one.

She frowned. "No, it's my second."

She could have sworn she'd told him that last night.

"Ah. I see." He shifted his weight uncomfortably. "How is your season thus far?"

"Rather stressful, as I'm sure you're aware." He was, after all, in the same position she was, although the damage to his reputation wouldn't be as consequential as it would be to hers.

He winced. "Er, yes. Forgive me. That was an ill-conceived question."

Kate glanced along the room to where Sophie was quietly drinking her own tea and pretending not to listen in. She wished she had her friend's courage. No doubt Sophie would have made some kind of scathing remark if she were in Kate's shoes, but all Kate had been able to bring herself to do was glare.

"How long will you be in London, my lord?"

"Until parliament closes prior to Christmas," he replied.

It struck her then how very strained this whole thing was. Last night, he'd seemed reluctant to give her his name—and now that she knew it, she could understand why—but he'd flirted and been quite charming.

A possibility occurred to her, and her heart squeezed. It would explain the reason he hadn't recognized her and give him an excuse for forgotten aspects of their conversation.

She sighed. "I'm sorry to ask this, but were you soused last night, my lord?"

He stared. Blinked. Stared some more. "I beg your pardon?"

She ducked her head. "I don't mean to cause offense. I'd just like to know so I can better understand. Something about you seems different today."

"Oh." He looked taken aback but then schooled his features. "I may have been a little tipsy. I don't believe I was inebriated. Unless I... I didn't do anything to make you believe I was out of my mind, did I?"

"No, you didn't," she hurried to assure him.

"Good." He was visibly relieved. Perhaps he had been more drunk than he wanted to admit, if he was so concerned about his behavior. He ought to remember at least some of it.

Kate heard crunching and looked over her shoulder at Sophie, who pulled a face and stuffed the rest of a biscuit into her mouth.

Blackwell leaned toward her. "What do you like to do with your time?"

"I enjoy art." She was tempted to elaborate, but drunk or not, he'd hurt her pride by not recalling what she looked like, and she wasn't going to make this too easy for him.

He raised his teacup to his lips and drank. He must have found it to his liking, because he promptly took another mouthful. "What kind of art?"

"Drawing. Painting. Other types too."

He nodded, and his gaze flicked to the window. "It's no longer raining. Would you like to walk in the park with me?"

She hesitated. On the one hand, she should take advantage of this opportunity to get to know Lord Blackwell better so she could decide what to do next, but on the other... "We would attract a lot of attention."

The last thing she wanted was to feel everyone's eyes on

her again. Being stared at last night had been unpleasant enough.

But Lord Blackwell's mouth lifted in the barest hint of a smile. "Perhaps that would be the most sensible way to get ahead of this."

"How do you mean?"

He shrugged. "If we're seen together today, then surely it makes yesterday's incident seem less scandalous. We can act as if we're courting and show that neither of us are concerned by any gossip."

It was… actually not the worst plan she'd ever heard.

"Wait here," she said, then got up and marched down to the other end of the room. "What do you think?" she asked Sophie.

Sophie blew air out the corner of her mouth. "His idea has merit."

"I know," she murmured. "But it will also cement any rumors that we're courting."

"Which would be more scandalous in the eyes of the *ton*: a tryst or a broken engagement?" Sophie asked, her tone making it clear that she wasn't sure and the question was genuine.

"I don't know," Kate admitted. "But I'm not marrying him upon the barest acquaintance—especially not with his reputation—so I suppose walking with him is at least a way to deepen our relationship, regardless of any consequences it might have."

"I can be your chaperone," Sophie said.

"Thank you." Kate squeezed her shoulder, then rejoined Lord Blackwell. "I will walk with you, and Lady Sophie will chaperone us."

Blackwell rose. "My carriage is outside. Will you need much time to prepare?"

"A little while." Kate looked down at her dress. Her

current attire wasn't suitable for being outdoors during such cool weather. "I'll have to change."

"I'll wait here."

Kate sent a maid to inform her brother and mother of their plans, and she and Sophie went upstairs together. Sophie had brought a pelisse with her, and she wore walking shoes already, which was fortunate in the circumstances.

Margaret helped Kate change into a more appropriate dress and pelisse and don shoes that would survive the damp ground. She also packed an umbrella, since the last thing she wanted was to be soaked through if the weather turned again.

Back downstairs, Lord Blackwell was waiting for them patiently, but, to her surprise, none of her family had arrived to invite themselves along. She'd expected either Lady Drake or Andrew to have come snooping, but for some reason, they'd both kept their distance.

As Lord Blackwell escorted them out to his carriage, Sophie asked him how long he'd been in London and where his country residence was. He answered in clipped tones without offering any extra details. Sophie was a bright conversationalist, but beyond answering her questions, he didn't carry on the thread of conversation or give her much to work with.

They reached the carriage, and he took Kate's hand and helped her in. A frisson of awareness rushed through her as their skin brushed, but she did her best not to let it show on her face. She sat on the far side by the window, and Sophie took the spot beside her. Blackwell sat opposite, his back rigid. He was clearly uncomfortable.

The carriage rolled forward, jolting slightly before the horses found a smooth rhythm. Kate watched the streetside, wondering how many people had been peeking through their windows when they left the house, eager to spread gossip about her jaunt with Lord Blackwell.

Sophie remained uncharacteristically quiet, and Blackwell didn't speak either. After several minutes, the silence grew almost painful.

Kate itched to say something—anything—to break it, but she didn't know what. Blackwell was essentially a stranger to her. A stranger whom she might be forced by circumstances to marry. While she wasn't shy, this situation wasn't one she'd ever expected to be in, and she didn't know the proper etiquette.

The carriage stopped at Hyde Park, and they waited for a footman to open the door. Blackwell climbed down, his long limbs moving gracefully, and assisted each woman as they disembarked. As she drew near him, she noticed that he didn't have that little freckle she'd spotted on his chin last evening. Perhaps it had been a smudge rather than freckle.

Together, they turned and started along the pebbled path into the park. There were few others around, most likely because of the poor weather, but every person without fail stared at their little group when they noticed them coming.

"Don't pay them any heed," Blackwell said, loudly enough to encourage the nearest group to turn away, tittering and pretending they hadn't been gawking.

"The river has a good flow today," Sophie said, gesturing toward the waterway that ran through the park. The edges were green and grassy, and the flow was higher than usual. "Do you think it might flood?"

"I doubt it," Blackwell replied, glancing over. "From my understanding, the weather is expected to clear tomorrow."

Good lord.

Kate was on the verge of being ruined, this man had proposed to her even though he clearly didn't wish to marry, and they were discussing the weather?

How dreadfully British of them.

She looked around, searching for something of more substance to discuss, but stiffened as her gaze landed on

Lady Talbot, who was holding court among a group of women whom Kate recognized as the mothers of other debutantes, many of whom were also seeking husbands this season.

Sophie's arm brushed Kate's as she moved slightly closer. "Don't let her upset you. She's just a spiteful old shrew."

"Lady Talbot," Blackwell mused. "I should have known."

What on earth was that supposed to mean?

Kate glanced at the women again, noting that at least one of them had her daughter with her. The girl met Kate's eyes and grimaced, although she couldn't tell if it was with sympathy or disdain.

"Do you have children, my lord?" Kate asked. The rumors about him would indicate that he didn't, but if he hadn't intended to wed again, then perhaps they were false. Why would a viscount opt not to wed if he didn't have an heir?

"No, I don't."

She bit her lip to stop from asking further questions. His brusque tone didn't exactly invite them.

A speck of water landed on Kate's cheek, and she tilted her face up to the sky. Another drop landed.

"I suspect we ought to leave unless we wish to get wet," she said in case neither of her companions had noticed.

"Very well." Lord Blackwell stopped abruptly and turned.

Both women hastened to do the same.

They made the short walk back to the carriage without further conversation. They climbed into the carriage and drove back as silently as they'd arrived. When they parked outside the Drake residence, Lord Blackwell focused the full force of his dark gaze on Kate.

"Have you come to a decision?" he asked.

CHAPTER 9

THEO WATCHED THE PLAY OF EMOTIONS ACROSS LADY Katherine's face. They weren't very decipherable, but it was obvious that she was conflicted. His fingers tightened on his thighs, and he drew in a slow breath and forced himself not to fidget while he awaited her answer.

She glanced at her friend, Lady Sophie, and seemed to arrive at a conclusion. "May I think on the matter further? Not for long. Perhaps we could meet again tomorrow? I know that we're pressed for time, but I'd prefer not to rush into making a decision that could completely change my life."

He gaped. Exactly how terrible was his reputation that she was willing to risk a scandal to avoid marrying him?

He'd always known that the *ton* gossiped about him and that he wasn't a sought-after guest at their parties, but was his reputation really so dire that Lady Katherine would throw away her future rather than become Lady Blackwell?

It was, to a certain extent, the outcome he'd been hoping for, but it shocked him, nonetheless.

"My lord?" she asked, worrying her lip.

"That's fine, Lady Katherine. I'll call on you tomorrow." He got out of the carriage like an automaton, offered her his hand to help her down, and then did the same for Lady Sophie. He waited for them to enter the house, and when the door closed behind them, he got back into his carriage and called, "To the Regent."

This called for a drink at his club.

Upon arrival, he entered through a little-known side door and slipped silently down the corridor to the room Nicholas usually favored. He had a suspicion he'd find his brother here—if he'd managed to recover from the consequences of overimbibing the night before.

Sure enough, Nicholas was sprawled on a brown leather chair in the small room with white marble flooring, a handful of candles providing a little light, and faded brown columns in the Roman style. There was a decanter beside him along with two small glasses, indicating that his brother had been waiting for him.

Theo poured himself a drink and dropped onto the nearest chair. "Do people genuinely believe I murdered my wife in cold blood?" he asked before draining the drink and immediately wishing for more. He didn't refill it, though. However tempting it might be, getting drunk wouldn't fix what ailed him.

Slouched low in the chair, Nicholas looked over, squinting as if even the small amount of light in here was too much for him. "What happened?"

Theo turned the glass around in his fingers. "I went to offer marriage to Lady Katherine Drake."

Nicholas grimaced and sloshed more brandy into his glass. "Sorry. I can still—"

"She didn't say yes."

Nicholas's eyes widened. "I beg your pardon?"

"First, Longley told me that it was his sister's decision."

"Good for him."

"And then Lady Katherine said she wasn't sure and that she wants to get to know me. I have the impression that she thinks that if she accepts the offer, there's a possibility I may strangle her while she sleeps."

He didn't want her to agree to marriage. He'd even hoped she might turn him down. But he couldn't deny that it wounded his ego to have her be so openly anxious about the possibility of marrying him.

He wasn't a monster.

"My reputation must be dark if she isn't jumping to accept," he muttered, turning the glass again and debating whether one more drink would hurt.

"Well, it certainly isn't good," Nicholas said tactfully. "But I didn't think it was all that bad either. Most sensible people know that the rumors about you are nothing more than gossip. Did you agree? Will you court the chit?"

Theo sighed and pinched the bridge of his nose. "I don't see that I have much choice."

"There's always a choice," Nicholas disagreed. "I've offered you a way out, but you're too self-sacrificing for your own good."

"You make that sound like a bad thing."

"It can be if it's to your own detriment." He paused. "I'm so very sorry, Theo. I never intended for any of this to happen. I just wanted to help you, and I didn't know how."

"I know." Theo exhaled sharply, his shoulders slumping. "I just wish…. Well, I suppose it doesn't matter now. Anyway, to answer your question, I've told Lady Katherine that I'll call on her tomorrow."

"You should take her to the opera," Nicholas suggested. "It's a place to see and be seen, and you'll have the opportunity to converse with her more, but there won't be so much pressure to engage with others as there might be if you were to venture elsewhere."

"I'll think about it." It wasn't a bad idea, but considering the trouble Nicholas had gotten him into, Theo wasn't in a hurry to take any of his advice.

"So." Nicholas tugged his chair around so they were facing each other. "What did you think of Lady Katherine?"

Theo frowned, caught off guard by the question. "What do you mean?"

"She struck me as the sort of lady you might find interesting."

Ah. This was more of Nicholas's ill-guided matchmaking efforts.

"She was quite reserved," he said tactfully.

Nicholas lowered his gaze to his glass. "Odd. She seemed unconventional when we met and not exactly a wilting violet."

Despite himself, Theo chuckled. "Oh, she definitely isn't a wilting violet. More like a cool white rose. Elegant and rather thorny."

"Oh ho." Nicholas arched his eyebrows. "Did you do something to offend her?"

"I believe you did plenty enough of that when you fled and left her for the gossips to tear apart."

He winced. "Touché."

Theo wasn't about to admit that he'd misidentified Lady Katherine. While he was certain that his brother would understand the confusion, considering that he never met the lady in question, he'd also find it far too amusing for Theo's liking.

"Do you intend to stay here for long?" Nicholas asked.

"No, I'll go soon. You might want to consider leaving too. I think it would be wise not to overimbibe again anytime soon."

They sat together for a while longer, and then Theo saw himself out and took his carriage home. When he arrived, he asked his butler, Albert, to find out what would be showing at the opera tomorrow and then sent word to Lady Katherine that, should she be amenable, he would escort her and Lady Drake to the opera in the evening rather than calling on her during the day.

That done, he dragged himself into his office, sat at his desk, and reviewed the letter from Elizabeth's parents once again. Elizabeth's father was the vicar of South Wye, the town nearest to Blackwell Hall in Oxfordshire.

The vicar, Mr. Norman, was concerned about damage to the church roof. Had Theo still been married to Elizabeth, it would have been assumed that his patronage would cover the damage. They implored him to have the decency to fund the repairs in honor of his late wife whose death they held him accountable for.

Theo would, of course, pay for the repairs, if for no other reason than to get the vicar and his wife to leave him alone for a while. They often came asking for things, and he didn't begrudge them that because they'd lost their daughter thanks to him. Unfortunately, they never missed an opportunity to remind him of that fact.

He drafted a letter to his man of business, summoned Albert to get it in the post, and then crawled into his bed, still mostly clothed, and shut his eyes.

What a day.

He'd been threatened with a duel. He now faced the possibility of marrying again, which was the last thing he wanted to do. He honestly didn't know what tomorrow might bring.

What would Elizabeth think if she could see him now?

She'd been such a loving soul. So warm and passionate. He'd considered himself lucky to have her... until he'd smothered her spark.

Theo had seen Elizabeth around South Wye when they were children, but he'd never paid much attention to her. She'd been the wild-haired daughter of Mr. and Mrs. Norman who lived in the vicarage and nothing more.

The magic happened when he returned home for the

summer from Oxford and met her at a local dance. She'd smiled and her mouth had curled in a way that was somehow adorable and mischievous at the same time. He'd fallen for her on the spot.

They'd danced and talked, and he'd called on her the next day. He'd been smitten. Something about her had eased a tension he always carried within himself. Mr. and Mrs. Norman had been thrilled by the attention he'd paid to their daughter, whose other local marriage prospects weren't particularly impressive.

His parents, on the other hand, were rather displeased. The daughter of a local vicar wasn't exactly the grand match they wanted for their son. Especially when he wanted to marry her at once, schooling be damned. They'd agreed to a compromise: They would allow the marriage to go ahead provided he completed his university education first.

They'd made the mistake of assuming that Elizabeth was just a passing fancy and his interest in her would wane. To their surprise, he'd returned home following his graduation and promptly made her his wife.

He summoned an image to his mind of how she'd looked on their wedding day. His mother had been determined to make it clear that she was not embarrassed by her son's choice to marry a commoner. She'd ensured that his father paid for an extravagant dress and had hosted the grandest wedding that Blackwell Hall had ever seen.

Elizabeth had met his eyes as they stood opposite each other, and her gaze had gleamed with amusement. The dress was far too gaudy to suit her, but neither of them had cared because they were in love and getting married. That was all they wanted.

Over the following years, she'd become his best friend. They were there for each other through everything, and despite his mother's disapproval of the match, the families gradually began to accept each other. They figured out how to behave around each other. They never really assimilated though. Not truly.

Fortunately, Theo's father had come to dote on Elizabeth. He'd made sure she always had what she needed and that no one who visited Blackwell Hall ever made her feel unworthy of her position. They'd enjoyed playing chess together and had often passed afternoons in the sun with a chessboard and a tray of tea.

But then, the storm happened.

The worst weather any of them could recall swept through the countryside. Winds raged and sent doors flying through the air, tore walls from buildings, and made it impossible for anyone to venture outside without risk of falling.

Rain pelted down, forming channels through the dips and valleys of the land around them and creating streams where they never used to be. Lightning flashed in the sky, and thunder shook the ground.

Then, they'd gotten word that his father's favorite horse had broken loose. Their stable master had advised them to wait for the horse to return on its own once the storm was over, but the viscount had loved that horse, and he ignored the stable master's advice and went searching for her.

When they had found out where he'd gone, Elizabeth had begged Theo to go after his father. Reluctantly, Theo donned his jacket and his most waterproof trousers and ventured out into the downpour. After searching for over an hour, he'd found the mare standing at the top of a cliff.

As soon as he'd seen her, he'd known something was wrong. He'd approached slowly, holding his hands out to soothe the agitated beast. Her eyes had been wild, and she reared back as if she might strike out at him with her hooves.

As he'd drawn near, he realized why she was so upset. There, at the bottom of the cliff, was the crumpled body of his father. It was obvious that he was dead. No one could have survived such a fall.

It had taken Theo another hour to coax the mare away from the edge of the cliff. He'd considered leaving her, but his father had given his life to save her, and he couldn't let that be in vain.

When he'd returned to the Hall, his mother and Elizabeth were waiting just inside and rushed to him as soon as he entered. He'd pulled Elizabeth into his arms and buried his face in her hair, steadying himself until he had enough strength to withdraw and tell them what had happened.

After that, it was like a light dimmed in Elizabeth. It had happened so gradually that he didn't realize how bad it had gotten until one day she simply refused to get out of bed.

During the years of their marriage prior to his father's death, Elizabeth hadn't fallen pregnant. It didn't seem to bother her because they were young and there was no rush to produce an heir. But as soon as Theo became Viscount Blackwell, that changed.

With each successive monthly flow, Elizabeth's melancholy grew.

She became less and less the woman he'd fallen in love with. She obsessed over her ability—or lack thereof—to bear his children.

It didn't help that some unpleasant members of the community made it known that they thought she had gotten above her station and that she ought to at least have the decency to produce an heir.

It crushed her spirit.

Then, one fateful day, he'd lost her.

It almost would have made more sense for her to slip away unnoticed, as she seemed to have been slowly fading from existence, erasing herself from her own life, but instead, she left with all the impact of an explosion, upending his life entirely.

He'd never expected to bury his wife. At least not for many, many years. He'd stood there, numb, as they lowered her casket into the ground. The second funeral in his family in less than two years.

She was buried in the family plot, to which Mr. and Mrs. Norman had protested. They'd believed she ought to be buried at the church. They'd blamed him, as they rightly should, but he hadn't been able to let her go, even in death.

Now, he pictured her as she'd been those last few days, her features gaunt because she'd stopped eating, her eyes hollow.

"It's your fault," she whispered in his mind.

Maybe it really was.

CHAPTER 10

"Are you sure you want to do this?" Amelia asked as Margaret tugged a hairbrush through the length of Kate's hair.

Kate met her sister-in-law's gaze in the mirror. "I want to at least try to get to know Lord Blackwell. Perhaps the rumors are wildly untrue, and he would make a suitable husband."

Margaret began gathering the strands of Kate's hair and twining them together into a braid around the crown of her head. Kate flinched as she pulled one a little too hard.

Amelia pursed her lips. "Andrew and I will stand by you, whatever you decide to do."

George flailed about in her arms, and she lowered him onto the floor and watched as he wobbled to his feet and tottered toward the bed.

"Thank you. That's better than I deserve." She'd made a royal mistake when she'd pretended to trip and fall into Lord Blackwell's arms. There was no one else to blame for this situation but herself, and she was lucky that her family was being so considerate.

Margaret tied the end of the braid and pushed a jeweled

hairpin through to keep it in place. She smoothed the back of Kate's hair and then reached for a hot iron to curl the strands that hung loose around her face.

Kate sat very still even though she was aware of Amelia and George playing behind her. If she moved at the wrong moment, the hot iron would burn her cheek.

"What adventures are currently on Miss Joceline's horizon?" she asked Amelia, inquiring after the fictional character her sister-in-law had created. Amelia's first novel had been printed last year, and another one was soon to follow.

Amelia stopped George from pulling one of the drawers open and hefted him into the air, her expression easing. "Joceline has been sent to Russia to marry a prince. She was mistaken for a missing noblewoman and hasn't been able to figure out how to escape yet. Her companions will be most unhappy when they discover her true identity."

Kate grinned. "Joceline always gets herself into the most interesting situations."

When she'd first met Amelia, Kate had thought that perhaps she herself hungered for adventure, but it hadn't taken her long to realize that Amelia preferred her adventures to happen between the pages of the book. That suited Kate, as she was much the same, enjoying the comforts of home too much to be interested in real-life adventure.

Margaret released Kate's hair and tugged on the end of one curl, smiling to herself when it bounced.

"I'm debating whether Joceline ought to have a suitor," Amelia said, perching on the edge of the bed and resting a fussy George on her lap. He caught her necklace and studied it as if it was the most fascinating thing he'd ever seen. "He'd have to be a dashing sort, but I can't decide whether it would be best to give her a fellow adventurer or perhaps a pirate or some kind of nobleman who wants to save her but doesn't realize that she is perfectly capable of saving herself."

"Why not introduce one of each and see which character has the best chemistry with her?" Kate suggested.

Amelia's eyes widened and she extricated her necklace from George's chubby little hands. "I like that idea."

"I thought you might." Kate had long since realized that the less conventional things were, the more her sister-in-law tended to enjoy them.

Margaret backed away from Kate to let her see her reflection clearly in the mirror. "Would you like anything else done, my lady?"

Kate studied herself. The braid crested her forehead like a tiara, especially with the jeweled pin in place, and curls fell around the sides of her face in a nod to the current style. "No, thank you. I believe I'm ready to dress."

Margaret went to the wardrobe. "Which gown would you like to wear?"

"The buttery yellow one with green trim." Yellow didn't always flatter Kate, but this particular pale shade looked nice with her eyes, and the hints of green complemented her coloring. It would do well for the opera.

Margaret pulled the gown out and helped Kate into it. Amelia stood quietly as Margaret buttoned the back of the dress. Kate could tell she was deep in thought, but it was impossible to know whether she was considering the options available to Kate or plotting how to introduce her fictional heroine to a handsome pirate.

Once Kate was dressed, she added a simple necklace to make her neck feel less bare, thanked Margaret, and walked with Amelia and George down the stairs to the foyer, where Andrew and Lady Drake were waiting.

Kate's lips twitched with satisfaction when she realized that her mother was wearing a gown in colors Kate had recommended for her. Lady Drake thought the deep blue was too much for a woman of her age, but Kate had assured her that she would look lovely in it, and she did.

Although she knew it was unlikely—her mother had never shown any interest in remarrying—Kate lived in hope that she would meet a nice gentleman who could keep her company as she aged. She was too young to be alone, and once Kate was married, both of Lady Drake's children would have partners and families of their own.

Andrew glanced up. "Blackwell has just arrived."

Sure enough, there was a knock on the door, and Boden answered.

Andrew sidled closer to her. "It isn't too late for me to send him on his way."

"I know, but I want to find out whether we're compatible." After all, she'd thought they might be before everything had gone wrong. Lord Blackwell was resistant to marriage, but Andrew had been, too, and now he was ridiculously happy. The same thing could happen for them.

Boden turned. "Lord Blackwell is here for Lady Drake and Lady Katherine."

The door opened to reveal the viscount in a stark black suit that emphasized the sharp planes of his face.

He dipped his head respectfully. "Lord Longley. My ladies. A pleasure to see you all."

"Blackwell." Andrew nodded in return. "I expect my sister to be brought home unharmed."

Blackwell's lips thinned. "She will be."

Seeing the need to smooth things over, Kate glided across to him and smiled. "You look very debonair this evening, my lord."

His eyes widened almost imperceptibly. "And you are beautiful, as always."

It was interesting how easily those words had rolled off his tongue. Perhaps he'd been charming once upon a time.

"Shall we be on our way?" she suggested, eager to get away from Andrew's simmering dislike. Rationally, her brother knew that Lord Blackwell hadn't done anything wrong, but he was protective of her, and it showed.

Lord Blackwell escorted Kate and Lady Drake out to his carriage, and they drove through the crisp night air to the opera house.

The lower portion of the opera house had already filled, so there were only a handful of people around as Lord Blackwell helped both ladies down from the carriage. He took Kate's arm and together they passed through the entrance and climbed the stairs.

"I have a private box for the evening, so we won't be bothered," he said, stopping outside a door and gesturing for Kate to enter.

There were several chairs, and she claimed one right in the center. Her mother sat to her left, and Lord Blackwell sat to her right. A hum of conversation traveled up from below, and she gazed around at the other boxes, making eye contact with a couple of people who were doing the same thing.

Something brushed her thigh, and she jolted, surprised when she realized that Blackwell's leg had bumped her own. Awareness skittered through her, and her belly flipped over.

She hadn't been this close to him before—at least, not for any length of time. He was a large man, so it stood to reason that he occupied quite a lot of space. She stole a glance at him out of the corner of her eye.

While not classically handsome, he was far from plain. There was something about the slope of his nose and the contours of his mouth that made her itch to grab a pencil and start sketching him. He would be an intriguing subject. Especially with how the light and dark constantly played over his features. It would be a study in contrast.

Excitement flittered inside her like butterfly wings, and she forced herself to stop staring at him, even if she was doing so sneakily.

"Do I recall correctly that you hail from Oxfordshire?"

she asked, curling her fingers into her palms to prevent herself from silently tracing the clean lines of his figure.

"I do." He turned toward her, his expression unchanging. So solemn. There was such a veil of sadness that hung about him. "I was born at Blackwell Hall, which is a short distance from the town of South Wye. Longley Estate is in Suffolk, is it not?"

"It is." She wondered if he'd researched the family or remembered that fact unaided. "Do you like the country?"

"I like its peacefulness and how easy it is to recuperate there. London bustle can be exhausting. That said, there are aspects of London that I like too. And you, my lady? Do you have a preference?"

"I also find enjoyment in both." She considered her next question. She was doing her best to get a sense of the man—and whether he harbored any latent homicidal impulses—but it wasn't as if she could directly ask him whether he'd killed his wife and intended to do so again if the need arose. "Do you have family who reside at Blackwell Hall?"

"My mother stays there when it suits her. At present, she is in Oxfordshire, but I have no doubt that she'll visit London soon. She can never stay away from society for long."

There was a certain type of fondness in his voice. Certainly, a man who cared for his mother couldn't be a heartless murderer, could he?

Honestly, she was having a difficult time reading him, which was unusual. It generally didn't take much for her to get an inkling of what made others tick. It didn't help that he seemed different now than he had on the balcony. There had been something carefree about him then. A lightness he no longer possessed.

He confused her.

The show began, and she settled in to watch. She had a tolerable singing voice, but she'd always been amazed by those who could perform so flawlessly to such intimidatingly huge crowds.

She leaned closer to the edge of the box and hung on every word. She was pleased they were watching a comedy rather than a tragedy. She didn't have a taste for drama the way some people did.

No one in their box spoke until the intermission when Lord Blackwell stood and rolled his shoulders back.

"Would you like a drink?" he asked, focusing that dark gaze on her. "I can brave the throng while you remain here. Lemonade, perhaps?"

"Yes, please." She was a little thirsty.

Lady Drake requested a glass too. As soon as he was gone, she ducked her head near to Kate's. "What do you think of him?"

Kate grimaced. "I'm unsure what to make of him."

Lady Drake nodded. "He seems solicitous but aloof. He's certainly striking, in an unusual way."

"He is," she admitted. "Part of me wants to draw him."

Lady Drake nudged her. "Perhaps one day you will."

"Perhaps." But she wasn't rushing into anything.

Lord Blackwell came back a few minutes later, carrying a drink in each hand. He offered one to Kate and the other to her mother. Their fingers brushed as she accepted the glass from him, and a shiver rippled through her despite the fact that she wasn't cold.

Her eyes caught his, and her breath hitched. A slight narrowing of his eyes indicated that he'd felt the spark between them too. Neither of them acknowledged it out loud.

"What do you think of the show so far?" Kate asked, curling her fingers around the stem of her glass and savoring the tartness of lemon on her tongue.

"Miss Caradori is extraordinarily talented."

He sat, and she held her breath, almost hoping their legs

might touch again. Alas, he was careful to keep a small amount of space between them.

"She is," Kate agreed, disappointed that he had chosen not to comment on the storyline. Simply remarking upon something obvious gave her no insight into his personality.

"The costumes are wonderful," Lady Drake said.

Lord Blackwell only nodded.

The intermission ended, and Kate became absorbed once again. However, the feel of eyes on her prevented her from being able to relax completely. Several times when she glanced up, she found someone staring at her. When Blackwell had fetched their drinks, he must have attracted enough attention to divert some members of the audience from the show on the stage.

A sudden bang behind her made her flinch. Her hand flew to her chest, and her heart galloped madly.

"It's all right." A warm palm settled on her thigh and gripped it tight enough to reassure her. "Probably just a chair falling over or someone who had too much to drink tripping over their own feet."

Kate's gaze locked on the masculine hand that rested over her skirt. Blackwell stiffened, as if only just realizing what an intimate gesture it was. He snatched his hand away, but it was too late. Kate had already realized a stunning truth: She'd liked his touch.

Even through the layers of her skirt, the heat from his hand had reached her, and it settled something inside her. It felt like being wrapped in a hug from a friend, but more. There was a spark there that she'd never experienced with any friend.

By the time the performance ended, she'd completely lost track of the plot. They waited for most of the audience to disperse before venturing out of the box.

Blackwell linked his arm with hers and was the perfect gentleman as he walked her down the stairs, past the stragglers, and handed her into his carriage. Yet despite his good behavior, something hot and exciting fizzed low in her gut.

That must mean he wasn't responsible for his wife's death, mustn't it? Her instincts had somehow decided that it was safe to be attracted to him, and surely that wouldn't have happened if he were evil.

Unless, of course, she was one of those foolish young ladies who believed they could reform someone unredeemable.

A sobering thought.

Blackwell drove them back to Longley House and escorted them to the door.

"May I call on you tomorrow?" he asked.

She squinted at him in the dark, unable to tell whether he genuinely wanted to spend more time with her or if this was simply part of his restitution efforts.

"There's a musicale at the Harrods' residence tomorrow afternoon," Lady Drake said, thankfully taking the lead because Kate wasn't certain how to respond. "Perhaps you could attend with us?"

Blackwell bowed. "It would be my honor. Good evening, my ladies."

As he turned and stalked away, Kate watched him go, her emotions conflicted. He was an intriguing man, but even as she spent more time with him, she became no surer of his character.

He would want an answer soon, and she didn't have one for him.

CHAPTER 11

Nicholas handed Theo two small wads of cotton. "Use these to stuff in your ears."

Theo frowned, confused. "For what purpose?"

Nicholas looked at him as if he were stupid. "To protect them. Some young ladies play their instruments like a dream, but others wield them more like torture devices. They like to see how loudly they can make them scream. Trust me, you need to be prepared."

Theo put the cotton in his pocket and patted it to make sure they weren't visible. "It can't be polite to stuff your ears."

"The things they do to those instruments aren't polite," Nicholas muttered. "You can choose whether to be polite or to have an aching head. It's entirely up to you."

Considering himself duly warned, Theo thanked him and made his way slowly down the front steps to his carriage. Part of him was amazed that he and Lady Katherine were still going through this strange courtship, but another part of him, one that he'd prefer to keep buried, rather liked her company.

That wasn't the positive thing it might seem because while he didn't want to condemn any woman to a life of misery at his side, he especially wanted more for the women he admired and respected.

Never mind. Until Lady Katherine decided one way or another, he was at her beck and call. He had no intention of ruining her—unless she decided that was the preferred course of action.

He collected Lady Katherine and Lady Drake from Longley House and instructed the driver to take them to the Harrods' residence.

"I understand this is an informal musicale in which anyone may participate," he said as they bumped along the street. "Will you play, Lady Katherine?"

Lady Katherine smiled, showing a glimpse of the straight white teeth that were usually hidden by delicate pink lips. "I've been practicing a piano piece for the event."

"Do you enjoy music?" It had seemed as if she had enjoyed the opera, but listening and playing were two very different things.

She waggled her hand back and forward. "I find music beautiful, and I enjoy listening to those who are more talented than myself. I am a passable musician, which means Mother volunteers me for events such as this, but I'm more adept at art than music."

He nodded. It wasn't the first time she'd referenced her artistic inclinations. "I hope you will let me see your art one day."

"Perhaps." Her lips twisted in a hint of a smirk. "If I think you'll like it."

Somehow, that sounded less like she was concerned about protecting her ego and more like she was laying down a silent challenge. She was asking him to prove himself worthy of seeing something she considered personal.

What an intriguing woman.

They stopped outside a house on the fringes of Mayfair. It was an older building but well-kept. Theo hadn't met Mr.

and Mrs. Harrod before. Honestly, unless someone was an acquaintance of his parents, an old school friend, or participated in the House of Lords, there was a high likelihood he wouldn't have met them. Having married young, he'd remained mostly in the country and kept to himself.

A cluster of young ladies were gathered just outside the front door, and they all looked their way as the carriage door opened and Theo got out. He offered his hand to Lady Katherine and helped her down.

One of the women watching them hid her mouth behind her hand and giggled. He hoped she just happened to have heard a joke because he wouldn't tolerate anyone treating Lady Katherine less than respectfully.

Lady Drake led them up the stairs and greeted an older woman wearing a fussy purple dress. She introduced Theo, who murmured a few words of gratitude for allowing him to attend on such late notice, and then they walked farther into the house and veered left into what appeared to be a small ballroom.

Chairs were arranged in an arc around a low stage. Lady Drake went straight to the left-hand side and sat near the back. Theo guided Lady Katherine into the chair beside her mother, and he took the one on her other side.

As the seats filled, he noticed that the guests left a wide berth around them, as if concerned that either his reputation or her scandal might be catching.

An array of instruments was set up on the stage. A grand piano occupied the center with small instruments positioned around it. A cello, a violin, something in a case that might be a flute, and, by far the most beautiful of all, an intricately carved harp. He wondered whether these instruments belong to the Harrods or if the people intending to play had brought them.

Eventually, the doors behind them were closed, and Mrs. Harrod stood at the front to make a brief welcoming speech. When she was done, she introduced the first performer.

The young lady, who was a startling shade of white, picked up the violin, her hands trembling so violently that the bow kept catching the strings and making awful screeching noises.

When she began to play in earnest, Theo immediately dug into his pocket to retrieve the wadded cotton. He jammed tiny bits of it into his ears and prayed that no one around would notice his rudeness. He glanced sideways at Lady Katherine, but she was too busy trying to maintain a straight face to have noticed his poor behavior.

Thankfully, the song didn't last long. The young lady dashed from the stage and rushed toward the door as if intending to make a getaway. She was intercepted by Mrs. Harrod, who steered her toward a chair near the exit.

The next person to ascend the stage was also a young lady. This one, however, preened and made a show of smiling brilliantly as she sat behind the cello. Then proceeded to murder it.

There was absolutely no difference in the skill level between her and the previous performer except that the first had the common sense to know how terrible she was. The cellist reveled in her performance. She swayed with the music and made exaggerated hand motions with the bow as if carried away by passion.

Theo almost envied her. How nice would it be to have such delusions of grandeur? To never doubt one's ability? He certainly wouldn't mind such a boost of confidence.

Lady Katherine was the third to be summoned to the stage. She sat at the piano and rested her fingers on the keys. When she began to play, she was... not too bad. She certainly couldn't be considered a virtuoso, but the music that sprang from her fingertips was pleasant. He even removed the cotton from his ears.

The song she'd chosen was upbeat and made him think of fields of wildflowers blowing in a spring breeze. There were a few hesitations and perhaps a couple of missed notes, but he would gladly listen to her play again. The same couldn't be said for the first two performers.

As her fingers danced over the keys, her face was serene, her lips curved in the smallest of smiles. He took his chance to study her fully. He hadn't spent much time examining her over the past few days—not because he was uninterested but because staring was impolite.

Now, he was able to look to his heart's content. She was pretty. Her fingers elegant and nimble. Her hair thick and shiny. And her lips…

No, it was safer if he didn't linger on those attributes.

"Doesn't she play beautifully?" Lady Drake murmured, loud enough for only him to hear.

"She does. You ought to be proud."

She beamed. "I always have been. Even when she gets herself into trouble."

When Lady Katherine finished with a flourish, he applauded enthusiastically. He wasn't the only person in the audience who was obviously relieved not to have been subjected to another round of ear torture.

She bowed, returned to her seat, and folded her hands primly on her lap.

He leaned toward her. "You played well."

"Thank you, my lord."

A man approached the stage next. He played the violin much more skillfully than the first performer had. His movements were well practiced, and he made the strings sing like crystal.

There were nearly a dozen performances in total. Many of the musicians played decently well, and one, a female cellist, would have deserved a place in the national orchestra.

To Theo's relief, he didn't have reason to plug his ears again. Honestly, he was fortunate he'd managed to get through the musicale without anyone noticing he'd done so in the first place.

When Mrs. Harrod declared the musical portion of the afternoon to be at an end, servants carried platters of food into the room and laid them on tables along the back wall. The guests mingled and enjoyed refreshments among which were tiny sandwiches and biscuits.

He stood with Lady Katherine to the side of one of the tables while her mother fetched herself a drink. "Is there a reason why Lady Sophie isn't in attendance?"

She laughed. "Sophie has no interest in performing. Her mother displays her talents plenty at home during calling hours, but she prefers to play only for herself."

"Lord Blackwell, Lady Katherine," a neatly dressed woman said, stopping in front of them. She had shrewd eyes that darted between the two of them. "Do I hear church bells in the distance?"

Theo glanced at Lady Katherine. He had no idea who this woman was, so he was uncertain how to respond.

Lady Katherine smiled, but it didn't reach her eyes. "If there are banns to be read, you'll hear them, Lady Bowling."

Lady Bowling's mouth wrinkled like a prune. Apparently, she didn't wish to wait to find out what, if any, arrangements between them had been made. She wanted to know now.

"I'll keep my ears open," she said, gliding toward Lady Drake—presumably in the hopes she might have better luck getting the latest gossip from her.

Theo lowered his head. "Would you like to get tea and cakes elsewhere?"

He knew that she wanted to further their acquaintance, and it would be difficult to do that if they were worried about everyone staring at them.

"Where did you have in mind?" she asked.

"There's a small teahouse near Hyde Park that's very pleasant."

She nodded. "That would be most agreeable. Let me just rescue my mother first."

A short time later, they entered the teahouse and placed their orders. The premises was decorated rather plainly, with none of the frills of the more fashionable establishments. He'd always liked this place because the staff were polite but not nosy, and for the most part, the patrons left one another alone.

Unfortunately, he seemed to have attracted more interest today than usual. Not only were a group of women at one of the tables glancing at them every time they thought no one was paying attention, but so, too, were a pair of elderly gentlemen in the corner. Their expressions suggested that they found his presence about as tolerable as dog shit on the bottom of their shoe. They kept looking from him to Lady Katherine as if afraid he'd either do away with her or start undressing her right in front of them.

He didn't acknowledge either party because he didn't want Lady Katherine and Lady Drake to feel uncomfortable, but he was sure they'd noticed of their own accord.

Briefly, he considered that it might be in both their best interests to play up his poor reputation to encourage Lady Katherine to refuse him—he really didn't want to ruin her life by tying her to him—but for some reason, he just couldn't bring himself to do it.

"Do you enjoy reading?" Lady Katherine asked after they were seated in front of the window. The shop owner was crafty enough to realize that their presence would attract attention from passersby and draw them in.

The back of his neck prickled, but he focused on her and did his best to ignore it. "I do."

She smiled, and a jolt of lust shot through him. She was pretty no matter what she was doing, but when she smiled like that, she could surely entrance any man she wanted. It was strange that she'd entered her second season unmarried.

"The countess, Lady Longley, writes adventure novels. I live in awe of her skill and smarts."

His eyebrows flew up. "She does?"

It was unusual for an aristocratic woman to pursue a career, even one in the arts. Lady Katherine's eyes narrowed as if daring him to speak ill of the countess's exploits.

"We're all proud of Amelia," Lady Drake chimed in, her sweet expression at odds with the steel in her spine.

"I'm sure it's well deserved." He'd have to find out what she had published. "I'm afraid I don't recall hearing news of Lord Longley's marriage. Which family is the countess from?"

If possible, Lady Katherine's eyes narrowed further. "Amelia's father is a businessman, Mr. Hart."

Ah, that made more sense. She'd no doubt been raised to be industrious.

"Do you also enjoy reading?" he asked.

Surprise flashed through her eyes, as if she'd expected him to comment on the countess's lowborn status. He made it a rule not to remark on anything of that nature. Considering his own reputation, to do so would be rather hypocritical. If the earl and countess were pleased with the match, then it was no business of his.

The server brought over their tea and placed a delicate china teacup in front of each of them. Lady Drake took the initiative and poured.

"I prefer learning about Joceline's exploits directly from Amelia," Lady Katherine said, reminding him he'd asked a question. "I have patience for many things, but I'm afraid that reading long works isn't one of them."

"What about poetry?" he asked, warming to the subject. "Poetry is often in a shorter form."

Her cool gray eyes warmed. "I have to admit, I'm partial

to poetry, particularly the likes of William Blake, William Wordsworth, and Lord Byron."

His heart lifted slightly. Here, they had something in common. "I used to consider myself something of an amateur poet. I haven't written anything in years, though."

Not since before Elizabeth passed away.

He knew that some people used art—whether written or visual—as a way of getting through dark times, but he'd always expressed himself most effectively when he was feeling inspired or joyful. His best work had come during the early days of his courtship and marriage. Once Elizabeth descended into a state of melancholy, he hadn't been able to bring himself to continue.

"I'd like to read your poetry some time," she replied, a soft look in her eyes that absolutely terrified him.

That look?

It said she just might marry him, and there was nothing he could do to stop her.

CHAPTER 12

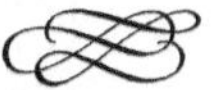

SEVERAL DAYS LATER, AT LADY HAMPSTEAD'S BALL, SOMETHING like sparks skittered over Kate's skin the instant Lord Black-well arrived. She watched him greet Lord and Lady Hampstead, and as her gaze traveled the elegant slope of his neck and the sharp edge of his jaw, her heart skipped, and her insides fluttered.

"He cuts a striking figure," Sophie said from where she stood beside Kate on the edge of the ballroom near a closed window covered by maroon curtains.

Kate opened her mouth to tell Sophie that she wasn't allowed to find Lord Blackwell handsome because he was hers, but she promptly snapped it shut. Lord Blackwell wasn't hers. She wasn't even entirely sure whether he'd warmed to the idea of marriage between them, although something had altered during their last encounter.

"He does indeed," she agreed instead and drew in a deep breath, ignoring the tickle in her nostrils. A fragrance she could only describe as "green" filled the room, courtesy of the many, many pieces of shrubbery and floral arrangements Lady Hampstead had used to decorate. There had already been a chorus of sneezes during the time Kate had been here, and it seemed to be getting worse.

"I expected him to be dressed more similarly to how he was at the Wembley ball," Sophie said.

"His attire is much more subdued tonight, it's true." Kate had noticed that immediately too. He wore predominantly black, with a white shirt and a simple tie. There were no flourishes or bursts of color. "There was definitely something different about him at the Wembley ball."

Perhaps it was simply that he'd overimbibed as he'd implied, but she'd spent hours with him since that evening, and he hadn't given her the impression of being a man who drank to excess.

Her thoughts halted when he turned toward the ballroom and his eyes met hers as if he'd known exactly where to look for her.

Her breath caught. "Oh."

Sophie giggled. "He's remarkably intense, isn't he?"

He was, and she liked that about him. Was that foolish of her?

Holding her gaze, Lord Blackwell cut a swath through the revelers and made his way directly to her. He took her hand, bowed, and brushed his lips over her glove. "Good evening, my lady. May I claim the next dance?"

"Indeed." She couldn't look away from those dark eyes of his.

"May I reserve a waltz later in the night too?"

Sophie squeaked and nudged Kate. They both knew that claiming two dances was akin to announcing a courtship.

"I'd like that."

Her hand remained in his, and she wondered whether she ought to draw it back, but then the song ended, and dancers began to ready themselves for the next one. He drew her onto the dance floor and stood opposite her as the music began.

His steps were slightly halting, and he paused a couple of times as if he couldn't recall what came next, but that was to be expected, as she doubted he'd danced for many years. As he gained confidence, his dancing became smoother, and she was able to relax into it and enjoy his closeness without fear of tripping or being trod on.

Each time he drew near to her, she caught the faint scent of peppermint. It was quite pleasant. The heat from his body practically radiated out, and she knew that a flush must be rising on her own cheeks.

Her dress swished around her legs, and she was grateful she'd worn one of her new, more extravagant designs. From the way his eyes dipped down every now and then, she suspected that he liked the way it looked on her.

"People are staring," he murmured, as if she could possibly not have noticed. She was aware of everything in this moment.

"Ignore them," she whispered back. That was what she was trying to do. At this point, everyone in the *ton* knew they'd been caught on a balcony together and were eager to watch the drama unravel right before their eyes.

He grimaced and flubbed another step. "Easier said than done. I thought I knew how it felt to be on the receiving end of a scandal, but this is something else."

She studied him, realizing that this was the first time he'd alluded to the rumors regarding his wife's death. She supposed he would know how it felt to be the subject of gossip, although according to her mother, he'd hidden away since then, so he'd probably never experienced the full force of social ostracism.

There was a groove between his eyebrows and strain lines at the corners of his mouth that showed this was weighing on him. That in itself told her something about him. He wasn't one to enjoy notoriety. Not that she'd thought otherwise, but one could never be certain until evidence was presented to the contrary.

She suspected that he was a kind man too. He was serious —there was no doubting that—but apart from that initial interaction when he'd run from her, he'd been solicitous and honest but never unkind.

Frankly, he didn't seem like the type of person who would murder his wife for failing to produce an heir. If he'd been seen carrying his wife's bloody body soon after they'd been heard arguing, there must have been an explanation. Perhaps London's gossips simply never shared that part because it would ruin a good story.

The dance ended, and he escorted her back to where Sophie waited, now with Lady Drake at her side. He thanked Kate for the dance, greeted Lady Drake, and turned to Sophie.

"Would you like to dance?" he asked her.

Sophie nodded and started to bounce toward him before apparently remembering her training and moving more gracefully instead. Kate's chest squeezed as she released Lord Blackwell and watched him walk away with Sophie. She was pleased to note that they stood farther apart than she and he had. She trusted her friend not to do or say anything untoward, but she was feeling oddly possessive of the viscount.

"Have you made up your mind about him yet?" her mother asked, offering her a glass of lemonade.

Kate accepted the glass and sipped as she continued to watch Lord Blackwell and Sophie. "I'm beginning to think that getting caught on a balcony with him might not have been the worst thing that could have happened to me."

"Really?" Lady Drake's eyes gleamed with something Kate couldn't identify. "You think you'll accept his offer?"

"I'm considering it." If she didn't, their invitations would likely dry up. The other gentleman whose acquaintance she'd made at the Wembley ball, Mr. Adair, had failed to call on her, and she couldn't imagine that any other men were likely to view her as a suitable match either. Especially when she only had a modest dowry as a result of the financial difficulties her family had experienced.

"What's your opinion of him?" She valued her mother's input, so if she had concerns, it would give Kate cause to reassess her initial thoughts.

Lady Drake set her empty glass down on a tray as a server walked past. "I expected someone with his reputation to be more hot-tempered. He hasn't raised his voice once in my hearing, and I'm inclined to think that Andrew might be correct in saying that he is probably blameless in his wife's death."

Kate nodded. While she wasn't certain of Lord Blackwell's true disposition, she'd come to a similar conclusion.

"He seems a very somber sort," Lady Drake mused. "He isn't who I would've envisioned for you, but from what I can tell, his estate is well maintained and profitable, his finances are in good order, and Andrew hasn't uncovered any dark secrets other than what we're already aware of. You could do worse."

Yes, she could, and Kate was beginning to think it likely she *would* do worse if she didn't accept him. If her choices were between men she'd already decided she wasn't interested in—whichever lechers or title hunters might stoop to marrying a disgraced debutante—or him, then he was probably the best of the bunch.

"Brigid, Kate, it's so lovely to see you."

Both women turned toward the speaker, a pretty blond woman with deep blue eyes and a shy smile.

"Emma!" Kate exclaimed, automatically greeting Sophie's older sister with a hug. "I didn't expect you to be here tonight."

Lady Emma Stanhope, the Duchess of Ashford, shuffled closer to get out of the way of a couple who were passing by.

"Vaughan and I have an agreement to attend three balls each season. I love to dance, but he wishes he could avoid society entirely, so it's a compromise that works for both of us."

Kate looked around, searching for the dark imposing figure of the duke. "Where is His Grace?"

"He's getting me a piece of cake," Emma said, and Kate could hardly be surprised. Emma was the reason that Sophie had such a sweet tooth. Emma looked around, her lip curling disdainfully. "Ignore them all. I know it's hard, but you should just do what's best for you."

It was on the tip of Kate's tongue to ask whether that was what Emma had done, given they both knew she'd married someone she didn't particularly want to marry in order to protect her family, but she adored Emma and didn't want to make her friend uncomfortable, so she kept her mouth shut.

It did remind her, though, that both Emma and Amelia had married men they were uncertain of, and those marriages had worked out well for them. Both women loved their husbands, and their ridiculous husbands were completely besotted with them.

That sounded rather nice. She'd be happy to tread the same path if it led to happiness.

"Thank you for the advice," she said. "I'll keep it in mind."

Lord Blackwell returned Sophie to them and took his leave. The Duke of Ashford brought Emma her cake, and after she finished eating it, he led her onto the dance floor. Kate watched them go, feeling wistful. What she wouldn't give for a husband who looked at her the way the duke looked at Emma. As if she was the only thing in the world that mattered.

Miss Francine Thompson, one of the girls she had been friendly with last season, joined them with a petite brunette who looked far too young to be on the hunt for a husband.

"Are you marrying Lord Blackwell?" Francine asked

beneath her breath. "Aren't you afraid he'll push you off a cliff or have you trampled beneath a carriage?"

Kate stiffened. "Lord Blackwell has given me no reason to fear for my safety. He's been perfectly polite every time we've interacted."

The looks they gave her reminded her that though nothing had happened between them, it wasn't what society believed. They thought he'd debauched her on a balcony.

"He *has* been," she insisted.

Francine's friend's eyes widened comically. Kate followed her gaze and found Lord Blackwell hovering behind Sophie, a glass in his hand.

"I thought you might like some lemonade," he said awkwardly, extending the glass to Kate.

She took the drink from him, pretending not to hear Francine and the other girl tittering.

"Is everything all right?" he asked, his eyebrows drawn together as he glanced between them.

"Entirely." She drank the lemonade and turned her shoulder to Francine, not cutting her but showing that she didn't approve of the other woman's behavior.

Blackwell bowed to her. "I believe the next dance is a waltz. Will you join me?"

"I would be delighted to." She handed Sophie what remained of her lemonade, smiled at her mother, who was engaged in conversation with Lady Villiers, and took his arm.

As they got farther from the others, he leaned close and said quietly, "I apologize if my presence is causing you any distress."

"It isn't."

The attention wasn't comfortable, but she could weather it, and, if he really were nothing more than a victim of vicious gossip and unsubstantiated rumors, then he deserved better than the treatment he received from others. He didn't seem concerned with making that happen himself, so if she were to marry him, it would have to be her job.

They moved into position together, and she breathed in his minty, fresh scent, grateful that he had better hygiene than some of the other men of the *ton*. It was somewhat stuffy in the ballroom, and even though the smell of the shrubbery overwhelmed most things, many of the men present still had a detectable odor of sweat.

The music started. Lord Blackwell waltzed more gracefully than he'd danced earlier, perhaps because there were fewer steps to remember. The heat from his body enveloped Kate, lulling her into a state of contentment she'd not expected to feel tonight.

She smiled to herself. If she could feel this way even in the midst of the scandal, then there was potential for her happiness to grow exponentially.

And that was how she knew.

She was going to marry this man.

She didn't tell him so right then, though. She waited until they had a moment to themselves on the edge of the dance floor with no one around to overhear them, or at least, no one paying quite so much attention.

She nibbled on her lip, a little nervous about how he was going to react. "If your offer still stands, I would like to accept and become your viscountess."

His eyes widened but he nodded. "It does. When shall I call on you to discuss the particulars?"

"Come by tomorrow. I'll have had time to tell my brother by then."

Hopefully, Andrew wouldn't react poorly to the news.

CHAPTER 13

Theo strode past Albert and went directly to his office, where he managed to find the brandy in the dark, pour himself a healthy portion, and toss it back. The brandy burned down his gullet, but it wasn't enough. He poured another and drank that too.

"Is everything all right, my lord?" Albert asked from behind him.

With a sigh, Theo turned toward him. Albert was silhouetted in the doorway by the faint flickering light from the hall. He couldn't make out many of his butler's features, but his hands were clasped nervously in front of his large belly.

"Come tomorrow, I'll be betrothed." Theo weighed the bottle of brandy with one hand, noting there was still plenty left, and considered pouring himself the third.

"Congratulations, sir!"

Even though he couldn't see Albert's face, he could tell that Albert was far more excited about the prospect of having a mistress of the house than he was. No doubt many of the household staff would feel the same. They liked having a lady around, and his mother didn't fill the role the same way she used to.

"Yes, well," he said distastefully. "Let's not get ahead of ourselves. There's still a chance she'll change her mind."

Albert pressed his palms together. "I'm sure she won't. What lady of good breeding wouldn't be thrilled to have Viscount Blackwell as a husband?"

Theo snorted. "You know my reputation just as well as I do, Albert."

"Perhaps, my lord. But I also know you don't deserve it. I look forward to learning more about your intended. For now, shall I have Barlow sent to your room?"

"No, thank you." Theo had dismissed his valet earlier in the day and told him to take the night off. He wouldn't disturb the man now even if it would be convenient to have his assistance.

He glanced at the bottle. Unless he wanted to down it all and wallow like a drunkard, he supposed there was nothing for it now but to go to bed and hope things looked better in the morning. He really, really didn't want to be responsible for ruining the life of another woman he cared about, and he'd already grown to like Lady Katherine.

Unfortunately, she'd made her choice.

He dismissed Albert, dragged himself to his bedchamber, and was relieved to find that a candle was burning on the nightstand and his nightclothes were set out for him. He began unbuttoning his shirt, his fingers fumbling thanks to the drinks he'd downed, but he stopped when he realized there was a lump on his bed.

He tensed and raised his fists, prepared to demand the intruder explain himself, but relaxed when he realized it was Nicholas. His brother lay face down, his cheek turned to the side, his mouth hanging open and his eyes closed.

Rolling his eyes, Theo leaned over and poked Nicholas. His brother jolted awake and scrambled into an upright position.

"You got what you wanted," Theo said, uncharacteristic

bitterness flooding him. "Come morning, Lady Katherine Drake will officially agree to become the new viscountess."

Nicholas grimaced, and his gaze was wary as he took Theo in. "I truly think this marriage could make you happy again," he said after a long pause. "I'm sorry for the way it happened, but won't you give it a chance?"

Theo sat on the edge of the bed and fought to remove his boots as he considered Nicholas's words. If he was backed into a corner, it made sense to try to make the most of it, but he wasn't sure if he was capable of that kind of optimism.

He wrestled one boot off and then the other and flopped onto the bed beside Nicholas. "I'm afraid I'll fail her like I did Elizabeth."

"Oh, Theo." Nicholas patted his shoulder. "What happened to her wasn't your fault. It wasn't hers either. It was just terrible luck."

Theo closed his eyes. "If I'd responded differently, then she might not have gone down the path she did."

"Or it might not have changed anything at all." Nicholas scooted back down so they were lying side by side. "No one can know these things."

"I just wish I'd…."

That he'd what, exactly?

That he'd stopped trying to manage the estate he'd suddenly found himself in charge of and fussed over her instead? He'd done his best to coddle and care for her regardless of his other obligations.

Perhaps he wished that his father had never gone over that cliff. He should have lived for years to come, but he couldn't deny that if he and Elizabeth were going to have difficulty conceiving, it would have eventually become an issue regardless of whether his father lived or died.

Nicholas sighed. "You know what they say. If wishes were horses, beggars would ride. You can't go back. Why not make this a fresh start?"

"Because I don't know how to do better." If he didn't know what he'd done wrong, he couldn't avoid repeating the same mistake, and he couldn't stand to see the light slowly fade from Lady Katherine's clever gray eyes.

"I have faith in you," Nicholas said.

"You'd be the only one."

In truth, Nicholas was the one who'd do better with a wife. Perhaps Theo shouldn't have been so quick to martyr himself. Nicholas was charming, and thoughtful when he wanted to be. Lady Katherine might have been happy with him, and given what he now knew of her guardian, the earl likely wouldn't have pressed for her to wed Theo for the sake of his title.

It was too late for that now though.

"Do you wish to marry?" he asked, sure he knew the answer but needing the confirmation to quiet his agitation.

Nicholas snorted. "Me? Dear God, no. I'm too much for any Mayfair miss to handle."

But Theo couldn't help noticing a trace of something unfamiliar in his voice.

"Did I make a mistake in offering for her?"

Nicholas huffed. "If you wish to get out of the situation, I will do my duty, but I have no desire for your future bride."

Theo fell silent. They lay together without speaking until, eventually, sleep claimed him.

He woke alone, with a bitter taste in his mouth. He was cold despite the fact that someone—presumably Nicholas— had pulled a blanket over him during the night. He stretched, wiped his bleary eyes, and called for his valet.

Barlow helped him out of his clothes with a raised eyebrow and a slightly judgmental look. He assembled a new selection of clothing—one that was fit for calling upon an earl—while Theo cleaned his teeth and performed his morning ablutions.

He dressed with a little assistance and wandered down to

breakfast, surprised to find Nicholas already seated at the table with a cup of tea in front of him. He'd assumed that his brother would be sleeping in his own bed for a few more hours.

"Have you thought about what I said last night?" Nicholas asked, pushing his chair back and rising to his feet as Theo entered.

"About what?" Theo asked, too emotionally exhausted to figure out Nicholas's meaning.

"About giving your marriage a real chance." Nicholas went to the sideboard and served himself eggs and sausage. "Don't dismiss the possibility that this could be a happy occurrence."

Theo fixed himself a cup of tea and followed suit. They sat opposite each other. Theo didn't reply to Nicholas. His brother already knew his thoughts on the matter.

Nicholas speared a piece of sausage on his fork and waved it at Theo. "You should at least throw an engagement ball to prove that you aren't ashamed of the match and that nothing nefarious has happened between you. Lady Katherine deserves that. Especially because the ball would ensure a delay before the wedding, which would show the *ton* that there's no reason to rush to the altar, thereby preserving her reputation."

Theo narrowed his eyes at Nicholas. His brother had a lot of suggestions for a person who'd gotten him into this mess in the first place.

Although… he had a good point.

If Theo threw an engagement ball and delayed the wedding for a few weeks while the banns were read and they made preparations, it would go a long way to mitigating any damage to Lady Katherine's reputation, which would, in turn, ensure their marriage started off on a better foot.

No, he did not particularly wish to marry, but he also

didn't want his future viscountess to be miserable if it could possibly be avoided.

"Fine, I'll host a ball." It was the only concession he'd make for now.

"I think that's wise."

Theo gave Nicholas a look, and he promptly shut his mouth. Theo turned his mind to the ball. He'd have to do this intelligently. They'd need to invite several core members of the *ton*, but he wasn't going to welcome any nosy gossips into his home if they might make Lady Katherine uncomfortable or try to pry into his personal affairs.

Nicholas would have a better idea than Theo of who might suit. If only he could introduce his brother to Lady Katherine and allow them to put together the guest list. Unfortunately, he had a suspicion that keeping Nicholas and Lady Katherine apart was the wisest course of action for now.

After breakfast, Theo summoned a carriage to take him to Longley House. His chest was tight and his heart heavy with an impending sense of doom as he marched up the stairs and knocked on the door.

The butler—whose sneer revealed he was unimpressed by Theo—took him through to the drawing room to wait while he fetched Lady Katherine. He sat on one of the chaises in front of the black-and-green marble fireplace and checked the time. It was slightly earlier than he'd usually make a social call, but his anxiety would have had even more time to build if he'd waited for another hour before coming.

When Lady Katherine walked in, she wore a simple blue day dress with her hair loose around her shoulders. It gleamed in the sunlight like burnished gold, and he wondered how soft it would be if he ran his fingers through it.

She curtsied. "Good morning, my lord."

He stood and bowed. "Good morning, Lady Katherine."

She crossed the room and sat opposite him, bringing with her the faintest scent of something floral. "Have you come to speak with Andrew?"

He nodded and lowered himself back onto the chaise. "Before doing so, I wanted to make sure you are certain of your decision and haven't had a change of heart overnight."

Please let her have had a change of heart.

She smiled, her expression serene. "I'm comfortable with my decision, but thank you for checking."

His breakfast threatened to rise up the back of his throat, but he tried to keep it from showing. "Very well, then. I will speak with the earl at once. Is he in his office?"

"He will be by now. Boden will have warned him of your arrival. Let me walk you there."

They both rose and strolled side by side out of the drawing room and along the corridor.

She paused outside. "Thank you."

He wasn't quite sure what she was thanking him for. Doing the honorable thing, perhaps. Whatever the case, he nodded in acknowledgement, then knocked.

"Come in," the Earl of Longley called from within.

Lady Katherine backed away, and Theo pushed the door open, the question flashing briefly through his mind as to whether it would be too late to drop this whole situation on Nicholas's lap and flee for the country.

He entered.

Andrew Drake sat behind his desk, his usually warm hazel gaze shrewd and assessing. "Please have a seat."

Theo dropped onto the visitor's chair and got straight to it. Better to get this conversation over and done with quickly. "I'm here to ask for your blessing to marry Lady Katherine."

Andrew tilted his head to the side. "She has made it clear to me that she's amenable to the match."

"Excellent."

Andrew rested his hands on the desk. "I'd like you to

know that I never believed that nonsense about you being involved in the deaths of your father or wife."

Theo frowned. That was an unexpected comment. "I'm glad to hear it."

Andrew cocked his head. "Quite honestly, I think it's ridiculous that anyone ever suggested you might be involved in your father's death. I suspect it never would have happened if not for the unfortunate circumstances of the former Lady Blackwell's demise. Once the gossips sink their teeth into something, they love to make it seem as dramatic as humanly possible and that was fuel to a fire."

Theo thought much the same. There had never been any hint that people questioned his father's death until after he'd ridden into South Wye with Elizabeth's body that fateful day.

Andrew's eyes narrowed and his lips flattened. "That said, I get the impression you're somewhat of a reluctant groom. If you go through with this marriage, I don't want Kate to bear the brunt of that. I expect you to do everything you can to ensure her happiness."

"I will." Theo may not want a wife, but he'd do his best to provide and care for one. He wasn't cruel, just jaded.

Andrew held his gaze for a long moment before nodding. "Then I consent to the marriage. What time frame do you have in mind?"

"Perhaps a month," Theo suggested. "If we marry in early December, we'll still have time to travel to the country before Christmas, and wedding preparations won't be too rushed either."

"Early December is acceptable to me."

"Good." Theo's head spun. Was this actually happening? "I'd also like to host an engagement ball. Perhaps that could be a week or two prior to the wedding?"

"Interesting idea." Andrew sounded like he approved. "That will certainly make all of this seem less scandalous. I'll call for Kate. It would be a disservice to discuss her wedding without her present."

Once again, Theo was caught off guard by the other man's attitude toward his sister. He wasn't trying to make decisions for her and was actively involving her in things that would affect her life. Theo respected that.

Perhaps, after all of this was done, he and Andrew could be friends. Although he had a feeling that it would take a lot to make up for jeopardizing Lady Katherine's—Kate's—reputation to begin with.

Andrew circled the table and opened the door. Kate must have been hovering not far away, because she joined them a moment later. Theo forced himself to smile at her as she pulled up a second chair and Andrew returned to his seat behind the desk.

Andrew cleared his throat. "Kate, I have given Lord Blackwell permission to ask your hand in marriage. Do you still want to go through with this?"

Kate lit up, her smile radiant, her eyes bright. The expression—full of hope—hit Theo right in the chest and knocked the oxygen from his lungs.

Hell.

What on earth had he gotten himself into?

CHAPTER 14

Nerves clustered in Kate's gut as she knocked on the front door of Lord Blackwell's London residence with her sketchbook under her arm and waited for a response. It was the Monday after they'd come to an agreement about marriage, and the viscount had offered to show her and Lady Drake his ballroom so they could begin planning the engagement ball.

Kate was excited to see inside the house, since it would soon become her home whenever they stayed in London. She hoped it would be nice.

The door swung open, and the butler filled the frame. He was a short, rotund man with fluffy gray hair around the sides of his head and a shiny dome on top.

"Lady Katherine Drake and Lady Brigid Drake for Lord Blackwell," she said, handing him a calling card.

He smiled broadly, giving her the impression that he was the cheerful sort. "It's a pleasure to meet you, my lady." He bowed low. "And your esteemed mother too. I'm Mr. Albert Smith, but you may call me Albert."

Kate smiled back, charmed. "Lovely to make your

acquaintance, Albert. I'm sure we'll be seeing much more of each other."

He looked positively giddy. "Indeed we shall."

Kate's heart warmed. It was nice to know that even if Blackwell himself was hesitant about their nuptials, his household would likely be welcoming. She hadn't known whether they would be pleased to have a new lady of the house or if they'd feel she was replacing someone they cared for and give her the cold shoulder.

Lord Blackwell appeared behind Albert. His expression was difficult to read, as usual, and he inclined his head in greeting. "Good afternoon, Lady Katherine, Lady Drake."

She frowned, confused by his quick arrival, and before Albert had gone to fetch him too. Had he been waiting for them? Staying near the door, eager for their arrival? Such ponderings were likely nonsense, but it was sweet to imagine.

"Allow me to show you the ballroom," he said.

He gestured for them to follow him past an impressive staircase and to the right, where a pair of double doors opened onto a ballroom. The space wasn't as large as the one at Longley House, but it was lavishly appointed with a royal-blue-and-white patterned carpet and numerous shiny candelabras.

The walls were cream colored up to the tops of the windows and powder blue above, with octagonal white-and-blue tiles on the ceiling and elaborate white molding in the center with a chandelier hanging from it. Thick curtains, a shade between cream and gold, framed each window, and there was decorative metalwork forming a floral design above each that was similar to the one on the carpet.

Light streamed in, and the air was warm, as if it captured heat from the sun and held it. There was an ornate fireplace set into one wall.

Kate loved the room on sight. Blue was one of her favorite colors, and, given the way that color combined with the shades of cream and gold as well as the quality of the furnishings, she knew she wouldn't change a thing even if she were given leave to redesign the space from scratch.

"You may decorate however you see fit," Blackwell said, interrupting her silent appreciation. "Please don't worry about the cost. While Blackwell isn't the wealthiest estate in the country, you certainly won't want for anything."

Kate's heart sang. While she knew he was referring to material items, his words still made her feel like he cared for her. He might not show it in typical ways, but nor did the Duke of Ashford, and Emma was blissfully happy with him. Perhaps Kate could have that too.

Lady Drake wandered the length of the room from one end to the other. Kate circled around, feeling in her soul that this was exactly where she was supposed to be. Perhaps her first meeting with Blackwell and their subsequent courtship had been unconventional, but all of her instincts said that this was right.

"What do you think?" she asked her mother, interested to hear her opinion.

Lady Drake ran her fingers over one of the silken curtains. "This is your engagement ball, which means you get to make the decisions. If it were me, I'd keep the decor relatively simple. No dragging in entire shrubs. Perhaps some elegant roses or, depending on how difficult they are to source, snowdrops."

"I agree." Kate put her hand on her hip as she evaluated the room with a critical eye. "If we were to introduce too many other elements, it would look busy. I think snowdrops or white roses would suit nicely. The guest list could be reasonable but not massive. Perhaps a hundred people."

Lady Drake turned to Lord Blackwell. "What do you think?"

His gaze was dark and unfathomable. "Whatever you think is best. I know that balls here have hosted upward of one hundred guests in the past, provided the connecting room is open, so you need not worry about that as a limitation."

"Whatever we think is best?" Kate made her way toward him, a mischievous smile lifting her lips. "That's an awfully dangerous promise to make, Lord Blackwell. What if I were to suggest several dozen arrangements of lilies and an indoor koi pond with real fish?"

Such things had been known to exist. Kate had always thought it ridiculous, although she did concede that the goldfish were very pretty and nice to watch.

One of his eyebrows inched up ever so slightly. "Then I would do my best to make that happen."

"And what if I were to decide I wanted everything in brilliant shades of pink and orange?" she challenged.

He tipped his head. "If that was your wish, I would honor it."

"Hmph." She wasn't sure why she'd expected a different answer except that she'd have thought that the gentleman with the fashionably colored cravat she'd first met at the Wembley ball would have at least some kind of opinion about the decor for his engagement ball—or perhaps some basic concerns about good taste. He'd seemed the type.

Just another way Viscount Blackwell confused her.

"Perhaps we could have musicians in that corner," Lady Drake said, diverting Kate's attention from the viscount.

"Let me draw it out." There were chairs along the far side of the room, so Kate sat on one and perched the sketchbook on her knee. With a few simple lines, she sketched the general layout of the ballroom. She added basic figures for the musicians in the corner her mother had indicated and drew small floral arrangements where she thought they might best be placed.

Lady Drake stood near her shoulder. "I think that will do nicely."

"May I see?"

Kate jolted, surprised to realize Lord Blackwell was standing right in front of her. He extended his hand, and she passed him the sketchbook.

He made a sound in the back of his throat. "This is very good. You're quite talented."

Heat suffused Kate, and her stomach flipped over. She ducked her head, noticing that her mother was watching her in a knowing way.

"Thank you, my lord."

He handed the sketchbook back. "I look forward to seeing more of your drawings."

She was oddly excited to show him. He seemed as if he'd be an appreciative audience.

"Would you like a tour of the rest of the house?" he asked as she added another embellishment to one of the flower arrangements—the centerpiece.

"Oh, yes, please." She hurried to her feet and dropped the sketchbook to the side, worrying belatedly that she'd smudged it, but when she checked, the lines were still clear. Not that it mattered. The drawing was purely practical. She'd just rather not realize later that her hands were covered in gray and she'd accidentally gotten it on her face.

"As you can see, there's a room adjoining this one that can be either used as an extension of the ballroom or closed off as a smaller room for entertaining guests." He led them through the second room and back into the hall. "My study is at the end of the corridor."

They followed him back into the foyer and down a hall on the other side of the main staircase. He opened each door as they passed and let them look inside. There was a drawing room, a morning room, a formal dining room, and a more casual family room. The rooms farther along were used by staff.

As he guided them up the stairs, Kate tried to recall the basic layout of the rooms so she wouldn't get lost in future. It seemed straightforward enough.

"The family rooms are to the left." He gestured along the corridor. "To the right is the library, upstairs family room, and the room where my mother likes to sit in the window and embroider as she watches the world go by."

Kate frowned. She didn't think she'd met the dowager viscountess. "Is your mother currently in London?"

"No, she's at Blackwell Hall in Oxfordshire. She usually resides there unless she's visiting friends in London or Bath. It's where she feels closest to my father."

Her heart squeezed. "That's sweet."

The viscount shrugged one shoulder. "She'll come to London for the wedding, if not beforehand, so you can meet her then."

"Will she want to attend the engagement ball?" Lady Drake asked.

Blackwell pursed his lips. "I'll invite her, but I can't be certain."

Kate didn't understand that. Surely most mothers would be eager to celebrate their child's engagement. If her father were alive, no one would have been able to stop him from being there, but not all aristocratic families were as close as hers. In fact, many weren't.

It made her a little sad for him to think that his might be one of them. Never mind. When they were married, he'd have her family to make up for any shortcomings.

They wandered into the family wing, and Blackwell pointed at each door in turn, indicating which were guest bedrooms and which were reserved for particular members of the family. They didn't enter any, but Kate hadn't expected to. That would come after they were married.

"What about that one?" she asked, realizing that he hadn't mentioned one of the doors they'd passed.

He hesitated. "Uh, that one is my brother's."

"Oh." She'd almost forgotten he had a brother. He never mentioned it, and she hadn't thought to ask for details. "Is he in London too?"

A long pause followed her question.

Finally, Blackwell said, "Yes, but he's currently out, so unfortunately I can't make introductions."

"I'm sorry to hear that. I hope I'll meet him before the wedding."

"We shall see." His tone became brisk. "Let's return to the ballroom and discuss the wedding itself."

He started back along the corridor, and she hurried to keep pace with him, glancing at her mother over her shoulder. Lady Drake arched an eyebrow inquisitively. Kate widened her eyes in response, relieved to know that she wasn't the only one who'd found Blackwell's reaction strange.

There was something off about this family. She just couldn't put her finger on what it was. Perhaps once she met his mother, everything would fall into place.

"Would you like a large or small wedding?" Blackwell asked as they started down the stairs.

"I'd prefer it to be small." She lifted her skirt with one hand so as not to trip over it. "Family and close friends. Do you have a preference?"

He looked over at her. Some of the tension had left his features, and his crooked smile made her insides fizz. "I agree. Small would be best."

"Not a society wedding at St. George's?" Disappointment laced Lady Drake's voice.

Kate sent her an apologetic look. "No, but regardless of how many people we invite, I'd like a beautiful gown. Something I've designed myself."

"Then you shall have it," Blackwell declared. "I'd love to see what you come up with."

This time, Lady Drake's arched eyebrow had nothing to do with strangeness and everything to do with the unspoken implication of Lord Blackwell's words. He supported Kate's hobbies, and he didn't think less of her for being so interested in something that could be seen as either trivial or beneath her status.

Kate hid her smile. She was still nervous about marrying him, but every time they were together, she became more certain that she was making the right decision. Her instincts told her that despite his dark reputation and stoic demeanor, Lord Blackwell was a good man.

He led them into the drawing room, and they all sat. She wished he hadn't left such a space between them, as she enjoyed the tingles and flutters his presence caused in her.

"You should also give me a list of what will make you more comfortable here," he continued as if their conversation had never paused. "I want you to feel at home."

Joy bubbled inside her. Yes, the viscount would be an excellent husband.

"I'll do that," she said warmly.

A figure walked past the open doorway. She only caught a glimpse of him, but something about him seemed out of place. He wasn't dressed in the servant's uniform, and his upright bearing suggested he was someone important. But who would be here other than the viscount?

"Is that your brother?" she asked, curious.

"Where?" Blackwell's gaze flew to the open doorway, and he paled. "I'm sure it was just one of the footmen."

"He wasn't wearing a uniform."

Blackwell went to the door and closed it. "Perhaps he was off duty."

A furrow formed between her eyebrows. That man hadn't been a footman—she knew he wasn't—and the fact that

Blackwell closed the door so she wouldn't see him pass by again was concerning.

What was Lord Blackwell hiding?

CHAPTER 15

London
December 1822

KATE COULDN'T TELL WHETHER THE TANGLE OF KNOTS IN HER gut was caused by excitement or nerves. Their carriage stopped outside Blackwell House, and she waited for Andrew to get out first and then help Amelia, their mother, and herself down.

Goose bumps prickled her skin, and she rubbed at her bare upper arms. It was a cold evening, already dark because of the heavy cloud cover, and a light drizzle fell as they strode to the front entrance, which stood open.

Albert hastened them inside to escape the inclement weather. He closed the door behind them and bowed low. "Lord Blackwell is in the ballroom."

At that moment, the man in question entered the foyer, giving the lie to Albert's words, and paused, his gaze caught on her. She squirmed as his dark eyes heated.

"You are exquisite, Lady Katherine," Blackwell said.

She shivered, and not from the cold this time. He had a

way of making her feel like the only thing he saw. "Thank you, my lord. You look very handsome."

It was true. He'd dressed in a suit she suspected was new, although it was as monochromatic as the others she'd seen him wearing since the Wembley ball. From what she'd come to know about him, it truly was strange how flamboyant his attire had been that night.

His gaze lingered on her dress, and she wondered what he thought of it. She'd designed the mint green gown with pale blue trim to complement her coloring and emphasize her slim waist, but she had no idea whether he noticed any of that.

"Is this one of your designs?" he asked.

"Yes, although Madam Baptiste helped. I showed her drawings of my vision, and she made it a reality." Kate truly appreciated the modiste's patience with her. She knew that most young ladies tended to give her far fewer instructions or suggestions, but Madam Baptiste had never made Kate feel like a nuisance.

He met her eyes again, and something in them softened. "It seems I'm to have an extremely talented wife."

Kate's heart lifted and she smiled so widely it almost hurt. She really was fortunate to have found such a man, however it came about.

He turned to her family. "Thank you for coming, Lord Longley, Lady Longley, Lady Drake."

"I'm glad to be in out of the cold," Andrew said. "It's deuced bad weather."

"Well, it is winter," Amelia pointed out. "It's only to be expected."

Albert cleared his throat, and Blackwell glanced over. The butler had been joined by a woman of average build, slightly soft around the middle, with well-worn features and neat brown hair.

Blackwell gestured to them. "Please allow me to introduce my butler, Albert, and the housekeeper, Mrs. Taylor. If any last-minute changes are needed prior to the ball, Mrs. Taylor will be able to assist."

Mrs. Taylor curtsied. "I'm more than happy to help. It's a right pleasure to know that Blackwell House will have a mistress again."

Kate nodded to her. "Lovely to meet you, Mrs. Taylor. I look forward to speaking with you more in future."

It was important she establish a good relationship with the housekeeper as soon as possible, as the servants would largely take their cue from her and Albert, who'd thankfully already made his approval clear.

"Let's go through." Blackwell backtracked to the ballroom.

Kate watched him go, wondering at the figure beneath his well-tailored clothes. He had broad shoulders and a trim waist, but she had no idea what to expect beyond that. She'd never seen an undressed man before. Hopefully he wasn't the sort to be overly formal with his wife, because she was rather eager to learn.

As she entered the ballroom, a wall of warm air greeted her. It emanated from a fire that burned from within a gilded marble fireplace and from the dozens of candles that illuminated the space, casting the blue and cream carpet and curtains in a golden light.

Bouquets of white roses and sprigs of snowdrops were positioned around the arches and doorways and on some of the small tables around the edges of the room. Space had been cleared in one corner for the musicians, who were in the process of tuning their instruments. The soft tinkle of piano notes and the rich chords of a violin thrummed in the air.

Kate adjusted a sprig of snowdrop that was slightly askew and wandered to the adjoining room to check the refreshments table. The food hadn't been brought out yet, but lemonade and ratafia were waiting by a tower of delicate wineglasses for guests to help themselves.

"We'll put the fire out after the first few guests arrive."

Kate jumped at Blackwell's voice so close to her. She hadn't heard him approach.

"It'll be too hot once everyone is here otherwise. Especially after the dancing begins."

She nodded. "It was a good idea to light it for long enough to warm the ballroom."

He shrugged. "It was Mrs. Taylor's suggestion. I'm not sure I'd have thought of it."

Somehow, Kate suspected that he wasn't giving himself enough credit.

"It came together well," Kate said, referring to the decorations.

He smirked. "You have a good eye. With you and Lady Drake in control, I never expected anything less."

She rolled her eyes. "You flatterer."

She couldn't deny the way his compliment made her heart skip. He'd always been polite and solicitous with her, but she didn't get the impression he was one to say things he didn't mean.

"Would you like a drink before we start?" he asked. "If you don't feel like lemonade or ratafia, there's sherry in my office. I think we deserve it."

"Sherry?" Lady Drake appeared beside them. "I'd appreciate a glass."

Kate giggled. "I'll have one too."

She still wasn't sure whether she actually liked the sweet burn of sherry, but she certainly didn't *dislike* it. She thought she might acquire a taste for it if she gave it a chance.

Amelia and Andrew joined them, arm in arm. It was the first time they'd both been away from George in the evening since they'd come to London. It was unusual for parents of their class, but they enjoyed spending time with him in the nursery and tucking him into bed. Kate was glad they'd offered to come tonight, though. Her family shouldn't miss her engagement ball.

Amelia pulled a face. "I think I'll just have lemonade, thank you."

"What about you, Longley?" Blackwell asked.

"Sherry sounds brilliant," Andrew replied.

Blackwell called Mrs. Taylor over. "Could you please fetch us four glasses of sherry."

"Of course, my lord."

"Will I meet your brother tonight?" Kate asked Lord Blackwell.

His eyebrows knitted together. "Unfortunately not. Nicholas traveled to Oxfordshire to escort Mother to Town, and they have not arrived yet."

Kate hid her disappointment. She was yet to meet any of Lord Blackwell's family, and she was eager to learn more about him.

When Mrs. Taylor returned with the tray of drinks, she offered it to Blackwell first and then Kate. She took her glass and raised it to her lips, catching Blackwell's gaze as she tipped the glass back. He raised his glass in a silent toast, never taking his eyes from hers. Her heart lifted, and she felt lighter than air.

Albert interrupted the moment. "Lord and Lady Carlisle have arrived with Lady Sophie."

Kate emptied her glass and placed it back on Mrs. Taylor's tray. "We should welcome our first guests."

They made their way to the front door, where the Carlisles were waiting. Sophie beamed and waved at Kate when she caught sight of her.

"Hi, Sophie," Kate said, gliding over to her. "I'm so glad you're the first people here."

It would be reassuring to know that they had some support present before the rest of the *ton* descended. Not that anyone had made untoward comments or implied the betrothal was anything less than *de rigueur*—at least, not to her face. She still couldn't help but feel that they were whispering about her behind her back.

"I could hardly be late," Sophie exclaimed, looking around with interest. "You're essentially the hostess of this event. How exciting is it to have that role when you haven't even married yet?"

Kate tried not to smile too widely. "It's quite amazing."

She liked that she was permitted to play hostess tonight. If the dowager viscountess had arrived in London, that would be her role, but she was yet to turn up.

Kate turned her attention to Lord and Lady Carlisle only to find that her fiancé was welcoming them with that slight upward tilt of his mouth that passed for a smile.

The rumble of carriage wheels signaled the arrival of more guests, and Kate positioned herself to Blackwell's right, ready to fulfill her welcoming duties. She half expected Andrew and Amelia to join them, but they walked with the Carlisles into the ballroom, leaving Lady Drake with Kate and Blackwell.

"I'd better follow them," Sophie said, nodding toward her parents. "I'm under strict instructions to behave myself tonight. Who knows? Maybe I'll meet a handsome rogue on a balcony too."

Kate snorted. "Not tonight, you won't. The external doors are remaining firmly closed. It's far too cold out there to have them open."

Not to mention the fact that she'd rather her friend not get herself ruined at her engagement ball.

Sophie hurried to catch up with Lord and Lady Carlisle, and Kate fixed a smile on her face to greet Francine Thomson and her mother. She narrowed her eyes, silently warning Francine not to make any comments like the one she previously had about Lord Blackwell tossing people off cliffs. If they'd been alone, she'd have come straight out and told the other woman to keep her opinions to herself.

She and Blackwell stood in place at the entrance for far too long before joining the merriment in the ballroom. Once they were free of their duties, Kate got herself a lemonade and drank it quickly, her throat parched after talking so much.

She was grateful to be done with that part of the evening. Even though everyone had been polite, she could tell that some of them thought she was a fool for marrying Blackwell, and others thought she was a harlot for trapping him in the first place.

The people in the refreshments room parted as Blackwell walked in, clearing a path for him to walk straight to Kate. He didn't even seem to notice, his dark eyes never wavering from her.

He offered her his hand. "I've asked the musicians to play a waltz for the next dance. Would you like to join me?"

"I would love to." Kate laid her gloved palm on his and allowed him to draw her away from the table.

As they entered the ballroom, the song ended, and they found an empty patch of floor and arranged themselves while they waited for the next song to begin. When it did, she found herself being swept into an easy dance.

Blackwell moved gracefully, with no hesitation, and she wondered if he'd been practicing. He was rusty the last time they danced.

She peeked up at him and found him already watching her. Those dark eyes should have been cold, but somehow, they flooded her with warmth. His touch on her side was gentle but firm. They swayed together as if each one knew precisely where the other was about to put their feet.

It was enchanting.

She really had gotten lucky.

Even though they didn't speak, the silence didn't feel

awkward. As the dance ended and they linked arms and left the dance floor, she turned to him and asked, "Are all of your suits black, or do you have them in different colors?"

One corner of his mouth curled, as if he were amused. "Most of them are black. I have one gray and one dark blue. Does that bother you?"

"No, it just surprises me. I could have sworn you were wearing bright blue and pink when we met." Although perhaps he had cravats in other colors and just used them to bring more life to his darker suits. "You were quite unlike yourself that night."

Again, she got the impression there was something she was missing. Something important and right under her nose.

His expression didn't change, but he became almost preternaturally still. "As I said, I was a little inebriated."

She hesitated before asking the next question on her mind. "Is that something that happens often with you?"

She didn't think he would be an angry or violent drunk, and he came across as being too meticulous to allow himself to become sloppy, but if that was what she was getting into, she ought to know.

"No. I had some things on my mind that evening. It was nothing you need to be concerned with. I promise it won't affect our marriage."

She drew back, feeling slightly rebuked. It wasn't as if he'd told her not to pry, but she'd received that message anyway, loud and clear. She didn't like it, but she did believe him when he said that he didn't make a habit of becoming intoxicated.

"Would you like to dance again?" he asked, and she couldn't help but think that it was a distraction to end this line of questioning.

"No, thank you." She tried to smile but knew it didn't land quite right. "I'm a bit overheated. I might get another drink."

"Allow me to keep you company."

He escorted her to the drinks and offered her a lemonade, which she took and drained rapidly. It hadn't been a lie—she was thirsty. Unfortunately, the lemonade didn't take away her uncomfortable suspicion that Blackwell was keeping something from her.

"Please excuse me," she said. "I need to visit the retiring room."

She left before he could offer to walk her there or before he asked any other questions. She didn't go directly to the retiring room, though, but paused on the way to touch Sophie's arm and murmur in her ear that she needed to talk to her.

Sophie finished a conversation with a blond gentleman that Kate didn't recognize and fell into step beside her. Kate didn't speak until they were inside the retiring room and she had checked that they were alone.

"I think Blackwell is lying to me about something," she whispered, her eyes darting around to make sure no one could sneak up on them. "I don't know what, though."

Sophie's smile faded. "Do you want to call off the engagement?"

Kate considered that. "No, I don't think so, but it's making me uneasy. What if it's something serious, and I don't find out until after we're married? I'll have no way out."

Perhaps she was making this all sound a little bit more dramatic than it was, but her future was on the line. If Blackwell was keeping secrets, there was no knowing what they might be.

CHAPTER 16

Rain thundered down as Theo guided the horses along the
muddy road between Blackwell Estate and South Wye. Even
though it was only afternoon, the darkness from the storm clouds
above made it difficult for him to see.

A gust of wind dislodged a branch from a tree and hurled it
toward the carriage. The horses reared back and the wheels skidded
in the mud. Theo's heart lurched. Another branch followed, and a
moment later, the entire carriage toppled over.

Theo thudded to the ground, the impact driving the breath from
his lungs. He rolled over, groaning at the ache in his ribs, and froze
when the horses took off, dragging the overturned carriage behind
them. Even from here, he could see that part of the wood was
smashed in.

Frantic, he looked around for Elizabeth, but there was no sign
of her. She must still be inside.

He rushed after the carriage, making shushing noises to soothe
the horses. It was all he could do to keep up with them, but eventually, they stopped. He freed each one from their harness immediately to prevent them from doing any damage should they take off
again, then dropped to his knees. Water from a puddle soaked into
his trousers as he grabbed the window and ducked to look inside.

His stomach dropped as he struggled to absorb the sight before him. Elizabeth was wedged in the doorway, her lower body inside the carriage while her upper body must be on the other side of the door, having been dragged between the carriage and the road.

He got out and struggled to shove the carriage off her, to free her from its weight. He was too weak, so he grabbed a fallen branch and used it as a lever. When he finally pried it up, he used every ounce of strength he possessed to heave it off her.

The door opened, and she flopped onto the ground.

"No," he sobbed, his breath catching in his chest.

Her clothes were torn and shredded, stained with both mud and blood. Her face was scraped on one side, and blood soaked her hair and trickled down her forehead. Her eyes—usually such a rich shade of brown—gazed sightlessly into his own, a faint glassy sheen proving that he was too late.

She was already gone.

He clambered over to her and felt for a pulse. When there was nothing, he put his ear to her mouth, desperate to feel her breath on his cheek, hoping with every fiber of his being that he was wrong. But as he drew back, her features changed. They formed a pointed chin and high cheekbones, the blank eyes switching from brown to gray.

Lady Katherine.

Dear God, she was dead. He'd lost her just as he'd lost Elizabeth.

He bolted upright, his shirt clinging to his torso, which was drenched with sweat. His heart hammered wildly, and he looked around, unable to relax until he'd confirmed that he was in his own bedroom.

"It was just a dream," he whispered to himself. The words didn't make him feel any better, though. This time, it had been a dream, but there was nothing to say it wouldn't come true in the future.

Needing a physical release, he got up, wiped the sweat from his body, dressed in his boxing clothes, and made his way through the silent house. The gray light of dawn lit his way as he walked to the room where he went to wash away his sins.

He wrapped his hands and beat the boxing bag until his fists ached, his muscles screamed, and his breath came in ragged bursts. Slowly, the gray light brightened, and the faintest hint of blue sky became visible through the windows.

Mopping the sweat from his brow, he slunk to the stool and dropped onto it. He stared into space, willing the image of Lady Katherine's blank eyes to disappear from his mind. When that didn't happen, he undid his wraps and took them with him back to his bedchamber.

The sheets had been stripped from his bed and his bathtub had been filled while he was gone. One of the maids must have heard him in the boxing room—or, more likely, Mrs. Taylor had, since she seemed to know everything that went on in the house at all times.

He undressed, relieved that his blood was pumping from the exercise he'd just done, otherwise it might have been too cold in his room for comfort. He tossed the clothes where he'd discarded his fist wraps and got into the tub.

The water was warm but not hot, and a cake of soap had been left beside the tub. He washed himself with brisk movements, grimacing when he noticed that one of his knuckles had split. Hopefully no one would notice at the wedding tomorrow. The last thing his reputation needed was for him to look like he'd been in a brawl.

As it was, he'd noticed that Lady Katherine hadn't been herself at the engagement ball. They needed to hold everything together until after the wedding, which meant he couldn't draw attention to anything that could be considered inappropriate.

He stood, water sluicing from his body, and dried himself quickly as the droplets cooled on his skin. The hairs on his arms stood on end, and he rubbed them, then wound the towel around his waist before summoning his valet.

Barlow was a tall, thin man with a thick mustache and sideburns, his clothes as impeccably maintained as Theo's own. He helped Theo into his clothes for the day—he had to dress well, as he would be calling on his fiancée—and tsked at the sight of his knuckles.

"Would you like me to bandage that?" he asked, his nose turning up in clear disapproval. "If you leave it as it is, you might bleed on your white shirt."

Theo shook his head. "If you bandage it, then it will draw attention. I'd prefer no one to notice."

Barlow pursed his lips. "Then at least allow me to apply a salve to reduce the risk of bleeding."

"Thank you, that would be appreciated."

Theo sat on the end of the bed while Barlow pulled a small vial of salve from his pocket and knelt in front of him. Barlow smeared the clear salve over the cut on Theo's knuckles, then wiped his hands on a handkerchief and returned the vial to his pocket. Mrs. Taylor must have warned him that the salve might be needed in order for him to have been so prepared.

Theo thanked Barlow, dismissed him, and made his way downstairs for breakfast. Footsteps thumped on the stairs behind him, and he glanced over his shoulder as Nicholas hurried to join him.

"Excited for the big event tomorrow?" Nicholas asked, keeping pace as they reached the foyer and turned toward the dining room. He was, in fact, not on the way to London with their mother as Theo had told Lady Katherine. He had simply decided to lay low until they were wed so as not to confuse matters.

Once they were married, Theo would make introductions. Fortunately, Nicholas was in the process of growing a short beard so as to look as different from Theo as possible and please their mother.

"I'm not sure that 'excited' is the word I'd use." More like terrified. Stricken. In denial. "I can't believe I'm marrying again."

Theo's first wedding had been huge, with all of his family and many others in attendance. He was relieved this one would be smaller.

Back when he'd first married, Lady Blackwell had made a fuss about him and Nicholas both being at the wedding. She hadn't wanted them seen side by side in case her lie came out, but she was the one who'd insisted on a large wedding, and Theo wasn't marrying without Nicholas there.

It helped that they'd had their father around then. He'd simply reminded their mother that no one would be looking for evidence of a twenty-year-old deception and had suggested that Nicholas grow his hair and beard so they were not so obviously identical.

"I hope you won't regret it." Nicholas's smile disappeared. "I feel awful. It's my fault you're doing this."

"I made a choice," Theo reminded him. He could have simply ignored the whole thing, or forced Nicholas to wed Lady Katherine, but he hadn't. Ergo, he had no one to blame but himself.

They entered the dining room, and each fixed themself a plate of food from the side table. A pot of tea had been brewed and was sitting between their two place settings.

In an effort to distract from the impending nuptials, they discussed horses as they ate their breakfast. Nicholas enjoyed riding, although he did it far less frequently in London than he did in the country.

Theo was preparing to leave for Longley House when Albert tracked him down to his office.

"My lord, your mother is here," he said, wringing his hands.

Theo's head fell back, and he groaned. "Will she notice if I leave via the back exit?"

"Yes, I will," a firm female voice said from behind Albert. "Don't even think about running away, Theodore. We have matters to discuss."

Pulling a face, Theo gathered himself and nodded to Albert. "Thank you. Please inform the driver that I'll be delayed."

"Yes, my lord." Albert bowed and trotted away with more speed than he usually displayed. The butler had served his mother and father before serving Theo, and he hated any tension between the family members.

Lady Blackwell swept into the room, clad in a thick purple traveling pelisse. She'd worn shades of purple and gray ever since the death of his father despite the fact that the appropriate mourning period had long since passed.

She looked down her nose at him, which was a remarkable feat considering he was several inches taller than she, and narrowed her dark eyes. "What is the point of sending me an invitation to your wedding if you leave it so late that I'm unable to participate in the planning of the event?"

Theo darted a look at the drawer where he kept the brandy, wishing he'd had a nip to prepare himself for her interrogation. Leaving it too late had been precisely the point. Yes, he wanted his mother present at the wedding, but he hadn't appreciated her stance with regard to his marriage to Elizabeth and would prefer her to have as little input into this wedding as possible.

He'd never forgiven her for making such a display of the event in an attempt to prove she didn't care about the lower status of Elizabeth's birth when everyone knew she did.

"And what's all this about having a small wedding?" she demanded, putting her hands on her hips. "Your bride-to-be is an earl's sister. We should be celebrating the joining of our bloodlines in the most impressive manner possible."

He rolled his eyes. Of course she was happy to celebrate *this* marriage. It could only make their family look better in the eyes of the *ton*.

"Lady Katherine wants a small wedding, and that is what she'll have." He may not be able to give her everything he wanted to, but some things were within his power to provide, and he'd do so to the best of his ability.

"It is a shame you didn't summon me earlier. I could have talked her around. You know how adept I am at handling large affairs." Her gaze raked over him, and she finally seemed to notice he was dressed to leave. "Where are you on your way to, then?"

"I'm to call on Lady Katherine to confirm our plans for tomorrow. Mrs. Taylor has prepared your room for you if you wish to retire to catch up on rest. I'm sure your travels were wearying."

She looked at him as if he were crazy. "I'm coming with you. I must meet Lady Katherine. It wouldn't do for our first acquaintance to be after you're already married."

He swallowed. The last thing he wanted to do was inflict his mother on Lady Katherine at a time when she was probably already stressed. "I won't be staying for long. I'm sure they're quite busy today."

She flashed her teeth. "A quick visit is fine with me."

Damn, it seemed he wouldn't be getting out of this.

"Fine. Be ready to go in five minutes."

A short time later, Longley's butler showed them into a receiving room where Kate and Lady Drake were waiting for them. There was a tray of tea with three delicate teacups. Upon seeing his mother, Lady Drake rose and called for a maid to bring them another teacup.

Theo bowed. "Good afternoon, my ladies. May I introduce you to my mother, Lady Blackwell. Mother, meet Lady Drake and Lady Katherine Drake."

His mother nodded to them both respectfully. "I am so

pleased to meet you. I feared my son would never marry again, so it is a relief to know that his future is now in safe hands."

Kate smiled warmly. "I'm glad you were able to arrive on time. Would you like tea?"

"Yes, please, Lady Katherine. I take it with milk but no sugar."

Kate poured tea for each of them, proving silently that she remembered his preference before handing a cup to each of them. They sat opposite her and Lady Drake, and Theo could tell his mother was practically vibrating with excitement. Not only was Lady Katherine a member of the aristocracy, but she was also beautiful and poised.

She was practically Lady Blackwell's fondest wish for a daughter-in-law.

"Shall we run through the order of events for tomorrow?" Lady Drake suggested.

"I would be delighted to," his mother replied. "I have some suggestions if it's not too late to incorporate them."

An hour later, they'd gone through the necessary details, and, to his eternal gratitude, his mother hadn't made any unreasonable demands. She must have realized that it was too late for any significant changes, so she had only suggested ones that she thought they might agree to.

A maid came in with scones, jam, and clotted cream, and they took a break to eat. As Lady Drake was spooning jam onto a scone, Lady Katherine excused herself for a few minutes and Lady Blackwell took Theo aside, outside of Lady Drake's hearing range.

"She's very charming," she murmured, her eyes sparkling with excitement. "She's smitten with you too."

His blood froze. "Don't be ridiculous," he snapped. "She is not."

"Oh, but she is." His mother looked so very smug. "As a woman, I can read these things."

He bit his lip—hard—to avoid barking out the instinctive "She can't be."

She *could* be. They both knew it. He just didn't want her to be. If she wanted more than he was capable of giving, then she'd be miserable, and he would find himself in the same place he'd been before, with an unhappy wife and no idea of how to fix it.

The last thing he wanted was for history to repeat itself.

There was movement in the corner of his vision. Kate wandered back into the room, her eyes finding his immediately and a sweet smile crossing her face.

Oh no.

His muscles tensed. That smile wasn't one of someone who didn't care a whit for him. It was the smile of someone who—at the very least—*liked* him.

This was bad.

His mother squeezed his shoulder. "I told you so."

All of a sudden, he wished he was in his boxing room, where he could beat the stuffing out of the bag and find a way to feel better. Unfortunately, there was no escaping this.

His mother rejoined Lady Drake, and he forced his feet to follow her. He picked up a scone and took a bite of it, but it was all he could do to swallow. There was certainly no chance of him enjoying the treat.

They stayed for a while longer and made polite conversation. Every time he met Kate's eyes, he was viscerally aware of the fondness in them.

With each meeting of their gazes, he felt worse. This wasn't how it was meant to be. She hadn't liked him in the beginning, and while that was hardly an ideal state of affairs, he preferred it to the tentative hopefulness he saw in her expression now.

He had to get control of this. There had to be something he could do to ensure a safe emotional distance remained between them.

Then, it struck him.

As they were leaving, he took her aside and summoned all of his courage, hoping this wouldn't upset her. Whatever the case, it would be better to get it over with now and set the expectation between them rather than blindside her later.

"What is it?" she asked, a mix of curiosity and caution on her face.

He drew in a slow breath. "I think that perhaps after we're married, you should remain in London over Christmas. That way, you can be closer to your family. I intend to retire to the country estate in Oxfordshire."

She looked stricken. "But why? My family won't be here anyway. They're also going to the country."

Drat, he hadn't considered that possibility.

"You could go with them," he suggested.

Her eyes widened and her lower lip trembled. "Don't you want me to come with you?"

His heart squeezed. She was taking this as a rejection, and it killed him. "I just think it's for the best. Will you?"

Her lips pinched together, and she stalked away from him without a word.

CHAPTER 17

"WHAT ARE YOU IN A SNIT ABOUT?" AMELIA ASKED FROM where she stood in the doorway of Kate's bedroom the night before her wedding.

"Nothing," Kate replied irritably.

Amelia took a step inside. "Brigid and Andrew are worried about you. I am too. It's not too late to change your mind."

Kate crossed her arms, feeling far too vulnerable for this conversation. She'd already changed into her nightgown, and her hair had been brushed and hung loosely down her back. "So they sent you to figure out what's wrong with me?"

That was surprising, since communicating about feelings wasn't exactly Amelia's strong point.

Apparently reading Kate's thoughts, Amelia laughed. "I know, it seems strange, but Andrew is a man and doesn't understand the problems women face. He can't imagine what's going through your head right now. I can. I married someone I was uncertain of."

Ah, that made more sense.

"And Mother?"

Amelia raised one shoulder and dropped it. "She loved

your father dearly. She can relate to womanly problems more than your brother can, but she's never been in the situation we have. I know they aren't the same, but there are similarities."

That was true. Amelia's parents had forced her to marry. Her options had been few because most members of the *ton* looked down on her because she was the daughter of a businessman and not of their class. Andrew might not have even considered marrying her if he hadn't needed money to bail him out of a difficult financial spot.

Kate sighed. "When he visited earlier today, Lord Blackwell said that he would like me to remain in London or go with you to the country for Christmas rather than travelling to his estate in Oxfordshire. I know that he didn't plan to marry, but I didn't think he disliked me so much that he wouldn't even want me near him."

Amelia wandered over and sat on the edge of the bed. Kate sat beside her but kept a little distance between them, choosing to lean on one of the posts of the four-poster bed rather than on her sister-in-law. She felt too raw for any closeness right now.

She noted that Amelia's expression hadn't changed, and she frowned. "You expected this?"

"Not this, exactly," Amelia said, looking down at her hands. "But men can be foolish when their hearts are concerned."

Kate scoffed. "I don't think his heart is involved."

And that hurt. Not only her ego, but her feelings too. She'd thought they really could build a solid relationship, but if he wasn't willing to, then any efforts on her side would be doomed from the start.

Amelia turned to her. "Did you ever hear what happened between Emma and Ashford when they were first married?"

Kate cocked her head. "No. What do you mean?"

Amelia hesitantly reached out as if to place her hand on

Kate's, but then she stopped and withdrew it. "Ashford tried to leave her in the country while he returned to London. Emma was quite upset about it."

"What did she do?" It was difficult to believe that Ashford would ever want to be away from his wife. He doted on Emma.

"She told him that if he was going to be stubborn and go to London without her, then she was going to visit her sister, not sit around waiting for him to return when it suited him."

Kate grinned, pleased that Emma had stood up for herself. Their friend was lovely, and she deserved better than to be abandoned. "Good for her."

Amelia nodded in agreement. "In the end, Ashford came to his senses and won her back, but she didn't make it easy for him. My point is that Blackwell's suggestion today doesn't mean that he doesn't care about you, just that he doesn't know how to process his feelings."

"That does help, actually," she admitted.

If Emma and Ashford had gone through something similar and emerged with a happy marriage, then perhaps the same could happen for her and Blackwell, but only if she stood her ground and didn't let him dictate their future just because he was afraid of his emotions.

"Thank you."

"You're very welcome." Amelia's smile turned devilish. "If you really don't want to go through with the wedding, we can sneak you onto a ship bound for the Americas."

Laughter burst from Kate, and she didn't even try to stifle it. That was such a characteristically *Amelia* thing to say.

"You know what? I think we're going to be fine."

Amelia shifted closer. "I think so too."

Amelia left a short time later, and Kate put out the candles and got into bed, closing her eyes and wallowing in the familiarity of the soft mattress beneath her, the faint smell of flowers, and the way the house creaked as people moved around it.

Tomorrow, she'd be somewhere new. Somewhere with different noises and smells and feelings. She was nervous, but excited too. Her entire life was about to change, and her instincts told her she could be happy if she tried—provided Blackwell didn't let his reservations get in the way.

She dreamed of children with black hair and gray eyes.

In the morning, she rose early and ate breakfast, then retired to the bedroom with Margaret to prepare for the wedding. She studied the pink-and-white wallpaper, wondering how her new bedchamber would be designed. Perhaps it would be timeless and classic, or perhaps the previous Lady Blackwell had decorated to her tastes.

Whatever his hesitations about their marriage, Blackwell had given every indication that he would make things as comfortable for her as he could, so hopefully that extended to her being able to redo the room if it wasn't to her liking.

"As we practiced, my lady?" Margaret asked, picking up the ornate hairbrush from the dressing table and coming to stand behind Kate. Their gazes met in the mirror.

"Yes," Kate said. "You had it exactly how I pictured it."

She'd had Margaret dress her hair earlier in the week so that they could discuss any changes that might be needed if she didn't do it how Kate had envisioned. Fortunately, Kate's thorough description and the sketches she'd done had been enough for Margaret to get it right the first time around.

"Are you terribly excited?" Margaret asked, beginning to brush the length of her hair.

"I'm excited to wear the dress." Kate hadn't quite decided how she felt about the rest yet.

"I'm sure you'll be a beautiful bride."

"Thank you. I hope so."

Kate sat still as Margaret collected hairpins and held them in one hand as she gathered Kate's hair. She pinned it in place on the back of her head, leaving sections along the front and each side untouched. Once the majority of the hair was secure, Margaret wove a braid around it and added more pins to ensure that nothing would fall apart.

That done, the maid grabbed the heating iron and used it to curl the locks of hair along the side of her face, sweeping her fringe into the curls as well. Kate closed her eyes and held very still, aware of the heat emanating from the iron, warming her skin. She didn't want to twitch and inadvertently burn herself.

When Margaret was finished, Kate smiled at her reflection. Once again, Margaret had proved her skill. Curls framed her face and fell around her shoulders, while the back of her hair was up and off the nape of her neck. Rather elegant, if she did say so herself.

"Perfect," Kate said as Margaret held up a second mirror behind her so she could see the back.

Margaret grinned and stepped away to give Kate room to stand. With her hair done, all that remained was for Kate to don her wedding gown and jewelry and ride to the small church they'd chosen for the ceremony.

Margaret positioned the gown so that Kate could step into it and lifted it to help her slide her arms through the sleeves. Kate stood still while Margaret drew the laces tight and secured them down her back.

She hauled in a deep breath, surprised to find that her bosom looked larger than usual with the laces so tight around her waist. Fortunately, the constriction wasn't enough to hamper her breathing.

She watched her reflection as Margaret fussed about, ensuring the gown sat as it should. The layers of fabric against Kate's skin were relatively robust and a delicate shade of pink, while the upper layers were gauzier and floated around her. She'd had to have the fabric imported from the Continent, as it wasn't yet popular in England.

The sleeves were capped, and elaborate beading on the bust elevated the gown from eye-catching to stunning.

She loved it.

And she had just the right necklace to accompany it, thanks to Andrew and Amelia. When they'd seen the design, they'd bought her a three-tiered pink pearl necklace in the exact same shade as the dress.

Margaret fastened the pearls around her neck and then motioned for Kate to tilt her head so she could add the matching earrings. The last touch was a gold bracelet that encircled her right wrist. She was choosing to keep the left wrist bare, the better to emphasize her new ring.

Kate rolled her eyes at herself. She may not be selfish, but she could admit that she was a tiny bit materialistic in that she liked to look nice and put a lot of thought into her appearance. It wasn't the worst trait she could have, surely.

"Lift your foot so I can help you with your slipper?" Margaret asked.

Kate raised one foot and then the other, holding them aloft while Margaret slid the shoes—also pink—onto her feet. That done, she turned to her maid.

"Thank you, Margaret. You've gone above and beyond."

"You're welcome, my lady. If I may say, you look lovely."

"Thank you." Kate studied her for a moment. "I'll see you at Blackwell House tonight?"

"Indeed. My bags have already been sent over."

"I wish you all the best with settling in." Kate meant the words with every fiber of her being. She'd asked her maid to shift households with her, and to her delight, Margaret had been amenable. It was nice to know that she would have at least one familiar face in her new home.

Kate made her way downstairs to where her family awaited.

Amelia came over to greet her and offered her a sapphire hairpin. "Something borrowed, old, and blue to accompany your new necklace. If you'd like it. I know it may not suit."

Kate's heart warmed at the gesture. "I'd love to wear it. Will you pin it into the braid?"

She turned so Amelia could reach her hair and held still while she slid the pin into place.

"Now, are we ready to go?" Lady Drake asked, sweeping her hair off her shoulder. It had been pinned back, similar to Kate's, except where hers was held off her neck, her mother's cascaded down in loose ringlets.

"I believe so." Amelia circled around Kate to stand beside Andrew. "George is with the nanny, everyone is dressed, and the carriage is waiting."

"No second thoughts?" Andrew asked, his serious eyes conflicting with the light tone.

Her insides went soft. "No."

If she gave even the slightest impression she didn't want to go through with this, she had no doubt that he'd spirit her away. She was so lucky to have him as her guardian. She just hoped he was prepared for the little favor she'd be asking of him soon.

As they left the house, Boden called a blessing after them. She smiled to herself, pleased the overly proper butler cared enough to say anything that went beyond carrying out his duties.

Pink ribbon adorned the carriage, and it was warm inside, courtesy of the hot bricks beneath the seats. Considering the cool temperature outside, Kate was grateful for that.

She gazed out the window as they trundled down the street toward the church. People paused to watch them pass, knowing from the ribbons that they were headed somewhere important.

They stopped outside the church. It looked no different than usual. From outside, there was no way to tell that wedding guests waited in the pews. The church was stone, with an arched entrance and a decorative round window above the door.

"Ready?" Andrew asked.

"Er." Kate opened her hand to reveal the note she'd palmed prior to leaving her bedchamber. "Would you mind running this to Lord Blackwell for me?"

Andrew stared at her, his eyes wide. "I beg your pardon?"

"There's something I must know the answer to before we wed. I've written it on this note. Won't you take it to him please?"

Lady Drake groaned. "Please don't tell me you're going to stand him up at the altar."

"That isn't my plan." Although it might happen, depending on what Blackwell's response was. "Please, Andrew."

Andrew sighed and took the folded paper from her. "Is he going to flatten me when he reads this?"

"I don't think so." There was no way to know for sure.

He looked up at the ceiling as if begging God for patience. "The things I do for my family."

With that, he got out of the carriage and hurried through the arched entrance.

"What on earth are you about, Kate?" Lady Drake asked, her eyes narrowed.

Kate chose to look at Amelia rather than her mother. "I'm making a stand."

She wouldn't be separated from her new husband for whatever ridiculous reason he'd deemed necessary. She would do her best to make this marriage work.

Barely a minute later, Andrew jogged back out of the church. He gripped the sides of the carriage door and leaned in.

"Blackwell says, 'Very well.'"

Kate grinned. "Excellent."

She offered him her hand and used the other to lift her dress enough to descend from the carriage without tripping over its hem. Releasing his hand, she stepped aside so Amelia and Lady Drake had room to leave the carriage too. Once they were down, Lady Drake and Amelia joined arms and walked into the church together.

Andrew blew out his breath. "Now, can we do this?"

"Absolutely." She took his arm and raised her chin as they moved together across the paved ground and through the doorway.

There were only a handful of guests present. Less than twenty. But all eyes were on her as she glided along the aisle toward the altar with Andrew at her side. She met Blackwell's dark gaze and steeled herself to make the most significant commitment of her life.

Hopefully it wouldn't be a mistake.

CHAPTER 18

Oh no.

He was in deep trouble.

They weren't even married yet, and he couldn't tear his gaze from Kate. She was exquisite, her cheeks flushed from the cold, her gown fit for royalty. She made it difficult for him to think. Made him foolish.

This wedding was a terrible idea.

Her eyes met his, the gray irises sparkling with something he didn't recognize, and his rib cage constricted. Her perfect pink lips tilted up in a smile, and his trousers tightened in a way that was wholly inappropriate.

He barely noticed her brother as he moved to take her arm, figuratively taking on the responsibility for this beautiful woman who was going to turn his life upside down.

As they turned away from the flower-lined aisle, he couldn't help wondering if he'd made a mistake in agreeing to her last-minute change of terms. She was enough of a temptation already. If she insisted on accompanying him to Oxfordshire, and he couldn't get enough space from her to clear his mind, he was doomed.

She was too. She just didn't realize it yet.

She might have high hopes for their marriage, but she didn't know what a failure of a husband he was. Unfortunately, she'd learn the truth soon enough.

She disengaged her arm from Andrew's, and she pivoted to stand opposite Theo. The neckline of her dress cut low across her chest, drawing his eyes to the smooth porcelain skin it exposed. His mouth went dry, and he forced himself to lift his eyes to focus on her face.

He could have used her note—and the request contained within—as a way to escape this marriage, but he hadn't had the heart to do so. It was too late now. Calling things off would be a mistake. What remained of her good name would be in tatters.

The clergyman began to talk. Theo listened but he felt detached from his body, as if he were looking down on himself from above. Despite being able to feel the cold draft that whistled through the church and the firmness of the ground beneath his feet, he was strangely disconnected.

When it was his turn to speak, he recited the words, his voice impossibly loud to his own ears, as if it was echoing around the vault of his skull.

This couldn't be more different from his first wedding.

There were no mischievous smiles exchanged between the bride and groom, no ridiculously extravagant decor designed by his mother, and most of all, no love between him and Kate. The only thing the two events had in common was that they were legally binding… and that there was a glint of hope in his bride's eyes.

He really wished he hadn't noticed that. He had no desire to disappoint Kate, but he knew beyond a shadow of a doubt that he would. He didn't know how to be what she wanted.

He watched her lips move as she recited her vows, and then he slid his grandmother's ring onto her finger. This was one of the concessions he'd made for his mother. She hadn't allowed him to use his grandmother's ring when he married Elizabeth, but it pleased her to know it would be on the finger of an earl's sister. Someone who, according to her, was a worthy viscountess.

He noticed Kate studying the ring and he hoped she liked it. While he thought less of his mother for the games she played, he didn't feel any bitterness or resentment toward Kate for being allowed to wear the family heirloom. In fact, it suited her. The emerald went well with her reddish hair.

The clergyman announced that it was time to kiss his wife, and Theo moved closer to Kate, noting the way her eyes widened as she looked up at him. He placed his hand on her hip and dipped his head, brushing his lips to hers. They were petal-soft and parted on a surprised exhalation. He was tempted to press closer and learn how she tasted but forced himself to release her and back away again.

She stared at him with dilated pupils, and her tongue darted out to touch her lips. A bolt of lust shot through him, and he tamped it down quickly. He couldn't allow himself to feel such attraction to her.

When the ceremony ended, they accepted congratulations and solicitations from the guests. He made the briefest possible introduction to Nicholas, who had grown his facial hair and was dressed in a style that made him appear as different from Theo as possible, the better to avoid upsetting their mother *and* Lady Katherine until after all was settled.

It was possible she'd learn the truth of who had actually been on the balcony with her at some point, but it would be better for everyone involved if that didn't happen with an audience.

Once the stream of well-wishers had all left, Theo and Kate got into his carriage to follow those bound for the wedding breakfast at Longley House. They were both quiet during the drive, perhaps overwhelmed by what they'd just done.

He paused before helping her out of the carriage. "You've outdone yourself with the wedding gown. It's spectacular."

A shy smile touched her lips. "Thank you, my lord."

"We're married now, so please call me Theodore when we're in private."

Her smile widened. "You may call me Katherine."

He took her hand, enjoying the brush of her soft skin against his, and escorted her into the formal dining room, where everyone was seated around the table. There was a space left for him at the head of the table and one to his right for her.

He rested his hand on the small of her back as he guided her over. As the highest-ranking family member present, Longley was seated to his left with his wife on the other side of him. Lady Drake was beside Kate. She looked up and beamed at them both. The affectionate expression couldn't be more different from the cool smugness of his own mother, who was seated to the left of Lady Drake.

Nicholas had excused himself from the breakfast citing a headache, eager to avoid giving Lady Blackwell any reason to harass them both about how terrible they were for her nerves.

At this point, Theo thought the situation had gone on for too long. They really ought to have started attending events together as young men and simply made their mother deal with the consequences of her lies.

Unfortunately, because they both cared for her, and their father was no longer around to make her see reason, they still participated in this ridiculous ritual of minimizing public appearances together so no one would guess they were actually twins and she wouldn't be "ruined."

Honestly, he very much doubted that she'd be ruined even if they went directly to the gossip rags and confessed everything, but there would be whispers and disapproval and if there was anything Lady Blackwell hated, it was being the subject of public censure. While the actual ramifications probably wouldn't be severe, she'd be miserable, nonetheless.

The meal passed quickly. He struck up a conversation with Longley while keeping an eye on Kate to make sure she was having a pleasant time. After dessert, some of the men retreated to another room, but Theo stayed near her. He wasn't sure if it was the ring on her finger or the way her smile hit him in the gut every time it crossed her face, but he didn't feel able to leave her.

He made the mistake of stepping away to pour himself a drink and immediately regretted it when, upon returning, he found her deep in conversation with another gentleman. He was crossing to them before he even thought about it, possessive thoughts racing through his mind.

She was his wife, and this was their wedding day. He wouldn't tolerate anyone flirting with his bride.

It was only as he reached her side that he recognized the gentleman in question as the Duke of Ashford and recalled that he was happily married. It bothered him how relieved he was. He shouldn't be getting jealous over his wife. He should be keeping his distance and doing whatever it took to make her happy. Certainly not dragging her closer and burdening her with all of the complicated emotions she brought out in him.

The last part of the celebration was the cutting of the cake. Longley's cook had created an impressive tiered cake that was frosted in pink and matched Kate's dress so well that it couldn't be accidental.

He and Kate stood behind the cake, and they both held onto the knife as they pushed it through the frosting and into the dense, fruit-laced center. He released the knife first, his fingers sliding alongside hers as he reclaimed his hand. She completed the cut and wiggled the piece of cake loose.

Then, in a move he never would have expected, she broke off a piece and held it up to him. He resisted the temptation to close his mouth around her fingers and instead plucked the piece of cake from her and popped it into his mouth, his heart hammering wildly.

God, if she kept doing things like that, resisting her was going to be the challenge of his life. He had to succeed, though. He couldn't lose her the way he'd lost Elizabeth. If he did, there was every chance he'd come apart at the seams.

No, it would be better for everyone if he maintained a healthy distance. She'd be happier that way.

A server took the knife from Kate and continued cutting the cake into small portions. The Duchess of Ashford was first in line for a piece, with Lady Sophie close behind her.

Kate broke off another small portion and nibbled on it. It must have met her approval because she went back for more, then wiped her fingers clean and looked around as if to see whether anyone had noticed. When their gazes met, her eyes sparkled with mirth.

He shook his head. She was definitely going to test his restraint.

An hour later, they were back in his carriage on the way to Blackwell House. He'd sent word ahead, so when they arrived, the staff were gathered in the foyer to meet their new mistress. He glanced over to check on her, but she looked perfectly composed as they went to the head of the line to start the introductions.

"You've already met Albert and Mrs. Taylor," he said as the butler and housekeeper bowed and curtsied, respectively.

"It's a pleasure to see you again," Kate said with the faintest tilt of her head. "I look forward to discussing the running of the household with both of you."

Theo stood back and allowed Mrs. Taylor to introduce Kate to each of the household staff members. There was an unfamiliar maid among the group, who he assumed was the one Kate had brought with her from Longley House.

When all the introductions were made, he dismissed everyone but Mrs. Taylor.

"Is the viscountess's room fully prepared?" he asked.

"Yes, my lord. Everything is as you asked."

"Good." He turned to Kate, noting the curious scrunch of her brows. "Please let me show you to your new bedchamber. Do you recall the tour from the last time you visited, or do you wish to circulate again?"

She nodded. "I remember. If I ever find myself at a loss, I'm sure Mrs. Taylor will be able to assist me."

"Gladly," Mrs. Taylor said, her chest puffing out and her eyes lighting up.

They made their way up the stairs and to the family wing, where they stopped in front of the viscountess's room, and he drew in a deep breath. When he'd gone in to determine what changes might need to be made before Kate arrived, it had been the first time he'd entered the space since Elizabeth died.

Honestly, he hadn't been ready, but he didn't think he ever would be. Sometimes, people had to move forward regardless of their emotional state.

Mrs. Taylor opened the door, and the breath whooshed from him as the bed came into view. Fortunately, the purple bedspread that Elizabeth used to favor had been removed and replaced with a white one scattered with embroidered flowers.

His late wife's belongings had all been put into storage long ago, which made it easier to forget that she'd once haunted this space, as much a ghost while alive as after she'd passed. Kate's belongings had been unpacked, and an array of items he assumed she used for her artistic pursuits were spread on the small writing desk to the right of the window.

"I'll leave you to get comfortable," he said, then fled like the coward he was. His shoes thudded on the stairs as he made his way down them before rushing into his office and closing the door.

"I thought you might be here soon," Nicholas said from where he sat behind the desk, his stockinged feet resting on top of it. "I don't understand why, though. You have a beautiful new wife that you ought to be bedding."

Theo's fists clenched at his side. "Don't you ever talk about Kate like that again."

Nicholas's eyebrow arched. "Kate, is it?"

Theo grimaced at his slip. He went to the sideboard, found the brandy, and poured himself a healthy portion. He shot it back and then dropped onto the visitor's chair, since Nicholas showed no sign of leaving Theo's preferred seat.

"Why aren't you with your wife?" Nicholas asked.

Theo stuffed his hands into his pockets, his chest tight. "I can't go through what I did with Elizabeth. Not again."

Nicholas cocked his head. "So, what? You're just going to leave the marriage unconsummated and avoid her for the rest of your lives so you don't end up caring for her?"

Theo huffed. "I already care about her. I'm not protecting myself. I'm protecting her. We both know how things will end if I let her get close to me."

"No, we don't." Nicholas dropped his feet to the floor and crossed his arms. "Why don't you tell me what you think will happen?"

"Don't do this." Theo was too exhausted to play along with Nicholas, but he eventually answered, nonetheless. "She'll become miserable, and I won't know how to help, and then we'll both end up wishing our lives away."

"And what does she think of that?" Nicholas asked.

Theo tipped his empty glass back, enjoying the drop of brandy that landed on his tongue. "Of what?"

"Of your asinine plan to run away from your feelings."

Theo shrugged. "She doesn't need to know."

It wasn't as if this marriage was one of love. It had been born out of the need to avoid scandal.

Nicholas leaned forward and clasped his hands together. "And what about me? When will you tell her I was the one on that balcony?"

"Never, unless I have to." There was no reason to upset her unnecessarily. She'd agreed to marry him, not Nicholas, and she seemed pleased enough with her decision.

"I think that's a mistake," Nicholas said.

"The past month has been a lot for anyone to handle. There's no need to tell her something that might cause her more distress."

"Bollocks," Nicholas said. "You just don't want to deal with the consequences."

In this case, his brother had a good point. Kate was bound to be unhappy at learning that she'd been on the balcony with one brother and ended up married to another.

He'd thought he was doing the right thing. Everyone had assumed Nicholas was him, the guest list had his name on it, and most parents would insist on marriage to a viscount over a second son if it was an option.

Most.

How was he to know that the Drakes might be one of the rare families who would value the truth over convenience? His stomach twisted. If they hadn't deceived Kate, she might have made a different choice, but he couldn't risk her learning the truth now. As far as she was concerned, it had been him on that balcony.

"That's true. Perhaps I should confess, but not now. I ought to give her time to settle into married life."

"If she finds out before you tell her, the continued deception will only make her angrier," Nicholas said. "I think it's a mistake to wait. You should tell her now."

Theo closed his eyes. "I need time."

He prayed he was making the right decision.

CHAPTER 19

THE DAY AFTER THE WEDDING, KATE WAS PACKING A PENCIL and paper into a small carry bag to take with her in the carriage when Blackwell—Theodore, he'd told her his name was—knocked on the bedchamber door.

Her heart hitched at the sight of his expression. His mouth was turned down at the corners, telling her that she wasn't likely to appreciate whatever it was he intended to say.

"Are you sure you want to travel to Oxfordshire with me?" he asked, looking away from her, toward the window. "Even my family are remaining in London. You'd probably get more enjoyment out of spending the holiday here or with your family."

Kate straightened and put some steel into her spine. "Are you going back on your agreement to allow me to accompany you?"

When she'd sent in her note advising him that she'd only marry him if he allowed her to go with him to Oxfordshire, she hadn't thought she'd have to deal with any further discouragements such as this.

He blanched. "No, of course not. I'm a man of my word. I

just thought it was possible you might have had a change of heart."

"I haven't."

While it was true that she might be more at ease with her family, she needed to do everything she could to set herself up for a happy future, and that meant persisting with Theodore until she'd overcome whatever was holding him back from pursuing a meaningful relationship with her.

"I see."

She laced her fingers together in front of her, needing to keep her hands under control. If she let them do whatever they wanted, she worried they'd end up tangled in her travelling dress, and she didn't want to give away how nervous she was.

"The only parts of England I've seen are London, Bath, and the area surrounding Longley Estate." She did her best to smile. "I'm eager to see more of the country."

That was true, although she'd never been driven by a desire to travel. She was simply curious about where Theodore had grown up and how it had shaped him. She was also keen to discover new subjects to paint in the countryside of Oxfordshire.

"I hope Oxfordshire will be to your liking." He looked around the room, which was bare except for the bed and cabinets. "Are you ready to depart?"

"I am."

She closed her bag. He picked it up with one hand and offered her the other arm. She took it, and he escorted her along the corridor, down the stairs, and out through the front entrance where his carriage was waiting for them.

As he helped her in, his touch was warm and firm. She instinctively leaned closer, but he cleared his throat and shifted away. Her stomach soured. He hadn't come to her room last night as she'd expected him to. She didn't think he found her repulsive. In fact, his gaze had felt admiring at times.

Perhaps he simply wanted to take things slowly. After all, he'd lost a wife before, and she could imagine that it was difficult for him to suddenly be saddled with a new one.

She sat facing forward in the carriage and was pleased to find the seats were plushly padded, which would make the journey more tolerable. They were red velvet, as was the lining on the lower part of the walls. The curtains were crimson and thick. She kept them open, keen to watch the countryside pass by. She occasionally became ill during travel, and watching the scenery helped.

A cold wind whistled through the open door and she shivered, grateful for her thick woolen traveling coat and fur-lined gloves. Outside, Theodore spoke briefly to the driver before climbing in and sitting opposite her. A carriage had gone on ahead of them with the rest of their bags and the members of the household who'd be accompanying them— Margaret and Barlow.

"Tell me about Blackwell Hall," Kate said as the carriage began to move.

Theodore met her gaze. "The manor was rebuilt around fifty years ago. It's large but relatively unpretentious. The building is constructed from brick and stone. There's a main central portion, where the public-facing spaces and the rooms most commonly used by the family are located. Then there are smaller wings jutting off each side. The east wing houses the servant quarters, and the west wing is mostly guest rooms. It remains unused a lot of the time, but it's cleaned periodically."

"Is it...." Kate trailed off, unsure how to ask whether Blackwell Hall was comfortable and how much he enjoyed spending time there. "Do you prefer Blackwell Hall or your London residence?"

To her surprise, he grinned. The corners of his eyes crinkled, making him seem younger. She wondered how much older than her he was. She would guess not more than ten years, perhaps less, but it was difficult to know for sure, and one generally wasn't encouraged to enquire as to other people's ages.

"While I enjoy both the city and the country, if pressed, I must concede that I prefer Blackwell Hall," he said, looking somewhere over her shoulder, his gaze distant. "There's something very peaceful about it. That's why I return when I get the opportunity."

Kate nibbled her lower lip before venturing into dangerous territory. "Did you and your late wife spend most of your time there?"

Something dark flashed through his eyes before he refocused on her. "Yes, we did."

She hesitated, put off by his no-nonsense tone, but she couldn't tiptoe around the matter of his late wife forever. "Will you tell me a little about her?"

"I didn't kill her," he snapped, his fists clenching, the knuckles white.

"I didn't think you did," she said, remaining outwardly calm even though knots were tangled in her gut. "I'd just like to know what she was like."

After all, the other woman had played an important part in Theodore's life and, possibly, factored into his reluctance to embrace a marriage with Kate.

His hands loosened. He inhaled slowly, then scratched the back of his neck. "All right. My apologies. I tend to leap to conclusions where questions like that are concerned."

"Understandable." He'd been vilified, after all.

"Elizabeth was the local vicar's daughter. I saw her and simply knew I had to marry her. I'm not going to say it was love at first sight, but we fell for each other quickly. Not everyone approved, including my parents, but they came around enough to allow us to wed—or at least, my father did."

The harsh lines of his face softened as he spoke about Elizabeth, and if Kate had harbored any doubts about his part in her death, they were firmly put to rest. This man had adored his wife.

Her heart twinged. Hopefully, one day, he could feel that way about her too.

"Did you know each other for long before you married?" she asked.

"About two years. My parents insisted I complete my schooling first, and, in hindsight, that was a wise decision."

"Yes, I imagine once you'd married, you wouldn't have had any interest in returning to university."

She didn't ask more questions, not wanting to push him to share more than he was comfortable with. They'd have a lifetime together for her to get the full story. She didn't need it now.

After a while, the buildings outside became sparser until, eventually, they were driving through the countryside. They passed a folly that would likely be charming during summer but had a strangely ominous air about it silhouetted against the gray sky. Kate peered through the window, absorbing as much of it as she could until it disappeared from view behind them.

She withdrew a paper and pencil from her travel bag and set to work sketching the folly. She had to look up every couple of minutes to reorient herself with the view outside, otherwise she might become ill, but the distraction made time pass more quickly.

"May I see what you're working on?" Theodore asked.

Kate handed him the paper, feeling uncharacteristically shy about her work.

His eyes widened. "You're very talented."

"Thank you." Her insides fluttered. "I'm no artist, but I

enjoy re-creating the same subject across multiple mediums. For example, if I make a note of the colors present in the landscape around the folly, then I can later paint it or render it by needlepoint."

"If you do so, you'll have to show me. You've piqued my curiosity."

Her cheeks warmed, and she hid a smile as he passed the paper back, pleased by the comment. Surely his interest in her passions boded well.

They didn't speak much during the rest of the day's travel. The journey to Oxfordshire was too long to be made without stopping overnight, so they called in at an inn in a small town Kate had never heard of before. There was little more to it than a butcher's shop, a blacksmith's, and the inn.

When they were shown in, Kate took a moment to gather herself, certain that she was about to share her first night with her new husband.

Alas, she was taken to a separate room, and, except to join her for dinner, he kept his distance. She didn't know what to make of it. Surely they ought to have consummated the marriage by now. She wasn't entirely sure of the logistics, but Amelia had explained the basic details to her.

She didn't dare raise the subject with Theodore. She wasn't bold enough for that. Not upon such a limited acquaintance.

Thus, she kept her mouth shut.

Snow fell overnight and blanketed the earth, which slowed their travel the following day so that they only arrived at Blackwell Hall in the late afternoon.

She fell in love at first sight.

Despite the cold winter weather, the sun shone brilliantly overhead, making the building seem warm and welcoming. As Theodore had said, the place was constructed from brick and stone, and there was a winding road leading up to it covered in tiny yellow stones. Snow-covered lawns stretched in both directions and she could imagine how green they would be come spring.

The land around the Hall was flatter than she'd expected. Golden light danced over the shrubbery surrounding the lawn, which had been slightly flattened by the snow, and a few white clouds bobbed overhead.

"It's beautiful," she breathed, leaning close to the window to get a better look.

"It's home," Theodore said.

She supposed this *was* her home now.

It wasn't a particularly elaborate building. There were no turrets or spires. And there was just something about it that made it feel like she wouldn't have to stand on ceremony. Perhaps its attraction was in its simplicity. Sometimes the simplest things were the most beautiful.

Her fingers itched to paint it. She already knew what shades of color she'd like to combine for the surrounding scenery. She had a terracotta red that would be perfect for the brickwork, but she didn't often paint stone—at least not basic gray stone—so it would take some experimentation to get that right.

The other carriage had no doubt arrived already, so it was possible that her paints had been unpacked in her new bedchamber. If she went straight there, she could capture this light before it changed, as good light inevitably did.

But... she had duties. She was the mistress of this home now. She couldn't just ignore everything and do what pleased her. There would be time to paint later. First, she needed to meet the staff and explore the manor.

As they reached the stone-chipped area directly in front of the manor, she realized that she didn't have any choice other than to begin her duties immediately anyway. The staff were already gathered and waiting. There were more here than there had been at the house in London, but that made sense considering the Hall was much larger and there were also extensive grounds and stables to be cared for.

Kate did her best to remember names as she was introduced to each and every person present, but there were a lot of them, so she focused on those members of the household she was most likely to interact with regularly. There was Mrs. Tubbs, the housekeeper, Mr. Giles, the butler, and Mrs. Franklin, the cook.

Mrs. Tubbs was a slight, thin woman with wild gray hair, eyes that looked slightly too big for her face, and a disposition much more pleasant than one would expect from looking at her. Mr. Giles was young for a butler, and Theodore informed her that he had replaced his father, who had retired only a few years earlier.

Mrs. Franklin was a ruddy-faced, plump woman, which Kate found promising. If the cook had had a similar figure to Mrs. Tubbs, she might have been concerned about the quality of the food served at Blackwell Hall. A plump cook was never a bad thing.

Once the introductions were made, all the staff except for Mrs. Tubbs were dismissed.

"Are you ready for a tour?" Theodore asked. "Or would you prefer some time to recover first?"

"A tour now, please," Kate said.

Her mother had long since prepared her to take over a household. First, she needed to see what she was working with. Then, she needed to make sure the key staff were amenable to her management. Only after she had secured their respect and come to grips with the situation she found herself in should she try to implement any changes.

As it was, she suspected she'd need to tread more carefully than usual because she wasn't the only mistress this house had seen during Theodore's tenure as viscount. They might be used to doing things in a particular way, or, despite how favorably the London staff had reacted to her, these people might view her as an interloper.

Kate had no desire to erase Elizabeth's impact or replace her. That said, she wasn't about to be uncomfortable in her own home either. If something needed to change in order for her to feel like part of the household, it would have to happen.

They made their way up the stone stairs and into a foyer that was smaller than she would have expected from the outside. It had a white marble floor that looked like it had been recently cleaned.

"How much has Master Theodore told you about Blackwell Hall?" Mrs. Tubbs asked.

"He described the basic layout," Kate said. "He didn't go into a lot of detail as to the individual rooms or the grounds."

Mrs. Tubbs nodded. "The grounds are extensive. I'd recommend looking around the house today and keeping the grounds for tomorrow or later in the week. It would be a lot to take in all at once."

Kate inclined her head. "I'll take your advice. I trust you to know best in this."

Mrs. Tubbs looked pleased. "Excellent. Let's begin with the formal receiving rooms, since they'll be where you'll receive any guests or callers who come to wish you well."

The tour lasted long enough that Kate's feet ached by the time they were done and her stomach was hollow. Fortunately, they detoured to the dining room, where a meal had been served. She and Theodore ate silently, both of them hungry from the journey. Once they'd had their fill, he showed her to her bedchamber.

As soon as she entered, a sense of heaviness descended over her. It was obvious that the bed had recently been changed and the lack of dust on the dresser indicated that the room had been cleaned as well. She wondered whether the space had remained undisturbed after Elizabeth's death until now.

A door near the bed connected the room with Theodore's, and all of a sudden, this whole thing just felt too awkward. The meal she'd just eaten sat like a lump in her gut.

Theodore had loved Elizabeth. If he'd kept her room as it was all this time, she doubted that he'd grieved her as fully as he should have. It didn't feel right for Kate to move in when she knew she wasn't the one he would have wanted to be there.

"Would you like me to take another room?" she asked softly, turning to look up into his eyes.

He stared at her, askance. "Why would you do that?"

"This was Elizabeth's room."

"Is it not to your liking?" Mrs. Tubbs's tone was laced with concern. "We can make any changes you want."

She shook her head. "It's not that. It's just… won't it be strange for you to have me in here instead of her?"

The corner of Blackwell's mouth twitched. "No. You're the viscountess now. It would be stranger for you not to take this room."

She tilted her head back. "Are you sure?"

"Yes."

Well, that was that.

Somehow, the firm answer helped, although it didn't ease the awkward feeling of having put her nose where she shouldn't. She grimaced to herself. If she retired to her room now, the tension between them would linger, and she couldn't allow that.

"I know you advised me to leave the grounds until tomorrow, Mrs. Tubbs, but I couldn't help noticing through the rear windows that there seems to be a garden out the back. Could we walk through that? The fresh air would be nice after being cooped up in the carriage."

Mrs. Tubbs deferred to Theodore. "His lordship is likely

better situated to show you the gardens than I am. I don't venture outside much. The late viscountess had a real knack for growing roses. His lordship would often spend time in the gardens with her."

Theodore stiffened, and she wondered why. Did he not want the staff telling her about Elizabeth?

Perhaps she should find out because she wanted to cause as little distress as possible. Now wasn't the time to ask, though.

"I can walk you through the gardens, but there isn't much to see at this time of year," he said.

"Then you can describe it for me as it appears in summer."

He nodded briskly, dismissed Mrs. Tubbs, and led Kate down the stairs and out through a back exit. Immediately behind the house, there were several rows of rose bushes, their bare limbs jutting from the snow, in a holding pattern until spring arrived.

"Each garden is a different color when the flowers bloom." Theodore stood and gazed out at them, his expression distant. He interlaced fingers behind his back, and she wondered if he was thinking of a time when this garden had overflowed with color and he'd shared picnics between the rose beds with his wife.

Her heart ached for him. It couldn't be easy to lose someone you loved. Especially not someone you expected to walk through life with.

"This is really all there is to see." He turned in each direction and then looked out toward the horizon. "There's a pond a short distance away that's likely frozen now. The gardens around that are lovely in spring."

A pond. That sounded nice. Perhaps she could paint it come spring.

She moved closer to him. "Thank you for showing me. I look forward to seeing them when the seasons change."

"Perhaps you can paint them," he suggested, echoing her own thoughts and catching her off guard. She thought he was lost in a world of his own.

"I'd like that."

He turned back to her, and their gazes caught. "I want you to be comfortable here. I know the situation probably isn't what you imagined when you thought about getting married, but the world had other plans, and now we must make the most of it. If there's anything you need—anything —please don't be afraid to let me know."

Touched, she rested her hand over her heart. "Thank you, Theodore. I think I'm ready to retire now."

He escorted her back to the viscountess's bedchamber, and she closed the door behind him.

She flopped onto the bed and shut her eyes. She was grateful the room had been cleared out, but she couldn't help feeling like an intruder. Theodore had said she could change anything, but if she did so, would that be disrespecting Elizabeth's memory?

She sighed. Perhaps she had been wrong to insist on accompanying him here. Perhaps she'd been wrong about the entire marriage.

CHAPTER 20

Oxfordshire
December 1822

AFTER A NIGHT OF TOSSING AND TURNING, WAITING fruitlessly for Theodore to come to her bed, Kate needed a distraction. One that didn't involve him.

They shared breakfast, but then she excused herself, summoning Margaret and a footman to help her carry her paints, as well as a small canvas and an easel, to a drawing room that Mrs. Tubbs had assured her was rarely used.

The footman, Samuel, lay sheets on the floor so she wouldn't drip paint on it, then set the easel in place. She offered him the paints she was holding, and when he took them, she repositioned the easel so that it faced the window, then took the canvas from Margaret and affixed it.

"Thank you both," she said, grateful for the help. "It would have taken me several trips to get everything out here by myself."

Samuel bowed. "It's what we're here for, my lady."

She smiled at him. "You may return to your usual duties.

I'll send for help when I'm finished. There's no need for you to waste your time standing here with me."

He grimaced. "I don't believe his lordship would appreciate me leaving you alone when you've only just arrived. You don't know the household well yet, so I can help if you need anything you don't have on hand."

Kate's teeth sank into her lower lip, and she considered arguing. Being alone would give her more space to work through her thoughts, but she didn't want to get him in trouble with Theodore, and he was right in saying that she wasn't yet familiar with the Hall here.

"All right. Thank you, Samuel. I hope I haven't caused you any troubles by preventing you from tending to your other responsibilities?"

"No, my lady." He ducked his head respectfully. "Lord Blackwell assigned me to you for any tasks you may need assistance with today."

That was a relief. She'd hate to get off on the wrong foot with the household staff by interfering with their schedule right away.

She turned to Margaret. "Will you stay?"

"Yes, I'll remain with you, my lady," she said, her downcast eyes flicking in Samuel's direction.

Kate frowned, intrigued. Did Margaret not trust Samuel enough to leave them alone together, or was the maid romantically interested in the burly young man? "Very well."

Putting aside any questions about her maid's love life, Kate pivoted to study the landscape. She took a pencil and lightly sketched an outline of the horizon as well as the road winding into the distance. Once she had a basic idea of the layout, she began layering paints to form a background of white, brown, and gray.

A stormy sky would be the most dramatic background, so she used shades of gray, blue, and white to begin creating the impression of clouds and shadows near the top of the canvas.

She'd asked Samuel to pass her more brown so she could begin on the trees and shrubs when she noticed a carriage coming down the drive.

Curious, she watched as it stopped in front of the house and a warmly dressed, relatively unassuming couple disembarked.

Samuel stiffened.

"Who is that?" she asked him.

He pursed his lips and looked as if he might consider not replying. After a long moment, he said, "Mr. and Mrs. Norman, my lady. The late viscountess's parents."

"Oh." What on earth were they here for? Perhaps to congratulate them on their nuptials? That seemed an odd thing to do, in the circumstances.

"His lordship won't be happy to see them," Samuel muttered.

Stranger and stranger.

"Then I shall greet them first," she said, setting her paintbrush down and removing the smock she'd worn to protect her dress. She wiped her hands on a cloth but they remained speckled with paint. "Margaret, fetch my gloves, please. Bring them to the main receiving room."

As Margaret hastened to comply, Kate hurried down the corridor and met Mr. Giles in the foyer.

"Please have our guests meet me in the main receiving room," she said, noticing that Samuel was following her like a shadow. "And would you ask for a tray of tea and biscuits to be brought through?"

Mr. Giles bowed. "Of course, my lady."

Kate went directly to the receiving room, where Margaret waited. She took her gloves from the maid, put them on, and patted her hair to check that everything was in place, then she sat on a chaise and waited.

When Mr. and Mrs. Norman entered, they stopped and stared momentarily, as if surprised to be faced with Kate rather than Theodore. Mrs. Norman was thin, her lips pinched into a disapproving line and her gray-and-brown hair pulled back so tightly, her features looked gaunt. Mr. Norman, on the other hand, was slightly plump, with thinning gray hair in tight curls.

"Welcome," Kate said, rising to greet them.

"You must be the new viscountess," the woman declared, her voice as sharp as her pointed nose.

"I am. I'm afraid you have me at a disadvantage." She knew who they were, of course, but didn't like Mrs. Norman's disrespectful tone.

The woman's nostrils flared. "We are Mrs. and Mr. Norman. The late viscountess's parents."

"It's nice to meet you." She couldn't think of what else to say. Hopefully it would soon become apparent why they had come to call. Considering the poor weather, it wasn't an easy effort, even if they lived in the nearby town of South Wye.

She smoothed the front of her dress, wishing she were in better repair when meeting Mr. and Mrs. Norman for the first time. What must they think of her?

"Likewise." Mrs. Norman's tone belied that.

"I only arrived at Blackwell Hall yesterday, but it's already apparent that your daughter was adored by all who reside here," she said, pinching the skin between her thumb and forefinger in an effort not to fidget with her skirt.

Mrs. Norman snorted. "That can hardly be the case."

Kate cocked her head. "I don't understand."

"Of course you don't." Mr. Norman's voice was softer than his wife's, and something about it made one want to lean closer and confess all of their sins. She could immediately tell why he was a vicar. "Lord Blackwell was responsible for Elizabeth's death. Even if you believe that there was an accident, he was driving the carriage, which seems awfully suspicious. Why him and not a driver? Something nefarious was going on."

A breeze stirred Kate's hair, and she brushed it behind her ear, at a loss as to how to respond. From what Theodore had said, he'd cared greatly for his wife. He'd married her despite the fact that his parents would have preferred a different match. If he had been driving the carriage, it was strange, but not completely unheard of. She highly doubted he had anything to do with Elizabeth's death. Perhaps Mr. and Mrs. Norman were still blinded by grief even years later.

"And even if we look beyond that, the only reason they were out in that storm was because of the pressure she was under to conceive. They were visiting the doctor on just such a matter," he continued. "A friend of mine saw them arguing outside the establishment following their appointment."

Ah, that made more sense. Even if they didn't believe Theo murdered Elizabeth, they still felt that his choices had killed her. She didn't share their view, but she understood why they might need someone to blame. That said, she wouldn't allow them to speak ill of her husband while in her presence.

"No one here has talked about the late Lady Blackwell with anything other than the warmest of regard," she said, grateful that her voice didn't wobble. "The viscount included. I do not believe him to be responsible for her death."

"You're naïve, then," Mrs. Norman spat, her eyes narrowing into slits. "They might like to paint a pretty picture, but while she was alive, Elizabeth was treated with far less respect."

Someone moved in the periphery of her vision, but Kate didn't look around. She didn't want to turn her back on the pair.

"I'm very sorry to hear that." It wasn't a surprise. People could be cruel, especially when they believed that others had gotten above their station.

Mr. Norman dipped his head, acknowledging her comment. "I imagine you're aware of how the world can be toward those who aspire to higher dreams than their humble birth would grant them."

"I am." Not that she'd experienced that firsthand. She was privileged to have been born into a wealthy and powerful family. She had no idea how it would feel to have been in Elizabeth's shoes.

He stepped closer. "If she'd provided an heir, perhaps she would have been treated more kindly. As it was, many of the people she'd considered friends turned on her because she not only married above herself, but she also failed to produce the next heir to the Blackwell estate. Lady Blackwell certainly let her displeasure with that state of affairs be known."

Kate's heart ached for Elizabeth. She could well believe what Mr. Norman was telling her, and her chest constricted at the thought of what Elizabeth must have been through. "I'm sorry that happened. She didn't deserve it."

"No, she didn't," he agreed somberly.

A maid entered, carrying a tea tray, which she set on a table.

"Would you like tea?" Kate asked.

"Thank you, no," Mrs. Norman said, moving forward. "We won't be here long. I just want you to take heed. If you can't give Blackwell what he wants, you may end up like Elizabeth did. You'd be best to put as much distance between him and you as possible."

Kate's hackles rose, but she pressed her lips together so as not to say something she'd regret. "Is that why you came here today? To warn me?"

Mr. Norman nodded. "We don't wish to see another woman suffer the same fate as our beloved Elizabeth."

"I thank you for your concern." She raised her chin. "However, Lord Blackwell doesn't seem at all to be the vindictive sort. He has behaved honorably toward me and gives every impression of being a caring and thoughtful man."

"It's a trick." Mrs. Norman wrung her hands and shifted her weight from one foot to the other. "Don't allow him to fool you."

Kate's patience waned. "Please don't continue to speak ill of my husband in my presence. I know your intentions are good, but I won't tolerate any further disparagement of his character."

Two figures appeared on the edge of her vision, moving quickly toward her. She looked over and her gut clenched. Theodore stormed into the room with Samuel close on his heels.

"Speak of the devil and he shall appear," Mrs. Norman muttered.

Kate half expected the woman to cross herself, but fortunately for them all, she didn't. That would have created a dreadful scene.

Theodore didn't stop until he reached her side. His arm came around her, his hand resting on the small of her back, and he faced off against his former parents-in-law.

"How is the new vicarage roof coming along?" he asked, ignoring the very obvious tension between them.

"It is... acceptable." Mr. Norman spoke slowly, and his eyes darted from Kate to Theodore and back. He shrank into himself a little. "My thanks for sending the necessary funds for the repairs."

"You're welcome." Theodore glanced down, his dark gaze meeting Kate's. "I see you've made the acquaintance of Lady Katherine, the new Viscountess Blackwell."

"We have." Mr. Norman's back straightened slightly. "We hope that Lady Blackwell will experience good health for many years to come."

"As do I," Theodore said.

"We've got our eyes on you," Mrs. Norman hissed, apparently having decided that subtlety was overrated.

Theodore's hand twitched against her back. "There's nothing you need concern yourself with. All is quite well."

"We'd best return to the vicarage," Mr. Norman said, taking his wife's arm and tugging gently. "Good afternoon, Lord Blackwell."

Mrs. Norman's thin upper lip curled back, but she allowed her husband to lead her out of the room.

"Please ensure the Normans leave," Theodore said to Samuel, who nodded and followed them.

Once they were gone, Theodore released Kate and put space between them.

"Are you all right?" he asked, his eyebrows knitted together.

She blew out a breath and then inhaled slowly, trying to calm her racing heart. "They said you drove their daughter to her death and that I ought to leave before the same thing happens to me."

He sighed and raked his hand down his face. "I should have expected this."

"Why would you?" she asked, stunned.

"They blame me for losing Elizabeth, and they've reason to. Usually, they're sensible enough not to personally confront me. They must hate me even more than I thought to approach you within days of your arrival. They certainly wasted no time, and it was bold of them to come to the Hall."

His voice was rough with emotion. And Kate had the strangest urge to embrace him. His relationship with the Normans shouldn't be like this. They'd all lost someone they loved. They should have been able to mourn together, but instead, he'd been denied the opportunity to grieve with those closest to her.

"I'm sorry," she whispered, knowing the words weren't nearly enough.

The furrow between his eyebrows deepened. "Why? It isn't your fault."

"That doesn't mean I can't be sorry for you."

He exhaled and rubbed at his chest. "You're right. I suppose I owe you a proper explanation."

She hesitated. Yes, she would like a full explanation of the circumstances surrounding Elizabeth's death, but based on the sheen in Theodore's eyes and the tense way he held himself, telling her the story would bring him no relief.

She made a swift decision. "You don't have to do or say anything you aren't ready to. Our marriage is still new. I don't mind waiting until you're more comfortable with me before we share confidences."

He shook his head. "It's best if we get it over with now."

Kate turned to Margaret. "You may leave us alone."

Margaret bobbed a curtsey and scurried out.

Theodore jammed his hands into his pockets and rocked on his toes, then stilled himself. "Have you heard of how my father passed away?"

"There was a storm…." She'd heard more but wasn't sure how much of it was factually correct, so she trailed off.

"Indeed." He stared out the window, and she wondered if he was looking toward the spot where his father had died. "His favorite horse got loose, and he went in search of her. Unfortunately, the wind was ferocious, and he was blown off a cliff. I was the one who found him, but he was long gone."

Her heart squeezed. She couldn't imagine how horrible it would be to discover her mother's body. She shuddered even to think about it. "I'm sorry. That must have been awful."

"It was." He didn't turn to her. She wasn't sure he was even fully aware of her anymore. "Elizabeth hadn't been in a rush to have children, as we were still young, but once he was gone, we needed an heir. I… I didn't put pressure on her, but my mother did. Hell, all the goddamn world seemed to think they had the right to share their opinion on the matter."

"They often do," Kate commiserated.

"I'd have happily fought anyone who dared to make an untoward comment in my presence, but the problem was that they did it behind my back. Elizabeth had grown close to my father, and she was grieving. Add to that the pressure to conceive, and she became more and more miserable every time we learned she wasn't with child."

"Did you tell her there was no hurry?" Kate asked, curious despite knowing she ought to just let him tell the story as he thought best.

"Over and over again." He closed his eyes, his fists clenched at his sides. "Three times, she lost a baby."

Tears stung Kate's eyes, and she didn't try to stop them. For what they'd been through, Elizabeth and Theodore deserved her emotion.

"She grew melancholy. Sometimes days would pass without her leaving her chamber. Occasionally, she'd get false hope, and everything would seem brighter, but then it would vanish, and she'd be even more desolate than before."

His jaw clenched, and when he opened his eyes, his eyelashes clumped together with unshed tears. "That last day... the day she... the day it happened, I caught her trying to sneak out to visit the doctor. She confessed that she was nauseated and her courses were a little late. She thought she might be with child, but she'd wanted to confirm that on her own before speaking to me." His shoulders slumped. "She didn't want to disappoint me."

Kate's insides churned and she was almost afraid to ask, "What happened?"

He looked at her, his dark eyes swimming. "The weather was turning. I asked her to wait, but she said she couldn't bear the not knowing. She begged me to drive her there. Just me, so no one other than us and the doctor would know her shame if she was wrong."

"She had no reason to be ashamed," Kate whispered.

His fists clenched. "I told her that, but she was worn down by the looks and whispers. In the end, I agreed, against my better judgement. I thought if there was a chance, even a tiny chance, that she'd conceived, the peace of mind it brought her would be worth the journey. Unfortunately, she hadn't."

"The doctor was certain?"

Theo nodded. "She was beside herself. I tried to assure her that all was well, but she screamed at me that it wasn't and that until she had a son, nothing would be." He closed his eyes and squeezed them shut, obviously holding back as much emotion as possible in order to finish recounting the events of that unfortunate day.

Kate laid her hand on his arm, needing to offer comfort but hesitant to interrupt.

"On the way home, the storm blew branches across the road, and they startled the horses. The road was muddy, and I don't know if it was the mud, the wind, or the horses, but the carriage toppled over and I was thrown clear. The horses took off with it and by the time I stopped them, it was too late for Elizabeth."

Choking back a sob, Kate wrapped her arms around Theodore and held him. He was stiff in her embrace, but he sniffled and softened after a moment.

"I pushed the carriage off the road as best I could to avoid causing another accident and then rode one of the horses bareback to South Wye, taking Elizabeth with me. I went directly to the doctor, just in case I was wrong and she wasn't dead yet, but he said he doubted she'd survived for long after… after her head hit the ground."

"I'm so sorry." The words could never be enough to account for the devastating loss he'd suffered—not to mention the trauma he'd experienced—but they were all she had to offer.

He drew in a shuddering breath. "I just wish we hadn't

argued before she died. I wish I'd instead told her I loved her one last time"

Kate's breath hitched, and the tears that had been slipping silently down her cheeks started falling in torrents.

This poor man.

He'd lost the woman he loved, and there had been nothing he could do to save her. What's worse, he'd had to watch her die, knowing her last memories were unhappy ones, and then he'd been blamed.

Poor Elizabeth too. Alone and alienated. Obsessed with doing her duty but unable to do so.

It was tragic.

Unnecessary and tragic, and she felt so helpless that there was nothing to be done about it. All of this had happened, and the only thing she could do was help Theodore recover in whatever ways he'd let her.

Kate hugged him again, burying her face in his shirt and immediately wetting it with her tears. "Wherever she is, I'm sure that Elizabeth is at peace now."

"I hope so." His tone was wistful, as if he didn't really believe that, and it made her cry harder. "But what if she isn't, and it's all my fault?"

CHAPTER 21

The whispered words soothed the jagged edges of Theo's despair even though he didn't truly believe them.

"You need to get that silly idea out of your head," Kate continued, holding his shoulders and locking her tearful gaze on his.

His heart clenched. How incredible she must be to cry over a woman he'd loved and lost. Especially considering he was now *her* husband. By all rights, she ought to be put out with him for still mourning Elizabeth, not sympathetic to his loss.

He searched her eyes, looking for any hint of deception, but he didn't find it there. "There are so many things I could have done differently. If it wasn't for me—"

She held up her hand to cut him off. "No more of that. We have many things to discuss, but first, we're going to go ask for some scones to go with that tea."

He catalogued her expression. The corners of her mouth were tight, and her nose and eyes were slightly red, but there was no sign of the disgust he'd expected upon making his confession. His breath temporarily bottled up in his chest.

Was it possible that she honestly didn't think less of him because of what had happened?

He was afraid to hope.

Theo allowed himself to be drawn to a chaise, where he sat at Kate's urging and waited while she left again and spoke to someone just outside the door.

When she returned, she sat beside him rather than opposite him, and, to his utter amazement, reached over and interlaced her fingers with his.

"I never met your late wife," she began quietly, her gray eyes still watery but no longer actively leaking. "I didn't know her. But as a fellow woman, I can understand why she felt like she had to provide an heir, especially if people were already saying she wasn't a good match for you and your mother was pressuring her. I'm sorry she went through that, and I'm sorry you did too. I'm sure it wasn't easy for you to see how unhappy she was when you weren't able to fix the problem."

"I tried," he rasped. "I told her there was no rush. I have relatives the title could have passed to." In fact, it could have gone to his own brother. "We fought over it. She was so desperate for a baby that she was willing to take risks that weren't necessary. I just wanted her to be happy."

"I'm sure she knew that," she assured him.

"But it wasn't enough."

She raised their interlaced hands and brushed her lips over the back of his. Her mouth was soft and left tingles on his skin. "I think you probably did all that you could."

Why would she believe that? She didn't know him well enough to make such judgement calls.

"Because you're a good man," she said.

Huh. He must have spoken out loud.

He was tempted to argue. To point out all the ways in which he *wasn't* good. He'd failed Elizabeth time and time again. But Kate's steady gray eyes shone with sincerity, and he didn't have the heart to reject the comfort she was attempting to offer him.

"The whole affair was tragic," she continued, looking down at their joined hands. "But you aren't to blame."

"I don't accept that," he gritted out, all mixed up inside. He wasn't sure whether to be irritated with her for pushing the matter or frustrated with himself for not being able to just give her the response she wanted.

"You aren't," she insisted, her eyes narrowing. "It was an accident. It's horrible, but accidents do happen."

His chin trembled. "It was preventable."

"I think you—" She cut herself off and drew in a long, slow breath, then opened her mouth as if to go on, but closed it again.

What did she want to say?

There was clearly more on her mind, but she didn't seem inclined to voice her thoughts yet.

"I should have refused to drive her to the doctor." His shoulders slumped, and he withdrew his hand from hers. "Or, if not that, then I should have ensured she never experienced such despair as she did those last months. It made her reckless. Perhaps I should have stayed away from her in the beginning, and she'd still be alive."

Kate was silent for so long that he raised his head to find her watching him closely. "She might be," she allowed. "But maybe it was her time to go. It's impossible for us to know. You were in love, and the memory of that time deserves to be cherished, not regretted. You do her a disservice by wishing your marriage away."

Her words hit him in the sternum, knocking the breath from his lungs.

She was right, he realized. By second-guessing his choices, he was disrespecting what they'd shared and the years when they'd been happy. He didn't want to do that.

The door opened, and he jumped, his heart leaping in his chest.

"Apologies, my lord," the maid murmured as she set down a tray laden with scones, butter, jam, and clotted cream.

"No apology necessary," he mumbled, rubbing his chest to dispel the sudden tightness.

"How do you like your scones?" Kate asked.

"With jam and cream."

She spread strawberry jam on both scones and added cream on top, then passed him one and took the other for herself. He held onto the scone but couldn't bring himself to take a bite no matter how good it smelled.

"Is there anything else?" the maid asked.

"No, thank you," Kate said.

The maid retreated, closing the door behind herself.

Kate devoured her scone as if she hadn't eaten all day. She glanced at him, and he realized the cream had started to drip from the scone and run down his fingers. He licked them clean and bit into the scone. It was warm and, surprisingly, didn't taste like ash in his mouth. His stomach grumbled, and he quickly ate the rest. The run-in with Mr. and Mrs. Norman must have made him hungry.

"So...."

Theo raised an eyebrow, his stomach roiling as he wondered what she might be about to say. Surely nothing good. "So?"

She nibbled on her lower lip and avoided his gaze, a hint of color on her cheeks. "I have to ask... with everything that happened between you and Elizabeth, I can see how you'd be reluctant to repeat history. But does that mean that you don't wish to have children?"

The scone sat heavy in his gut. He'd hoped to avoid this question for a while yet, but she deserved an answer even if it wasn't one he wanted to give.

"The truth is," he started, squirming in his seat, "that I would like children."

She brightened.

"*But*," he continued reluctantly, "I can't watch another woman I care about go through the same thing Elizabeth did. It's too painful."

She tipped her head, her lips pursed thoughtfully. "Many women become pregnant and give birth without issue."

He nodded. "But many also die in childbirth or from complications."

"That's true." She picked up her teacup and lifted it to her lips. She sipped, pulled a face, and set it back down. "Too hot."

Her lack of a reaction bothered him. He wanted to grab her and demand to know her thoughts on the matter, but she was clearly working through them in her mind, so he summoned every ounce of patience and waited.

Finally, she placed the teacup back on the table and said, "I've always wanted children."

That was hardly surprising. In his experience, most women did.

She tilted her chin up and met his gaze. "I'm willing to take the risk that I will fail to conceive or that something might happen to me in childbirth. I think you ought to take that into consideration. I can't make you consummate the marriage—for one thing, that wouldn't be fair, and for another, I don't know what it entails—but I'd ask you to factor in my ability to make my own decisions."

The back of his throat ached, and he swallowed with a wince. His shoulders climbed up around his ears, and he pointedly avoided eye contact.

She had a good point. It was unfair of him to make decisions about their future without taking her desires into account, but surely there ought to be some leeway if it was for her own good.

"I can't stand the thought of seeing you wither away," he said softly.

To his surprise, she moved closer, pressing herself against his side. He met her eyes, and she cupped his face and feathered a kiss over his cheek.

"I'd appreciate it if you'd at least reconsider your stance. I'm strong enough to know my own mind." Her eyes filled with emotion as she smoothed her palm over his jaw. "I won't push though. Not now."

He bit his lip, hating that he stood between her and something she wanted. Surely there was something he could offer her now, even if it wasn't children.

"There are ways we can share intimacy that don't carry the same risks," he blurted.

She dropped her hands, and he mourned the loss of her touch. "You're upset. You shouldn't be making any decisions. I'd hate for you to do anything you're uncomfortable with or that you'll later regret."

"I won't." Desperation clawed at his insides. Now that he'd mentioned it, his sense of urgency wouldn't abate. It was important that Kate realize he did care for her. Perhaps he hadn't chosen this marriage, but he had feelings where she was involved. A certain fondness for her. "I want to show you."

Her eyes widened and she paused. "Er, are you sure? Because the past hour has been overwhelming. We shouldn't rush into anything."

"I'm absolutely certain."

Or, at least, he knew he'd regret not giving Kate something. He couldn't provide everything she dreamed of, but he wouldn't leave her totally unsatisfied with her lot in life.

He cupped her face. "Would you like a kiss?"

"Yes, please."

He brushed his lips over hers, softly at first, but more firmly with every second that passed. She sighed and leaned into him, her breath gusting over his skin. He drew back, then kissed her again. This time, she hesitantly responded, her lips moving against his.

He dipped his tongue between them, and she stiffened before parting them to allow him access. The tip of her tongue touched his in a silken caress that sent heat curling through him. She tasted faintly of jam, along with something unique that was only Kate.

She grew bolder, tangling her tongue with his, and he smiled into the kiss, loving the way her tentative touch was becoming more certain. It reminded him of the quiet confidence she displayed in most aspects of her life.

Reluctantly, he pulled away. "How was that?"

She blinked slowly, her eyes glazed and her cheeks pink. "Wonderful."

His stomach fluttered pleasantly. "There is so much more I wish to show you." He dropped to his knees in front of her, ignoring the dull pain from hitting the floor. "May I?"

She frowned. "May you what?"

"Push this up." He inched the skirt up to reveal a thin band of porcelain skin above her ankles. "Touch you. Kiss you here in this most intimate place."

"Oh." Her eyes widened, but she nodded after the briefest hesitation. "All right."

He lifted the skirt, baring shapely calves. Her undergarments blocked him from seeing more, so he hiked them up and gazed hungrily at her soft, smooth thighs.

He ran his hands from her knees to the apex of her thighs, and goose bumps rippled over the skin beneath his palms. He brushed his thumb over the silken heat of her sex and delighted in the way she whimpered and parted her legs.

"This is where we join during intercourse, but there are many ways I can bring you pleasure here."

"Pleasure?"

"Yes." He forced himself to meet her eyes rather than

focusing solely on that tempting softness he longed to bury his face in. "I want you to let me know what you like and what you don't. This only works if you're honest with me."

Her breath hitched, and he realized he'd started stroking her gently.

"I will," she promised.

"Good. Lean back and enjoy. You don't have to do anything."

"Are you sure?"

"Quite."

She shifted, presumably to make herself more comfortable. Theo finally allowed himself to stare at her center. It was pretty and pink, with a dusting of reddish hair a shade darker than the hair on her head. He bent and kissed the small nubbin at the top. She made a startled sound in the back of her throat.

"All right?" he asked, blowing warm air on her, and enjoying the way she shuddered in response.

"Yes."

His tongue darted out, and he swiped the flat of it along her most sensitive parts. Her hips bucked, and he used his forearms to pin her thighs in place. Then, he licked her again and nuzzled his mouth against her, getting her used to the sensation.

Her small gasps and sighs urged him on, and he dipped his tongue into her wet heat, groaning at her sweet, musky taste.

"Oh!" she cried out, clutching her skirt around her hips and staring down at him, wide-eyed. "Is that something people do?"

He grinned wickedly. "If they value their wives."

She didn't seem inclined to argue, simply taking him at his word and bracing herself as he did it again.

He worked her over with his mouth and tongue, moaning his enjoyment so she couldn't doubt his enthusiasm. When she began to tremble, he focused his attention on her nubbin and kept up a gentle rhythm until she keened and shook with her release.

He sat back on his haunches and drank in the sight of her. Cheeks flushed, eyelids heavy, chest rising and falling as she caught her breath.

Stunning.

As she regained her composure, she sat up and pushed her skirts down, covering herself once again.

She leaned forward and kissed him, which shocked him given what he'd just been doing. "Is there some way I can… reciprocate?"

CHAPTER 22

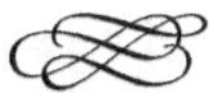

Theodore's mouth fell open, and the knots in Kate's gut tightened. Had she made a mistake to ask? Only, she'd never experienced anything like what he'd done to her, and she wanted to make him feel as lovely as he'd made her feel. How could that be wrong?

"Amelia told me that marital relations could be pleasurable, but I didn't fully believe her," she hastened to add. "I was wrong, and knowing how good it can be, I want you to feel the same."

He stared at her, apparently flabbergasted.

Heat throbbed between her legs, reminding her of the wave of sensation that had rolled through her only moments earlier, and she squeezed them together and savored the sweet pulse.

"Only if there's a way we can do it without creating a baby, of course." She didn't want him to think she was dismissing his concerns in that regard without further discussion.

He cleared his throat and the tips of his ears turned red. "There are, er, ways."

"Good." She grinned, pleased to hear it. She hadn't been

205

sure that sharing physical intimacy had been the best choice when they were both already emotional, but perhaps it would bring them closer together. She certainly didn't regret it. "Perhaps I could put my mouth on you the way you did with me?"

He sputtered, a blush spreading down his neck and disappearing beneath the collar of his shirt. "Let's, uh, save that for later." He hesitated. "Are you sure you want to do this? Don't feel obligated. What I did was for you, not because I hoped you'd return the favor."

"I want to," she assured him. "Please."

"Very well."

He got up and sat on the chaise beside her. She started to stand, ready to kneel in front of him as he had for her, but he stopped her with a hand on her shoulder.

"You can stay here," he said hoarsely.

"All right." She watched, fascinated, as he unbuttoned his trousers and shimmied them down far enough to reveal his drawers. He lifted himself up for long enough to pull his drawers down, and she stared at the flesh he'd uncovered.

She'd never seen this part of a man before. His thighs were covered with coarse, dark hair, and there was a patch of soft, springy hair at his groin in the same place she had hair, but that was where the similarities ended.

A thick, firm shaft thrust outward. It was red, with a shiny bulbous head and soft, large balls beneath.

This was the part that was supposed to go inside her? How on earth was it meant to fit?

Theodore grasped her hand and wrapped it around the shaft. It was hot against her palm and as satiny as the skin of her lower belly. Much harder though. He encouraged her to tighten her grip and move it along his length.

"Like this," he murmured.

She allowed him to guide her movements until she got the hang of it enough to brush him off and take over. She didn't want him to have to work for his own pleasure. He hadn't done that to her, after all.

"Is that right?" she asked as she tightened her hand on an upward stroke.

"Yes. Perfect. You're doing so well."

Smiling to herself, she kept going, using his breaths and the soft grunts and sighs he made to decipher what he liked most. Growing bolder, she used her other hand to play with the head. She ran her fingers over the taut skin and, when a bead of clear fluid appeared, she collected it on her thumb and studied it.

"That's my seed." His voice was strained, and she found she liked it. "When I orgasm—which is the peak of pleasure you experienced—I produce much more of it. The seed is what causes pregnancy if I'm inside you when I ejaculate."

How fascinating. It looked so innocuous, and yet this fluid could create life.

She resumed stroking him, determined to get this right. He'd suffered so much. He deserved to feel good.

His thighs began to shake, and she recalled how her own body had done the same thing soon before she'd... orgasmed.

Lord, his tongue had felt divine as it traced her most secret parts. Would he enjoy it just as much if she did the same to him?

Cautiously, she leaned forward until her mouth hovered only an inch over the head of his shaft. Another pearl of seed had appeared there, and she wrapped her mouth around it and licked the droplet off.

Theodore cursed and arched up. His shaft pulsed in her hand before ropes of translucent white shot from the end, landing all over her face.

She blinked, shocked, and her eyelashes stuck together. A musky scent filled her nostrils, and when her lips parted, she instinctively swiped them clean with her tongue. The seed was salty but not unpleasant, and she hummed, but as she realized exactly what she'd done, her insides turned to ice.

She backed away from Theodore, her hand flying to her mouth. He'd said that if his seed got inside her, she could end up pregnant. Did this mean…?

"I'm so sorry," she cried, horror twisting her gut. What a stupid mistake. He'd never trust her now. "I didn't mean to. I didn't think about it. Am I pregnant now?"

Theodore's brow furrowed, and then he chuckled. *Chuckled.* As if this were a laughing matter.

"It's all right." His tone was laced with affection. "You won't become pregnant from swallowing it."

The sudden tightness in her chest loosened. "Thank God."

"I'm the one who ought to be sorry," he continued, and something soft dabbed at her face. It traced over her nose, down her cheek, and breezed gently over one eye. "I spilled all over you. I didn't expect my response to be quite so… forceful. My apologies."

She giggled. "No need for apologies, my lord."

"Theodore," he reminded her. "Or Theo, if you prefer."

She opened her eyes and patted her face, noting that it was still slightly sticky. Ignoring that, she met his eyes, and her heart swelled at the fondness in them.

"Theo." She tasted the name. "I like it."

Calling him a diminutive was intimate. It implied closeness. And that made her feel special.

"May I call you Kate?" he asked, caressing her cheekbone and holding her gaze.

"Yes."

He grinned. He kissed the tip of her nose. "Excellent. Now, Kate, I suggest we take ourselves upstairs before the servants realize what we've been doing in here."

Her cheeks burned, and she glanced at the door. She couldn't believe she'd forgotten that any member of the household staff might have walked past it at any moment.

She hadn't tried to remain quiet at all. If they'd heard her, she'd never be able to meet their eyes again.

"Hey. Stop that."

"Stop what?" she asked, befuddled.

"Thinking too much." He tucked his handkerchief into his pocket and got to work fastening his trousers. "Husbands and wives are expected to do certain things with each other, especially when they're newly married. You have nothing to be embarrassed about."

She nodded. He was right, of course. Although that didn't mean she wouldn't be more careful in future. None of the staff needed to know what she sounded like in the throes of passion.

Theo stood and offered her his hand. She took it, and he helped her to her feet. Her legs were slightly weak, and she stumbled and landed against his chest while they steadied beneath her.

Once she was properly balanced, he led her out of the drawing room. She kept her head down, a little embarrassed regardless of what he'd said. They took the stairs to the second story, and he led her into the family wing and stopped outside her bedchamber door.

Only then did she realize that she didn't know what his intentions were now. Was she supposed to go inside and tidy herself up while he did the same in his own chambers?

Theo opened the door and kept his arm around her as they entered, preventing her from continuing to wonder. He led her to the chair in front of her dressing table and gestured for her to sit. When she did, he left the room.

Her heart sank. For a moment, she'd dared to hope that he might be going to stay with her for a while, but she should have known better.

She stared at her reflection, making a mental picture of her flushed cheeks and wide eyes, and wondered if anything inside her had changed now that she was no longer fully innocent of the ways of husbands and wives.

It felt so momentous that something ought to have happened to commemorate the occasion, but other than the awareness of a pleasure she'd never expected, all was the same.

It didn't seem right.

Kate stood, ready to summon Margaret to help her wash and dress for the first evening in her new home, but before she could do so, the door opened, and Theo stepped back inside, a bowl in one hand and a washcloth in the other.

He frowned. "What's wrong?"

"Nothing." A lump lodged at the back of her throat. He'd come back.

He tilted his head quizzically but didn't pry. "Sit. Let me clean you properly."

Promptly, she sat. He closed the door, made his way over to her and set the steaming bowl on the dressing table. He dipped the end of the washcloth into the water and wrung it out, then carefully used it to wash any remaining trace of his seed from her face.

She closed her eyes and basked in the attention. When he was finished, she expected him to leave once again, but instead he picked up her hairbrush.

"May I brush your hair?" he asked, a hint of vulnerability in his voice.

She was surprised by the request—at the intimacy of it— but loved the idea. "You may."

She held her breath as he unfastened the clips holding her hair in place and set them on the table one by one. She thought he'd be rough, but his fingers were surprisingly nimble.

When her hair was loose, he ran his fingers through it so that it flowed down her back, then he reached for her intricately carved wooden brush and began to drag it through her hair. The movement was gentle and soothing, and she closed her eyes and enjoyed the massage of the brush bristles over her scalp. Whenever he found a knot, he paused to undo it, always careful not to hurt her.

What a gentleman.

By the time he finished, her hair shone gold in the reflection, and she felt boneless.

"Can I hold you in bed?" he asked as he set the brush down and rested his hands on her shoulders. Their heat warmed her to her core, and she melted a little more.

"We haven't had dinner yet," she pointed out. Night hadn't fully fallen.

He smiled. "Later, I'll have them bring us something we can eat in bed."

Ooh, she liked that idea. It was naughty and delicious and something she hadn't done since she was a child unless she was unwell.

"Yes, please. I'll call for Margaret. Do you need Barlow?"

"No." He gave her shoulders a tender squeeze. "If you're comfortable with it, I'll undress you, and you can do the same for me."

Her stomach flipped over, and she barely concealed her surprise. Undressing him seemed even more intimate than what they'd already shared. Never mind the idea of allowing him to undress her. But as intimidating as the concept was, her blood buzzed with anticipation. She wanted to strip him and see what else his clothing covered.

"I agree." She moistened her lips. "May I undress you first?"

She would feel less exposed if he were already nude before he removed her dress and undergarments.

"Of course."

She stood and circled the chair to stand before him. She surveyed him from head to toe. Earlier, he'd unwittingly shown her how the fastening on his trousers worked, and the buttons of his shirt were clear enough.

Hesitantly, she took his top button between her finger and thumb and slipped it through the opening. The neck of his shirt parted, revealing a strip of pale skin. She moved down to the next one, her fingers clumsy as she fumbled with it. He remained still, being patient with her as she worked her way down his front until the sides of his shirt separated and she could see from his collarbone to his navel.

Tentatively, she pushed the shirt off his shoulders, her teeth sinking into her lower lip as she studied his bare chest. He had pink nipples, just as she did, but they were much smaller. Dark hair dusted his chest and formed an arrow down to his groin. His abdomen was firmer than hers, and the musculature of his upper arms was far more prominent.

He shrugged the shirt the rest of the way off, and it fell to the ground. Kate's gaze journeyed down his ropey forearms to his hands, and she noticed for the first time that his knuckles were slightly discolored, as if they'd been bruised and were in the process of healing. Had he been hurt somehow?

The need for answers burned inside her, but since the damage clearly wasn't recent and she didn't want to ruin the romantic atmosphere, she unfastened his trousers instead and watched as they dropped and pooled around the tops of his boots.

"Oh, dear," she said faintly. "I didn't think about those."

He laughed. "We can manage. Let me just shuffle over to the bed so I can sit."

With his ankles bound by the trousers, he awkwardly waddled to the bed and perched on the edge. Kate knelt in front of him and lifted the trousers off the laces of his boots. He took them from her and held them out of the way.

Kate studied the laces for a long moment before trying to untie them. It took several attempts, but finally, she was able to undo the knots and loosen the laces. She took hold of the boot and pulled it firmly. Thankfully, it came off with little effort. The second followed soon after, and he kicked off the trousers so that he was left in a pair of white drawers.

Kate giggled. "That didn't go according to plan."

A fond smile twisted his lips. "Indeed. Shall we move on from this before I lose all my dignity?"

Kate promptly turned her back to him, presenting him with her buttons. After seeing him with his trousers around his ankles, she was far less concerned by the prospect of being undressed in front of him.

His fingertips trailed down the center of her back as he unfastened her buttons. She toed off her slippers. When her dress fluttered to the ground, she stepped out of it, and he hung it over the back of a chair before helping her out of the petticoat.

He stepped up behind her, and she realized they were angled toward the mirror. From her viewpoint, she could see his reflection, broad-shouldered behind her, the harsh lines of his features softened somewhat as he gazed down at her. Compared to him, she looked small and delicate. The contrast was oddly stirring.

He cupped one of her breasts and ran his thumb gently over her nipple. She thought for a moment that he might suggest more pleasurable activities like the ones that he'd initiated in the drawing room, but instead, he released her.

"Which nightgown would you like?" he asked, striding over to her cabinet.

"Any will do," she replied, trying not to be too disappointed by his failure to ravish her.

He removed a white nightgown from a drawer and slid it over her head, then he settled on the bed, his long legs stretched out, and motioned for her to join him. Her heart beating a little too fast, she lay down alongside him, keeping a small distance between them.

He was having none of that. He dragged her against his body and slung one of his arms over her waist. Her back pressed to his chest, she was surrounded by warmth, held in strong arms, and she relaxed with a sigh of delight. She hadn't realized it could feel so lovely to simply lie with her husband.

She inhaled deeply, breathing in the faint scent of mint with... was that oil of wintergreen? Whatever it was, she liked it.

A deep sense of contentedness settled over her, making her unusually sleepy considering the time of day, but as she yawned and covered his hand with hers, an awful thought passed through her mind and served as a metaphorical bucket of ice water, jolting her out of her cozy cocoon.

She was falling in love with this man.

And she was reasonably sure that he was still in love with Elizabeth.

Oh no.

CHAPTER 23

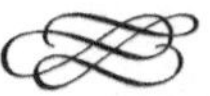

THEO SAW THE CARRIAGE ON THE HORIZON. IT WAS BEING
dragged behind a pair of panicked horses, the side crumpled in.

His heart in his throat, he pushed his legs to go faster. He was
fortunate the horses were so shaken up that they weren't moving
quickly. As soon as they drew near, he slashed out with a knife that
had somehow materialized in his hand and sliced the harnesses,
separating the horses from the carriage.

Theo scrambled over to the carriage, desperate to find
Elizabeth.

He crawled in through the window. This time, she lay face
down, her dark hair matted with blood. He grabbed her shoulder
and turned her gently over, the bottom dropping out of his stomach
when it wasn't Elizabeth's brown eyes staring blankly back at him
but instead, Kate's foggy gray ones.

"No!" he cried, pressing two of his fingers to the pulse point at
her neck, desperately probing for a heartbeat.

There was nothing.

He scooped her into his arms and tilted her head toward him.
This must be a mistake. Any minute, those glassy eyes would clear,
and she'd smile up at him.

But she didn't.

"No, no, no," he murmured, *fervently trying to get a response from her. "Wake up, Kate. Wake up. Please—"*

"Wake up, Theo," a feminine voice said from just above his face. "It's only a dream. You're having a nightmare."

He blinked blearily, and when the image of Kate's clear gray eyes, shining with worry, crystallized above him, a sob of relief burst from him.

Oh, thank God. She wasn't dead. She was still here, alive and well.

"You're all right," he whispered, fighting his way out of the blankets to wrap his arms around her waist. He buried his face against her belly and breathed in the scent of woman and whatever it was that made her smell like flowers. Her soap, perhaps.

She tensed momentarily but then relaxed and stroked his hair. "I'm fine. Everything is all right."

He clutched her tighter, unable to dispel the memory of her glassy eyes and pale skin. Even though she was with him in the present, he could recall the exact sensation of her lifeless body in his embrace.

He shuddered. He couldn't lose her too. Not like Elizabeth. He wouldn't be able to bear it.

Needing to reassure himself that she really was well, he rolled off her and stared at her face and neck in the dim light of dawn that filtered into the room around the curtains. She was unmarked, not a speck of blood on her. But seeing that wasn't enough.

He shoved the bedding off them and reached around until he found the hem of her nightgown. He tugged it up, baring her lower legs, and ran his hands up and down them, verifying for himself that there was nothing amiss.

But what if the damage was hiding underneath her nightdress? People did die from gut wounds.

Even though the rational side of him knew that she wouldn't have suffered severe abdominal trauma while in bed with him, he encouraged her to remove her nightgown so he could explore her torso.

He skimmed his palms over her belly and breasts, then around her back and down her arms. Finally satisfied that she was in no danger of sudden death, he stopped searching her, his breath coming in great heaves as he tried to get the ferocious hammering of his heart under control.

Sweat beaded at his temples, and he held Kate's hips more firmly than he probably should. His fingers formed indents on her lily-white skin, and he couldn't bring himself to move them in case she suddenly disappeared. Right now, he was anchored to her in a way that neither of them could deny.

He needed more, though. He kissed her, savoring her taste—sleepy woman with a hint of sweetness—and breathed in her scent, so warm and alive. Simply seeing she was well wasn't enough. He needed to feel her, smell her, taste her, hear her.

His tongue delved into her mouth, and he groaned, needing to be closer, but he didn't know how.

Kate turned her face away, separating their lips. "How are you feeling?" she asked gently.

He raised his eyes to hers and held her gaze, relieved once again by the spark of life he saw there. "I need..."

Her lips pursed, and she cocked her head. "What do you need, Theo?"

Suddenly, it was beyond obvious what would make this disconcerting panic go away. He needed to bury himself inside her over and over again, feeling her heat smother him and getting her scent so far up his nostrils that it imprinted itself on his brain. Surely, then, the nightmare would lose its hold on him.

"I need to make love to you," he rasped, removing one hand from her hip and slipping it between her legs. He caressed her until she moaned and then slid his other hand to her waist.

She frowned. "But didn't you say that's risky?"

"I changed my mind." There was nothing more life-affirming than sex. He needed it. Now.

He delved into her, finding a trace of slickness that proved she wasn't immune to his touch, and he pressed firmly against her, pleased when she trembled.

She circled her hips, riding his hand, and he supported her weight as best he could so she could get a better angle. Her head fell back, and his gaze finally dropped from her eyes to those perky breasts of hers. He knew the areolas were dusky pink, but they were shadowed in the darkness, the space between them a tempting valley.

She raised her head, her eyes slumberous, but there was a look of fierce concentration in them as she asked, "Are you sure?"

"Yes." Until he was inside her, he wouldn't rest easy. He needed the comfort her body would provide. "Do you want this?"

She watched him with hooded eyes, then nodded.

Thank God.

He continued caressing her until she was wet enough that he was comfortable giving her more. He kissed her to distract her as he pushed one finger inside her. She gasped at the intrusion, inadvertently exchanging breath with him.

"Does it hurt?" he asked through gritted teeth, praying that she'd say no.

"No, it's just… strange."

He tilted his hand to cup her sex, and she immediately rolled her hips, seeking friction. After a while, she'd relaxed enough for him to add a second finger, and then a third. He may be desperate, but he refused to hurt her.

After what felt like an eternity, he crawled over her and slotted his cock against her entrance.

"I'll go slowly," he promised. "If it's uncomfortable, tell me."

"I trust you."

Fuck, those words took the breath from his lungs. He couldn't help feeling that any trust she had in him was completely misplaced.

Nevertheless, he thrust the head of his cock inside her and paused for her to adjust. Her breath caught, and she tensed, clamping down almost painfully, but then her breathing eased, and she wriggled her hips, making space to accommodate him. He inched in bit by bit, pausing often so as not to rush her.

Finally, he was seated deep within her. All of the strain dissipated from his muscles.

She was here.

She was safe.

Most importantly, she was *alive.*

He began to move inside her and found her lips, claiming them with a kiss. Her lips parted and he rubbed his tongue against hers, pleased when she moaned and deepened the kiss.

Her inexperience was clear, but part of him was thrilled to know that she'd never been with another man like this. He was the only one who'd seen her eyelids droop with pleasure and her lips part on a sigh. The only one who'd felt her tight, hot heat clasp around him. The only one who'd tasted her sweet lips.

She wrapped her ankles around the backs of his thighs, holding him in place and opening herself to him even more.

Lord, she felt exquisite.

He kept up a slow, steady rhythm, the frantic edge of his need dulled with the evidence of her vibrancy. Her life.

Pleasure built at the base of his spine, and he rocked, making sure to bump against her clitoris with each thrust until she cried his name and clenched around him. Her orgasm drew his own from him, and he emptied himself inside her.

Immediately, he turned rigid.

Fuck.

What had he done?

He'd forgotten to pull out.

This was bad.

At this very second, they could be conceiving a baby together.

Or, worse, *not* be.

He should have pulled out. Why hadn't he thought about it? He was usually so careful. His goddamn emotions had gotten the better of him.

Now, she'd pay for his mistake.

God*damn* it.

His jaw locked, and he pushed off her and rolled onto his back beside her. He clasped her hand a little too tightly and gazed sightlessly upward.

He'd made love with her. His seed was inside her. If it took, he risked the agony of another miscarriage. If it didn't, there was the chance she'd walk the same path as Elizabeth and be stolen from him by melancholy.

Either way, nothing good could come of this.

"Theo?" Her voice was soft, hesitant. "What's wrong?"

He slammed his eyes shut and swore under his breath. Now, to add to his sins, he'd worried his wife at a time when she should be free to bask in the glow of their joining.

"All is well."

His tone was the last thing from reassuring, but he couldn't seem to fix it.

"Theo." He sensed her movement as she propped herself up on her elbow. "Tell me."

He opened his eyes. Her face hovered over his, a groove between her eyebrows and brackets of strain around her mouth.

"I'm sorry," he whispered. "I shouldn't have done that."

Her hand pressed to her throat, and she flinched. "Done what?"

"All of it." He started to reach for her but stopped himself. He didn't deserve the comfort of her embrace. "I shouldn't have risked what we just did."

She looked stricken. "Did you not want it? You said—"

"I did," he hurried to say, horrified by her distress. "I swear, I did, but it wasn't wise. What if something goes wrong? What if I lose you too?"

Her expression softened as understanding dawned, and she rested her head on the pillow beside him and cuddled up to him. "Whatever happens, it will be all right. You won't lose me."

"You can't know that."

She hadn't been through this before. He had. He'd thought to protect himself by refusing to remarry, and then, when that had fallen through, by keeping his distance from his wife.

Now, he feared it was too late to save either of them. Thanks to his selfishness, he might have doomed them both.

CHAPTER 24

Oxfordshire
January 1823

A knock on the door signaled Mrs. Tubb's arrival in Kate's bedchamber, and the knots in her gut tightened. She hoped she wasn't making a dreadful mistake.

It had been a little over two weeks since the night they'd shared their bodies. Two weeks, and one of the loneliest Christmases she'd ever experienced. The servants had put up decorations, and she and Theo had exchanged gifts, but the entire affair had been awkward, and they'd spent the day largely apart.

She'd tried to draw him into singing carols as she played on the piano, but he'd been preoccupied, and eventually she'd given up. It was far from the cheerful, festive holiday she'd hoped for.

Despite the time that had passed, she still couldn't get the memory of his horror-struck expression after he realized what they'd done after he'd woken from his nightmare out of her head.

She'd understood why he'd been upset—what had driven

his terror—and she'd tried to respond with kindness and sympathy. She cared for him and didn't want to see him in such a state.

But regardless of that, his reaction in the aftermath had felt like the worst kind of rejection. He'd been legitimately horrified by what had seemed to her like a beautiful, intimate shared moment… up until the end, at least.

Then, it had been all too apparent what it really was.

A mistake.

One he regretted wholeheartedly.

As awful as that was, what had been even worse was the sinking in her gut as she'd wondered whether she'd somehow taken advantage of him. He'd been in a weakened state, agitated by his nightmare and not in the most reasonable frame of mind.

She'd asked if he'd been certain he wanted to consummate the marriage, and he'd said yes, but she should have resisted anyway. The right thing to do would have been to dress and talk through whatever had plagued him in his dreams rather than allowing him to draw her into something he'd never have wanted if he had been thinking clearly.

The knock came again, and she snapped to the present.

"Come in!" she called, turning to face the door.

The handle turned, and Mrs. Tubbs entered, a friendly smile on her thin lips. "What can I do for you, my lady?"

Kate looked around, trying to find the courage she'd had when she'd initially summoned Mrs. Tubbs. She wasn't wrong to want to put her own stamp on this place, was she? Since she'd arrived, she'd been living with Elizabeth's ghost. The late viscountess's mark was on everything.

Kate didn't want to erase her or replace her, but she needed to do something to make it feel like she belonged. Everyone had treated her kindly, and she could tell they were pleased by her presence, but she felt like an intruder who'd stepped into someone else's life.

Theodore had told her that she could make whatever changes she wanted to, and she was going to do just that. At least within the safety of her own bedchamber.

"I would like to redecorate," she declared, injecting steel into her spine.

Mrs. Tubbs nodded as if this request didn't surprise her. "What would you like changed?"

Kate picked up a piece of paper from the top of her writing table and skimmed the items of the list. "I'd like new wallpaper, preferably something in a pale shade of pink. I'd like dark blue drapes and bedclothes to match."

"That's easily done." Mrs. Tubbs took the paper from Kate. "Would you rather choose your own wallpaper or have a staff member choose it for you?"

Kate considered this. "I'll choose my own. I'll take Margaret into South Wye to assist me."

"Very good, my lady. In the meantime, we'll need to shift you into another room while the changes are being made. Do you have any in particular in mind?"

When Kate shook her head, Mrs. Tubbs thought for a moment, and then her face lit up. "I have just the one." She bustled into the corridor.

Kate followed her down the hall to another room, which was decorated in feminine shades of lilac and cream with a frilly bedspread and a painting of a rose garden on the wall. It smelled slightly musty, as if it hadn't been aired out for a while.

Kate studied the painting, wondering at first if it was the rose garden at Blackwell Hall, but she quickly realized it wasn't. It was still pretty, though.

"I'll have your things moved in here temporarily, if you're satisfied with it?" Mrs. Tubbs asked.

"That would be helpful, thank you."

"Would you like that to be done right now?"

"Yes, please." There was no point in delaying. If she put it off, then she might talk herself out of it, and that would only end with her continuing to be uncomfortable in the space that should be her refuge.

Mrs. Tubbs backed out of the room, leaving Kate alone. She sat on the bed, pleased to find that the mattress was reasonably soft, then flopped onto her back. Gazing up at the off-white ceiling, she hoped she wasn't about to upset Theo. She really didn't want to do that. Nor did she want to disrespect his former marriage.

But she was lonely and felt out of place. He'd avoided sharing a bed with her again for the past two weeks, and seemed disinterested in doing so much as laying a finger on her lest he become overwhelmed by passion and make another "mistake." She couldn't do much about the loneliness, so her only recourse was to address the second problem and try to make Blackwell Hall feel more like home.

She closed her eyes when they began to burn and willed herself not to cry. She'd chosen this life, and she'd done so knowing that Theo hadn't intended to marry again. Naively, she'd thought that she would change his mind.

She supposed she could still do so, but she shouldn't have relied on that. While she honestly believed that he cared about her—he wouldn't be so distraught by the possibility of doing wrong by her otherwise—he was so caught up in the past that he couldn't see what joy the future could bring if he were willing to take a risk.

A knock on the door jolted her from her reverie. She got to her feet and opened it. Samuel stood on the other side, holding her writing desk.

"Can I bring this in, my lady?" he asked with a respectful bob of his head.

"Of course." She stepped aside, and he carried the desk over to place it beside the one already in the room. Kate's was made of darker wood, while the other was paler and intricately carved with a floral design.

Samuel straightened and backed away. "Would you like your bed brought in here, or shall we put it in storage?"

"Put it into storage, please." That would be easier than swapping the beds around. Especially since she doubted moving the bed would prove easy in the first place. "Or, if the renovations can be done without moving it, you could simply cover it and leave it there."

He nodded, his brow wrinkled. "I'll suggest that to Mrs. Tubbs."

He left, and Kate sat on the chair in front of the other writing desk. She studied the floral design and traced it with her finger. Curiosity got the better of her, and she opened the lid. The only thing inside was a small personal bible with a faded black cover.

She flipped through the pages, pausing when she noticed the tidy script in the margins. Whoever this had belonged to had cared enough about it to add their own thoughts about particular passages. The handwriting looked feminine, although she couldn't be certain.

She closed the book, feeling as though she'd intruded on its owner's privacy, but as she went to place it back inside the desk, a flower slipped from between the pages and landed on the wood.

Carefully, Kate picked the flower up between her thumb and forefinger. It must have been in there for years because it was so thin and dry that it was almost translucent. Her heart stuttered as a possibility occurred to her, and she dropped the flower as if it had burned her.

Had this bible belonged to the flower-loving Elizabeth?

She dashed to the door and called down the corridor for Mrs. Tubbs. The housekeeper emerged from the viscountess's bedchamber, her cheeks red and one eyebrow raised.

"Is something wrong?" she asked, her tone far warmer than her expression, as Kate had learned was usual for her.

The housekeeper's features never rested in a particularly welcoming way despite her kind nature.

Kate hesitated, feeling foolish. What did it matter if she'd found Elizabeth's bible? The woman had lived here for years. Of course traces of her personal life would remain. But she couldn't help being curious about her. She knew a little of her from what Theo and others had said, but she wanted to know more.

Mrs. Tubbs frowned. "What is it?"

"I found something. I just wanted to check who it belonged to."

"Oh." She nodded and marched along the hall more spryly than one would expect of a woman her age. "What have you found?"

Kate led her to the desk and showed her the bible and the flower. "Were these… Elizabeth's?"

Mrs. Tubbs exhaled softly. "Oh, yes. That was her ladyship's personal bible. Her father gifted it to her when she married his lordship. She was very fond of it."

Kate's heart squeezed. "Thank you for telling me."

"No trouble at all, my lady." She shifted from one foot to the other, obviously uncomfortable. "Do you want me to take it away?"

"No," Kate exclaimed, startled. "No, it can stay. I may want to make the bedchamber more to my liking, but I don't wish for Elizabeth's existence to be hidden away. If this meant so much to her, perhaps we could display it in the library."

Mrs. Tubbs beamed. "That's a lovely idea. I'll ask his lordship about it. In the meantime, I'll leave it in your keeping."

Kate glanced down at the bible, tempted by the idea of getting an unexpected insight into Elizabeth's innermost thoughts. It wouldn't be right, though. She ought not to pry where she had no business being.

"Actually, I've changed my mind. Perhaps you could give

it to Lord Blackwell for safekeeping until he's decided what he'd like done with it."

Mrs. Tubbs expression softened, and her eyes crinkled at the corners. "Indeed I will." She reached for the bible with gnarled hands and gently slipped the flower back inside. "You're good for our master. He may not see it yet, but I do. Have patience. He'll come around."

"I hope so." But she didn't have as much faith as Mrs. Tubbs. Theo had been through a lot. There was no guarantee he'd ever recover.

Mrs. Tubbs left with the bible. Kate shifted over to her own writing desk and withdrew a piece of paper and a graphite pencil from inside. She looked out the window, where bare rose bushes stood starkly against the snow. With pencil in hand, she began to trace the outlines of the plants, paying special attention to the contrast between the skeletons of the plants and the white powdered ground.

As she sketched, she allowed her mixed emotions to bleed into the picture. It wasn't a cheerful image, but then, she wasn't in a particularly cheerful mood. Instead, it was dark and moody—thought-provoking in a way she hadn't intended.

"Kate?"

She jumped and bashed her knee on the underside of the desk, biting down on her lip to prevent herself from cursing as her knee throbbed from the impact. She drew in a slow breath through her nostrils to gather herself, and, ignoring the new ache, turned toward the doorway.

Theo stood there, tears in his eyes and Elizabeth's bible clasped to his chest. "What did you mean by giving me this?"

She bit the inside of her cheek, wondering too late whether she'd overstepped and should have just pretended never to have found it.

"I thought you should have it," she said, not about to confess that she hadn't trusted herself not to peek inside in an effort to understand his late wife. That surely wouldn't be what he'd want to hear. "Should I… not have?"

He muttered something under his breath.

"I'm sorry." She stood and faced him. "I didn't mean to upset you."

"You didn't." He closed the distance between them with a few long strides. "I just…. I don't know what to do."

She cocked her head. "About what?"

"You." He gave a wobbly smile. "I feel something for you, and I shouldn't. Not when I don't know how to make you happy. You deserve better than a failure of a husband."

She gaped at him, at a loss for words. Was he admitting that he had romantic feelings for her?

He was clearly disturbed and conflicted about whatever was preoccupying his head and heart, but she got the impression his frustration was all directed inward. Perhaps he believed that he didn't deserve to be happy with another woman because Elizabeth would never have that option, or perhaps he genuinely thought he'd make her miserable.

"I'm going to make the same mistakes again," he continued, dragging his hand through his hair and turning to pace to the bed and back. "You'll be unhappy, and I'll be unhappy, and there will be nothing I can do.

"Hold on." She rested a gentle hand on his upper arm. "Stop this recrimination. I'm sure Elizabeth wouldn't want you to be so miserable. You haven't done anything wrong, and neither have I."

"But I have," he cried, emphasizing this with a wave of his free hand. "I wasn't enough to stop her from falling into despair, and I don't know how to do better with you other than to remove the stress of being pressured to provide an heir. If I don't learn my lesson, then history will repeat itself."

Kate narrowed her eyes. Yes, Theo had experienced more grief than most, but she'd had enough of this attitude. "How about you trust me to know what I need and ask for it rather than assuming you're solely responsible for my health and welfare and that I'm incapable of expressing myself? I'm a person with my own thoughts and agenda. I'm not a helpless child beholden to you."

His jaw dropped and his eyes widened. "I…. I…."

She crossed her arms and waited. "Yes?"

"You deserve better," he said, and turned on his heel and fled.

Kate sighed. "Well, that went poorly."

CHAPTER 25

"Have you seen Lady Blackwell this morning?" Theo asked Mrs. Tubbs as she walked past the room he was eating breakfast in.

After he'd made an ass of himself the other day, he'd apologized to Kate with a gift of special artists' paints delivered from London that he'd been assured were perfect for painting country landscapes.

She'd accepted his apology and told him he needn't have bought her a gift, but he'd seen the excitement in her eyes and the tiny smile she couldn't quite hide. It pleased him to buy her something she would take joy from.

They hadn't discussed any feelings between them further but seemed to have come to a silent understanding. They no longer avoided each other, and he adored being able to spend more time in her company.

Considering their tentative new closeness, it was strange that she hadn't joined him for breakfast.

"I haven't seen her, my lord," Mrs. Tubbs said, then hesitated.

"What?" Theo demanded, not liking that hesitation.

Mrs. Tubbs grimaced. "It's nothing, I'm sure."

He arched an eyebrow. "Why don't you tell me what's worrying you, and I'll decide whether I ought to be concerned or not."

She nodded. "Very well. I believe I heard Margaret telling Samuel that her ladyship is under the weather."

"Under the weather how?" he asked, his heart rate picking up. In the time since he'd met her, he hadn't known Kate to be sickly.

His mind flashed to memories of opening the viscountess's bedchamber and finding Elizabeth lying in bed, the curtains pulled, crying silently because her courses had arrived once again.

Perhaps Kate's monthly flow was here. He'd known since the night they'd been together that either her courses would come and he'd have to deal with the fallout of her not being pregnant or that his seed would take and he'd spend months in an agony of waiting, praying that they didn't lose the baby. There was nothing to be done about it now except wait and see.

"I don't know." Mrs. Tubbs lowered her gaze. "I didn't stay to listen."

"Thank you for telling me what you know." He dismissed her with a nod, and she hurried out.

He stared at his empty plate, relieved that he'd already eaten. If he'd waited, he'd likely have had no appetite. As it was, the food sat heavy in his gut like a lump of lead his body didn't know how to process. The back of his throat burned, and he drank the rest of his tea, hoping to soothe it, but the liquid didn't help.

He pushed back his chair, got up, and made his way through the house to the bedchamber Kate was staying in. He hadn't asked what changes she was making to the viscountess's chambers. Honestly, he didn't care. She'd done nothing but respect Elizabeth's memory, and she deserved to be comfortable in her private space.

He knocked. Seconds passed by, and no one responded. He knocked again. There was a muffled grunt inside. Concerned, he opened the door and stuck his head in.

The curtains were pulled, and the room was dim, but he could clearly see Kate huddled on the floor beside the bed with an empty chamber pot cradled on her lap. As he watched, she convulsed and retched into it, the sour stench of vomit permeating the air.

Wrinkling his nose, he hurried over and dropped to his knees beside her. He rested one hand on the back of her neck, and when she leaned over the chamber pot again, he helped hold her hair back as she emptied her stomach with a full-body shudder.

When she finished casting up her accounts, she turned to him, looking utterly miserable. "I'm sorry you had to see that."

Her cheeks were paler than usual, her eyes were watery, and when he touched the backs of his fingers to her forehead, she was hot and clammy.

"How long have you been feeling unwell?" he asked, waiting until it was clear that she wasn't about to be sick again before easing the chamber pot from her grip.

She closed her eyes and leaned back against the bed. "On and off for a few days, but this is the first time I've thrown up."

"You should have said something." Even as the words left his mouth, he knew why she hadn't. She'd been worried about his reaction. Hot shame coursed through him. His wife had needed a doctor but hadn't asked for him to summon one out of concern for him.

What a mess.

"I'm sorry," he said, not giving her a chance to respond. "I'll call for a doctor immediately. Wait here."

He went to the corridor and waved to Samuel, who was hovering nearby. The footman seemed to have taken a liking to Kate—or perhaps just to her maid—and could often be found nearby.

"Summon Dr. Hanson," he said, speaking low so as not to invite too much attention from other members of the household. "I'd also appreciate it if you could send in a maid to empty her ladyship's chamber pot and bring a glass of room temperature water, a bowl of cool water, and a cloth. Also, ask the kitchen to prepare a broth."

Samuel's eyebrows knitted together. "Is her ladyship ill?"

He nodded. "Be quick."

With a determined expression, Samuel strode away.

Theo returned to the bedchamber to find that Kate had made it back to the bed and crawled under the covers. He sat on the edge of the mattress and swallowed past the rock that seemed to be lodged in his throat. He knew what he needed to ask, and it was time to be a man and do it.

He held her gaze despite his churning gut. "When did you last have your monthly courses?"

She nibbled her lower lip, looking into space as she thought. "Not since before we married."

"Long before?" he asked, leaning forward. "This is important."

Ashen, she nodded. "Perhaps six or seven weeks. Might I be...?"

At first, his heart lifted—the instinctive reaction—but then a shiver ran through him, and his chest constricted.

Elizabeth had been pregnant three times. The first two times, he'd been excited to welcome his unborn baby into the world. By the third, all he'd felt was dread because he'd known how it would end.

"Then there's a chance you are with child." Theo inhaled and exhaled slowly and regularly, reminding himself not to lose his nerve. No matter how terrified he might be of losing any potential baby—or worse, Kate—she needed him right now, and he couldn't afford to fall apart.

"Do you think it's likely?"

Hope shone in her eyes, and he didn't have the heart to temper it.

"Perhaps."

A maid swept into the room with a glass of water in one hand, a bowl in the other, and a cloth tucked under her arm. She set the bowl and the glass on the nightstand and placed the cloth beside the bowl, then grabbed the chamber pot and took it out with her.

Theo passed Kate the glass of water. "Drink this. I'm sure your mouth doesn't feel very pleasant right now."

With a look of gratitude, she took the glass and sipped it. She paused, and, when her body didn't react negatively to the water, drank more. She half finished the glass before handing it back to him.

He dipped the cloth into the bowl of water, wrung it out, and dabbed her forehead. "How does that feel?"

"It's nice," she murmured, closing her eyes.

"Good."

He held the cloth to her forehead, refreshing it with the water every few minutes. He kept an eye on her in case she seemed ready to cast up her accounts again, but the fact that she'd already done so had apparently brought her a temporary reprieve.

Soon, the maid returned with the cleaned chamber pot and left it beside the bed in case Kate needed it. She had dozed off, but Theo didn't move from her side.

A while later, Mrs. Tubbs brought in a bowl of broth. Theo debated whether to wake Kate but decided not to. As it happened, she stirred when Mrs. Tubbs closed the door anyway.

"Would you like some broth?" he asked, gesturing to the bowl on the nightstand. "It's chicken, I understand."

"I'll try," she said tiredly. "I'm not sure if it will stay inside me."

She struggled to sit up, and he rushed to prop pillows behind her. He held the bowl of broth, dunked the soup spoon into it, and raised it to her lips. Her eyes widened, but her lips parted automatically, and she slurped from the spoon.

She hummed thoughtfully. "I think I'm all right to have a little more. Not too much, though."

He spooned more broth for her.

She narrowed her eyes at him. "I can feed myself."

"Let me. Please." He needed to make up for his previous negligence in whatever ways he could.

She searched his gaze, then tilted her head in silent agreement. This time when he tried to feed her, she didn't resist. There was something very intimate about feeding someone, and his heart filled with warmth as he helped her fill her poor unsettled stomach.

When the bowl was nearly empty, she shook her head. "No more."

"My lord," Mr. Giles called from outside the room. "Dr. Hanson is here."

"Bring him up, please," Theo called back.

Footsteps retreated down the hall, and a minute or so later, Mr. Giles showed Dr. Hanson into the bedchamber. The doctor was young, having recently inherited the local clinic from his father. He was fair-haired and bluff-faced with a genial personality well-suited to a man of his occupation.

Dr. Hanson placed his medical bag on the floor and bowed. "Good morning, Lord and Lady Blackwell. How may I be of service?"

"Lady Blackwell is ill," Theo said, standing to shake the doctor's hand. "Thank you for coming so quickly."

"Not a problem." Dr. Hanson turned to Kate. "How have your symptoms presented?"

"Uh…." She blinked as though focusing on him was difficult for her. "My stomach has been unsettled for several days, and I cast up my accounts this morning."

"It is… possible that her ladyship is pregnant," Theo said reluctantly.

"I see." The doctor gestured to her. "May I come closer?"

She nodded her permission.

He knelt beside the bed and touched her forehead. "You're hot. Have you experienced any headaches or dizziness?"

Kate glanced at Theo before answering. "A little dizziness."

Theo dug his fingernails into his palms as guilt clawed at his insides. No recriminations would help her now. All he could do was proceed with more care than he'd shown her so far and make it clear that she could come to him with anything.

"Have any smells made you particularly distressed?" the doctor asked.

"Hmm, no. I don't think so."

"When did you last have your monthly flow?"

Her cheeks flamed bright red, and Theo was tempted to snap at the doctor to not ask such personal things, but instead he simply answered for her, sparing her the embarrassment.

"Six or seven weeks."

Dr. Hanson made a sound in the back of his throat. "May I feel your abdomen?"

"All right," Kate said timidly, pushing the blankets down to reveal her nightgown-clad body.

Dr. Hanson ran his hand over her belly, stopping to push down a little in several places. After continuing for long enough that Theo wanted to rip his hands off his wife, the doctor backed away.

He asked a few more questions and then offered his conclusions. "I think it's very likely that you're with child.

Sickness is usual during the first months of pregnancy. You may experience nausea, dizziness, tiredness, and oversensitivity to particular smells or tastes. All of this is to be expected and is no cause for concern."

Sweat beaded on Theo's upper lip, and a wave of vertigo crashed over him.

Pregnant.

She was *pregnant.*

Well, they had the answer as to the outcome of their lovemaking. Now there was nothing he could do but keep her as safe and comfortable as possible and pray she wouldn't miscarry.

"Are you sure?" Kate asked, sneaking a glance at him.

His gut twisted. Under other circumstances, she'd no doubt be thrilled by this news but because of him, she mustn't know how to react.

Damn, he needed to make it obvious that he would stand by her through everything even if he was fucking terrified of losing both her and their baby. She'd brought so much color to his life. The thought of that ending…

He could scarcely countenance it.

"I can't be positive until you begin to show or have missed more of your courses, but I'm reasonably confident," the doctor said. "Do your best to eat and drink even if you aren't feeling well, and don't exert yourself too hard. You need to be careful."

Based on the way Dr. Hanson shot Theo a look, his father had told him exactly what kind of problems Theo and Elizabeth had experienced, and he, too, was concerned about Theo's frame of mind.

"If you need me, don't hesitate to call for me any time of day or night," he continued, smiling at Kate encouragingly. "If you have any general questions about pregnancy, you can have a letter delivered, and I'll respond promptly."

"Thank you," Theo rasped, burying his hands in his

pockets so he didn't wring them. If he gave Kate more cause for anxiety, he wouldn't forgive himself. He needed to be strong for her.

"I'll be on my way," Dr. Hanson said, standing and picking up his medical bag. "There's no reason for me to stay longer. If the sickness worsens, let me know."

"I'll walk you out," Theo said.

Dr. Hanson nodded and stepped out of the bedchamber. Theo hesitated before following, reluctant to leave Kate. It wouldn't be for long, though.

As they got farther from Kate, Dr. Hanson spoke.

"Just because pregnancy was difficult with the late viscountess, God rest her soul, doesn't mean your new viscountess is more likely to suffer the same problem," he said softly. "Chin up, Lord Blackwell. We'll do all we can to ensure your heir is brought safely into the world."

Theo's hands trembled, and he was glad they were still hidden from view. "Her safety is my priority." He would cherish a child, especially considering he'd thought he'd never have one, but he wasn't going to risk Kate to get one. "She comes first."

Dr. Hanson inclined his head. "Of course. I didn't mean to imply otherwise. Despite her nausea, Lady Blackwell seems to be of strong constitution. I see no reason to worry."

Theo was grateful to hear that even if it didn't completely reassure him. There had been no obvious reason for Elizabeth's difficulties either.

He escorted Dr. Hanson to the door and considered detouring to his illicit whiskey supply before returning to Kate but decided against it. Tempting as the thought might be, he ought to keep his wits about him, the better to protect her.

He made his way down a strangely silent corridor and couldn't help wondering if the household staff were hiding from him, uncertain whether he was about to lose his mind. He wouldn't blame them if they were.

He tentatively entered Kate's bedchamber and crossed over to sit on the edge of her bed.

"I'm sorry," she said, looking miserable. "I know you didn't want this."

He took her hand and gave it a squeeze. "I'm not angry. I've actually always wanted a child. I'm just... scared that something might happen to you."

She nodded but didn't seem convinced.

Sighing, he raised her hand to his lips and kissed the back of it, then turned it over and pressed his lips to the inside of her wrist, feeling her pulse flutter. "It was my choice to do what we did. This is the consequence. Honestly, it could end up being the best thing to ever happen to us, but I'm likely to be on edge until we come out the other side with both you and the baby healthy and happy."

Her expression softened, and she laced her fingers with his and tilted her chin up, a gleam of determination in her eyes. "I understand why you're afraid. I know it doesn't seem like it now, but I'm sure everything will be all right."

He hoped she was correct.

He sat with her until she drifted back to sleep, and then he did something he hadn't done in years. He got on his knees and prayed. He prayed for Kate and their baby to be well. For the pregnancy to pass without issue. For his new family to remain whole.

But in the darkest corners of his mind, he couldn't help wondering, if God hadn't listened to his prayers before, then why would He now?

CHAPTER 26

Kate glanced at Theo as he wrapped his arm around her back as if completely prepared to catch her if she were to swoon.

While that was sweet, he'd been much the same for the past two and a half weeks since they'd learned of the pregnancy, and between that and being confined to the house, she was at her wit's end.

As gently as she could, she smiled up at him and said, "If I don't see a little of the countryside soon, there's every possibility I might lose my mind. I've been cooped up for too long. I need fresh air and new sights."

His expression grew pained. "I know. I just worry."

She stretched up onto her toes and kissed his cheek, enjoying the faint flush that rose on it. "We'll be careful."

She had to admit, she liked him fussing over her… to an extent. It was nice to know he cared. After weeks of keeping a cool distance from her, his attitude had completely changed, almost as if one of his fears coming true was enough to bust through the emotional barrier he'd been trying to construct between them.

That said, she hated that his attention came from a place of fear.

Yes, she'd been unwell. Honestly, it was awful. She'd barely managed to keep any food down, and she ached constantly. But she didn't feel as if she was on the precipice of death, and he was treating her as if one misstep could be her last.

She wished she could prove him wrong but had quickly realized that the only thing that would erase his fear was delivering their child safely. Hopefully after that, he'd see that history wasn't going to repeat, and he'd allow himself to loosen his grip a little.

Theo helped her down the steps and across the graveled ground to the carriage. It had rained two nights ago and washed away the snow, clearing the road for the journey into South Wye. A small step was positioned in front of the carriage, and he assisted her inside. Her eyebrows rose at the sight of a cushion positioned on the bench beside the window on the far side of the carriage.

"I thought you might need extra padding in case we go over any bumps," Theo said as he climbed in behind her and ushered her to the cushion.

She sat on it and nodded approvingly. It was comfortable. "Thank you."

He sat beside her but left a disappointingly large space between them. "I've told the driver to go slowly."

One side of her mouth hitched up, and she looked out the window at the sky beyond so as not to let him see how endearing she found him. There was a cold breeze, and the clouds hadn't abated after the downpour, but she was grateful to be out of the house regardless.

The carriage began to roll over the gravel and toward the road leading away from Blackwell Hall. She rested against the wall to steady herself. The cushion made the seat softer, but it also rendered her less stable and therefore more prone to travel-induced sickness rather than the pregnancy-related nausea that had been her unwelcome companion.

As they trundled along the road toward the township of South Wye, she fixed her gaze on the horizon out the window and breathed slowly and deeply, doing her best not to show how badly her stomach was rolling. If she let on that she was unwell, Theo would have her tucked safely inside Blackwell Hall with all due haste.

She *needed* this outing.

She could sense Theo watching her out of the corner of her eye as they traveled. Eventually, she gave up pretending not to notice and took his hand, hoping that the physical contact would reassure him.

His palm was warm against hers. His knuckles were slightly scarred but didn't have any bruises like the ones she'd once seen, and she wondered what had caused that. Would he ever tell her?

During her exploration of Blackwell Hall, she'd been looking for spare thread when she stumbled into a room with a strange leather bag hanging from the ceiling. She'd never seen anything like it. Were the two somehow related?

She shook her head to clear her vision and blinked in surprise at the sight of a beautiful bare-branched tree set against the rolling fields. There was something about its gnarled branches and the way the shadows fell across it that would make it an excellent subject to paint. She'd have to return with supplies.

A while later, they arrived in South Wye. The town was small but not tiny. There were several shops on the high street, one of which belonged to the local seamstress. They'd visited the seamstress's shop when she and Margaret came to town, but the seamstress herself had been home unwell, leaving her daughter to manage the shop in her absence.

Kate had purchased a few ribbons and a bonnet, as much to endear herself to the local community than anything else, and had also dropped by the bakery, where she'd bought treats for herself and Theo.

She'd tried to make an appearance in every shop where she'd be welcome as a woman so the town locals would know who she was. She'd been especially thrilled when she'd visited the small bookstore attached to the post office and discovered a copy of Amelia's novel.

Today, they were primarily in South Wye to order new dresses from the seamstress.

The carriage came to a halt outside the seamstress's shop, and Theo disembarked and hovered at the door to help her down. She dragged in a lungful of fresh country air and studied the window display. There were perhaps two or three dozen bolts of fabric—not much compared to the offerings in London, but better than she'd expected to find in a town of this size.

"Shall I wait outside?" Theo asked, the purse of his mouth and the furrow of his brow making it clear that he'd rather keep close to her.

She looked up at the sky. There was a certain chill to the air that threatened snow, although they should have plenty of time to return home before it started. "You'd best come in. I'm sure she won't mind if you wait near the door." Most likely the woman would be thrilled by the local lord's presence.

He nodded. "Excellent."

She hid another smile. If he thought he was subtle in his hovering over her, he was deluded. She took his arm and they entered together.

Inside, she released him and approached a matronly woman with dark hair and a kind face who she assumed was the seamstress. The woman's eyes widened, and she sketched a quick curtsey.

"My lady," she said breathlessly. "It's an honor to meet

you. I'm Mrs. Halt but you can call me Annie. I believe you met my daughter a while ago. How can I help you?"

Kate greeted Annie warmly, confirming that she had indeed met her daughter, before addressing the reason they'd come—other than her intense need to get out of the house. "I'm increasing, and I would like to order new dresses that allow space for growth."

Annie gasped and clapped her hand to her mouth, obviously delighted to be blessed with this gossip, then seemed to remember herself and cleared her throat. "Whatever you need. Do you have particular fabrics in mind?"

Kate turned to study the display. "I've been unwell, so I'd prefer soft or light fabrics. I generally like to wear shades of blue, pink, and green."

Annie's forehead crinkled sympathetically. "Is the little one giving you trouble?"

"Only a little." Absently, she rested her hand on her mostly flat belly. "Some sickness, and I'm more tired than usual, but nothing to worry about."

Dr. Hanson had been summoned to reassure Theo of this fact several times. One night, when she'd been particularly ill, he'd even stayed at Blackwell Hall to monitor her and had reported that while she was dehydrated, her symptoms truly were nothing out of the ordinary so far.

"Have you tried eating ginger or drinking it with hot water and honey?" Annie asked, reaching for a pale green fabric that Kate had already decided she liked.

"I haven't."

"Worked wonders for me. Ginger settled my pregnancy sickness like magic. Try it and see what you think. If there's none out at Blackwell, I'm sure the grocer will have some."

Kate made a mental note to ask the cook about adding ginger to their meals. She'd never had it in a drink before, but if it would help, she was willing to try it.

She and Annie discussed fabrics and what styles of dress she might like. Kate kept it simple, unsure how far Annie's skills extended, and by the time she left, the seamstress was practically glowing with excitement at the idea of clothing a viscountess.

"Would you like to visit the bakery?" Theo asked as they stepped out onto the street. "I'm hungry, so I'm sure you are too."

"A bread roll or pastry might be nice," she allowed, knowing that there was no point resisting. She wasn't particularly hungry—her stomach was too unsettled for that—but along with keeping her warm and comfortable, Theo had also become obsessed with making sure she had enough to eat.

A snowflake landed on her nose, and she tilted her head back. Another melted on her forehead.

"We'd best be quick," she said, looping her arm through his. "The snow has come faster than expected, and we want to be back before it starts in earnest."

Theo dithered, visibly torn between feeding her and their unborn child and the need to get her home and out of the weather as soon as possible. After a moment, he nodded, and they hurried toward the bakery together.

Unfortunately, as they reached the bakery, a couple stepped out of it. Kate recognized them instantly and stiffened, almost tripping over her feet as she stumbled to a halt.

"Mr. and Mrs. Norman," she breathed, instinctively turning to Theo to see how he was reacting to this unexpected encounter.

He was pale, his lips thin, and he drew her closer to himself. "Good day."

"Good day?"

To Kate's surprise, it was the soft-spoken vicar who replied, his chest puffed out, his eyes narrowed, rather than the spiteful wife.

"Good day?" Mr. Norman demanded. "I say not, sir. Since

we first made the acquaintance of your poor wife, Mrs. Norman and I have discovered how you came to be married. You compromised an innocent and forced her into a wedding. Had we known earlier, I daresay we'd never have left Blackwell Hall without ensuring her safe passage somewhere away from you."

Kate eyed them with disbelief. "I beg your pardon?"

Mr. Norman turned to her. "I give you my word, my lady, we won't stand back and watch this cad ruin another young woman's life."

Instinctively, Kate's hand went to her belly.

Mr. Norman paled, and beside him, Mrs. Norman gasped and looked as though she might be about to pass out.

Mr. Norman sputtered for several seconds, and then, slowly, his face changed from white to an awful shade of red.

"How dare you?" He swaggered toward Theo more like a prizefighter than a vicar. "It wasn't enough for you to ruin her reputation and steal her future? You had to… to…. You are determined to make this sweet girl miserable, you utter swine."

A strong wind knocked Kate back onto her heels, and the sleeves of her dress clung to her skin, damp from the snow that was beginning to fall. She stared at Mr. and Mrs. Norman, and much as she felt for them because they'd lost the most important person in their lives, enough was enough.

It was no wonder Theo was such a mess. These people wouldn't let him move forward. They were grieving, but that was no excuse for destroying a good man.

Kate straightened her back and summoned her courage. "I am not miserable," she said loudly and clearly.

All three people turned to her. Excellent. They were listening.

"Lord Blackwell has *not* ruined me. He hasn't stolen my future. I care for him, and I respect him, and I'm truly sorry for your loss, but it wasn't his fault, and he isn't the demon you're making him out to be."

"You don't know how Elizabeth was treated under his care," Mrs. Norman said shrilly.

"I know that he loved your daughter." Kate held her gaze, silently daring her to contradict that. "I know that he grieved for her just as much as you did, if not more. But you had each other to lean on. Who did he have? He'd already lost his father, and then he lost his wife too. You should have been there for him, but instead you demonized him. If you want to talk about ruining someone's future, maybe you should look in the mirror."

Mrs. Norman's eyes were narrowed, color high on her cheeks, and she looked like she was thinking about slapping Kate, but Mr. Norman had paused and seemed to be listening.

"You're a vicar." Kate waited a moment for those words to sink in. "Shouldn't you be encouraging forgiveness, not blame and pointless anger?"

Mr. Norman nodded so subtly, she almost didn't notice it. "You've given me much to think about. You aren't unhappy?"

"No, I'm not," she said firmly, not allowing any room for misinterpretation.

"Very well, then." He backed away a step and tugged at his wife's arm. "If you ever need spiritual guidance, you're always welcome at the vicarage."

With Mrs. Norman protesting vehemently, he dragged her away.

"Kate?"

She turned slowly to Theo, hoping this whole interaction hadn't made him rethink the progress they'd been making in their relationship. "Yes?"

He moved toward her until less than a foot separated them and cradled her face between his hands. "Did you mean that?"

She gazed into his dark eyes, unable to read the emotion in them. "Which part?"

"All of it."

She smiled at him, hoping he'd be able to read the sincerity in her expression. "I did."

His thumb found the corner of her mouth, and he smoothed it over her lower lip. "I hope you know that I care about you deeply. More than I ever expected to."

Her heart lifted, and her chest felt light, but she hardly dared to dream. "You are so important to me," she whispered.

He glanced around, and she had the impression that he might've kissed her if they weren't standing on a public street. "It's always terrified me how easily I could fall for you, but I'm not scared of it anymore." He grinned, and it was joyous and bright and lovely. "I'm done fighting. I want us to be husband and wife in every sense of the words."

CHAPTER 27

KATE'S EYES BULGED AS SHE STRUGGLED TO PROCESS THEO'S proclamation. She could hardly believe what she was hearing. It was a dream. A fantasy. One she'd never expected to come true. At least, not this soon.

Perhaps Mr. and Mrs. Norman had done her a favor by confronting her and Theo, as their doing so had prompted her defense, which in turn had caused him to experience some kind of enlightenment.

How, she had no idea. But she wasn't about to question it.

"It's the wrong time for this." His expression shuttered, and he drew back from her. "I'm sorry, this is entirely inappropriate. It's cold, and we need to get you something to eat and make sure you're back in the manor, safe and sound, before the snow gets any worse."

"But—" She started to protest as Theo ushered her into the bakery and redirected his focus to the display of baked goods. She pressed her lips together, frustrated, but determined to speak to him properly as soon as they were alone.

"We'll have two slices of fruit pie," Theo said to the man Kate assumed was the baker.

The baker wrapped their slices of pie and Theo swept

Kate back out into the street where the carriage was waiting. The driver must have realized they would want to leave soon. Theo opened the door, mopping his snow-speckled hair off his forehead, and Kate clambered in past him and sat on her cushion.

Theo leaped in behind her, pulled the door closed, and offered her the wrapped bundle. "You should eat."

She raised her eyebrows. "Before I take a single bite, I'd like to know what you meant about being a husband and wife in every way."

He looked down at his hands, and a faint flush touched his cheeks. "Despite our growing closeness, I know we've both been holding back from being totally open with each other, and that's my fault. I let my past with Elizabeth cloud my present with you. I don't want that to happen again. I want us to embrace everything we could have together, even if it's scary."

She considered this for a moment, trying not to let her hope show on her face. She didn't want to get excited if she was only going to end up disappointed. "How are you going to handle it if the pregnancy doesn't run smoothly?"

He grimaced. "It won't be easy. All I can promise is to take each day as it comes. You're pregnant anyway, so whatever we decide to do now, it won't change that. We'll have to face it together."

"And intimacy?" Because she had enjoyed his attention recently, but though they'd shared kisses and cuddled together, they'd never revisited the pleasure they'd found together that first night she'd been in Oxfordshire.

His grimace transformed into a wicked smirk. "You're pregnant anyway. That's what I was most afraid of happening. I see no reason to hold back from intimacy unless…." His face fell. "It's not something you want."

"Oh, I want it," she assured him.

"Then we should start practicing as soon as we're back,"

he murmured, and for a moment, she thought he might attempt to seduce her right there in the carriage. Unfortunately, they then went over a bump, and her stomach lurched, and she had to thrust her head through the window in order to not cast up her accounts.

Instead of exploring intimacy somewhere as scandalous as the back of a carriage, Theo unwrapped the pie, and she ate as much as she could without being sick.

When they arrived back at Blackwell Hall, they retreated to his bedchamber, where he stripped her damp clothing from her until she was naked and reminded her exactly how lovely it was to feel him inside her.

At first, it was a little strange—although not painful because of the care he took with her—but with every moment that passed, she came to crave the way he filled her more. There was something incredible about being connected to him in such an intimate way.

He stroked her belly and held her close, warming her heart and making her feel almost... cherished. She was new to lovemaking, but she instinctively knew that what she shared with Theo was special. It wouldn't be like this with anyone else.

Afterward, she snuggled up to his side, listening to the rain drum on the roof, and smiled. This morning, she'd never have guessed the day would take this turn.

Her cheek rested over his heart, and she listened to the steady thump, a little relieved that he hadn't panicked the way he had last time they'd been intimate.

Eventually, they got hungry, so she called for tea and biscuits to be brought in. Indulgent, perhaps, but she was enjoying their quiet time together and didn't want to relocate. That said, she did get him to help her put her dress back on so that she wouldn't look completely debauched when the maid arrived.

There was a knock on the door, and she went to answer

it, expecting to find a maid on the other side, but instead, it was Theo. Startled, she spun around.

No, it wasn't Theo. It couldn't be. He was still sitting on the edge of the bed, waiting for her to return with the tray.

"Is something amiss?" he asked, looking concerned.

Kate turned back to the man. It must be Nicholas. When he was clean-shaven, he looked far more like Theo than he had with a beard.

"Good evening, Nicholas," she said and heard Theo swear behind her.

Nicholas wore a thick coat with snow dusted on the shoulders. He must have just arrived here from London. "Lady Katherine," he said, wiping his chin as water dripped off the tip of his nose and down his face.

That was when she noticed.

There was a small, sweet freckle on his chin.

A freckle she *recognized.*

A freckle that was not a smudge, and which her husband did not have.

"It was you," she breathed.

Nicholas's eyes widened, and he backed up a step. "I think I'd better leave."

"You were the one on that balcony," she accused, as he seemed to debate whether to stay or leave. "You were the one who fled and left me there."

"Get out!" Theo exclaimed, appearing beside her and ushering Nicholas away. He pushed the door shut and turned to Kate. "I can explain."

"It was *him*," she insisted, wrapping her arms around herself.

What in the lord's name was going on?

She'd met Nicholas. He hadn't looked that much like Theo, had he? But then, he'd had a beard and worn a hat, and she'd met him for such a brief time. It was possible she'd completely overlooked the degree of similarity.

Nicholas and Theo looked far more similar than brothers should.

Unless they were twins.

Not that it mattered what they were. What mattered was that *Nicholas* had been the one on the balcony with her, not Theo. Her stomach clenched, and nausea rolled through her. She caught onto the wall to support herself. Theo rushed toward her, but she held out her hand and stopped him.

Everything made so much sense now.

No wonder Theo had mixed her and Sophie up the morning after the ball. He hadn't met either of them previously. *Nicholas* had. He'd simply turned up to propose with no idea which woman he was supposed to be proposing to.

"Explain," she bit out, pushing off the wall and steadying herself. The last thing she wanted to look or feel right now was weak.

"Nicholas is my twin."

She waved her hand dismissively. "We'll get to that. First, I want to know why I met him and ended up married to you."

He started to reach for her but then stopped. "Nicholas thought I should consider remarrying. He tried to talk me into it, and I shot him down. Being the stubborn bastard he is, he decided to try to find a suitable bride for me behind my back. He attended the Wembley ball under my name. He pretended to be me to everyone he interacted with. That's how *my* name ended up in the scandal sheets alongside yours."

"How did you find out?" she asked, her temples throbbing.

He grimaced. "The first I knew of it was when he stumbled into my bedroom, blind drunk, and confessed that he might have ruined someone's reputation."

"So, what? You just decided that the fact you didn't want to marry was irrelevant and came right on over to propose to me? Why not make him do it?"

"Several reasons." His hands curled into fists at his sides. "First, because people might not have believed it was him. They might have thought he was trying to cover for me. Second, because even if people believed it, I was aware that a young lady's guardian would likely press for her to marry a viscount rather than a second son."

Enraged, she gasped, "I am not a—"

"Third," he continued, earning a glare, "If Nicholas told the truth, it would draw attention to the fact we're identical, which would make it obvious that we're twins."

Kate raised her eyebrow, still angry at the implication that she might have been a title hunter and bewildered by this whole situation. "And?"

"And we are, but my parents lied and said we were born a year apart. They thought it discouraged in-fighting over the title and inheritance. It was intended to be a minor, harmless deception, but then as we aged it became clear we were identical and Mother began to fear that society would recognize their lie and cast her out."

"But how have you hidden it?" she demanded, not understanding any of this. "Surely people at his school noticed, or friends of yours did?"

Theo paced the length of the room, agitation rolling off him in waves. "We attended different schools and did not move in the same social circles when we were young."

"What about after that? You're both expected to participate in society."

"I'm not much for social occasions." He pivoted toward her and tugged on the collar of his shirt, drawing her attention to the flash of skin visible because of the open top button. "I fulfil my duties in the House of Lords, but I don't participate in the sort of activities other men often do. Nicholas is fonder of socializing, visiting the club, and horse racing, so we rarely cross paths and few people notice."

Kate's temples throbbed. Logically, she followed the

meaning of his words, but her heart couldn't seem to make heads or tails of this. Her emotions were jumbled, the low ache of betrayal providing a backdrop to the heat of anger and the icy cold of disbelief. "All of this just to save your mother from being shunned by her peers for a season or two?"

Theo ran his hand through his hair, leaving it ruffled and standing on end. "It really hasn't involved much subterfuge, for the most part. As I said, we lead very different lives. But on the occasions when we are in the same place at the same time, such as the wedding, we take steps to differentiate ourselves as much as we can and to keep interactions brief. Otherwise, Mother becomes overwrought. I know it's ridiculous. We should have stopped years ago, but she's the only parent we have left and we don't want her unhappy."

Her heart gave a pang. No, she supposed he wouldn't want to see his mother suffer from social ostracism, even if it was of her own making, because her misery would remind him too sharply of what he'd gone through with Elizabeth.

Kate shook her head. "You had to know I'd learn the truth eventually. Why didn't you just tell me?"

"I intended to." He looked lost. "It never seemed like the right time. I came to… to care for you, and I didn't want you to be upset with me."

She pressed her fists to her eyes. "Upset?"

She was more than upset. Never mind the strange way he and Nicholas tried to shelter Lady Blackwell. For now, she could even forget the urge to wonder what on earth had possessed Lord and Lady Blackwell to make the decision to lie. But what she couldn't stop thinking about was that she'd met *Nicholas* at the Wembley ball, not Theo.

It cast their entire relationship in a new light. She'd known that Theo hadn't wanted to remarry—he'd told her as much. But she'd at least thought that he'd been the one on the balcony with her that night, so while she had harbored some guilt over her feigned trip, she had consoled herself with the fact that they were both victims of circumstance.

Now, he was telling her that it was his brother she'd chatted with. It was his brother who'd fled and left her there. Not him.

Everything she'd thought she'd known was false.

Theo's face was carved in harsh lines and he was breathing heavily but didn't seem to know what to say. She wanted to grab him by the shoulders and shake him. To demand to know why he'd had to be so blasted honorable and marry her to protect his family when he hadn't wanted to.

His brother had made a mistake, and he'd paid the price.

How lowering to realize that the "price" in this case was marriage to her.

She'd been blind not to realize it. He didn't want her. He never had.

"I need time alone," she said and rushed out of the bedchamber.

CHAPTER 28

THEO YANKED ON HIS SHIRT, FUMBLING WITH THE BUTTONS AS he raced after Kate. He had only made it a few steps outside his bedchamber when he crashed into Nicholas.

"Get out of the way," Theo growled, pushing Nicholas aside and running to the door of the bedchamber that Kate had been using while the viscountess's chambers were being renovated.

He grabbed the handle and tried to open it, but it was locked. He debated whether to bash on the door and demand she open it but figured that was unlikely to endear him to her at the moment, and he needed all the help he could get.

"I'm sorry," Nicholas said, resting his hand on Theo's upper arm. "I assumed you'd told her."

"I hadn't," Theo admitted, his gut tight with shame. "She knows now."

Nicholas grunted. "That much was obvious. It was unwise of you to deceive her for so long. I don't know her well at all, but I doubt any woman would be pleased by that behavior."

Theo gave him a look. The last thing he needed right now was to have exactly how big a mistake he'd made pointed out. He already knew. "I didn't mean to. I intended to tell her at some point, but I delayed longer than I ought to have. It's just that I got distracted, and it slipped my mind."

Nicholas snorted and rolled his eyes. "I can't see her accepting that excuse very well, brother. Why don't you come away from the door? I'm sure she needs a few minutes to herself."

"I...." Theo hesitated. He didn't want to leave Kate alone when she was upset. That said, she had asked him to do just that, and it wouldn't be right of him not to respect her request. With a sigh, he glanced over his shoulder and then reluctantly returned to his bedchamber.

Nicholas followed.

"Other than this, how have you been getting along together?" Nicholas asked, his nose wrinkling as he looked at the bed. He crossed to Theo's small private writing desk and sat there instead.

Theo stood. He couldn't bring himself to sit on the bed where, less than a few minutes ago, he had lain naked, holding Kate, everything apparently right with the world.

"It's been difficult, but we came to an understanding today. I... I told her I cared about her." He looked down at his hands, unsure what to do with them. "I think 'care' might be a misnomer. She makes me feel things I haven't in a long time."

"That's good." When Theo sent him a dubious look, Nicholas added, "No, it truly is. You deserve to have someone important in your life again. I'm just sorry I blundered in like a clumsy oaf without checking how much she knew first. Although, honestly, Theo, you should have been forthright with her sooner. If you've grown close, it's no wonder that she's hurt now."

Theo flinched. He hated the thought of Kate hurting and himself not only being unable to do anything about it but also being the cause of that hurt.

"Why are you here?" he asked.

Nicholas's shoulders slumped. "A matter of import came up in parliament. It relates to international diplomacy. It's going to a vote early next week, and I don't feel able to stand in for you. The documents they've provided for us to go through are dense. You know how I struggle with that type of thing. At the very least, I need you to review them and tell me how to vote. I don't want to get this wrong."

"Did you bring them with you?" Theo asked.

"I did."

"Good. I'll look at them soon."

Nicholas smiled tiredly. "Thank you."

Theo shook his head. "No, thank *you*. Because of you, I've been able to enjoy this time away from my responsibilities."

Nicholas had been acting in Theo's stead in the House of Lords. Provided he didn't speak up too much and wore the appropriate attire, no one seemed to notice the difference between them.

Nicholas dropped his gaze. "It was the least I could do after landing you in the parson's noose. I must say, I'm relieved to hear it hasn't been all bad."

"You were right about Kate," Theo admitted. "She's special."

"I'm glad."

"I'll attempt to return to parliament soon. The only thing that might delay me is the fact that we are expecting."

"Expecting? Expecting what?" Nicholas's jaw dropped. "Wait a moment. Are you saying that the viscountess is with child?"

Theo nodded ruefully. "I can't say I've been as calm about it as I should have been."

Nicholas whistled. "Of course you haven't. You've experienced several miscarriages and, well, with what happened with Elizabeth, it's hardly surprising that you'd be nervous. Don't worry about rushing back to the House of Lords. Provided you summarize the salient points to me and tell me how I ought to vote, I'm happy to continue as we are until the current session is concluded."

A knock at the door startled them both. Theo's heart rate picked up, and he lunged for the handle and pulled it open, hoping to find Kate on the other side. Instead, it was Mr. Giles. His stomach sank.

Mr. Giles dipped his head. "My Lord, I know it isn't for me to question Lady Blackwell, but she just summoned a carriage and went outside. She wasn't dressed for the weather, and even if she were, I don't think anyone ought to be venturing out. The snow is falling thickly, and the wind…."

Theo's throat tightened, and he tried to draw in a slow breath but found himself gasping for air. "Lady Blackwell has gone out into the snow?" he choked out, rubbing his chest to ease the pain.

"Yes," Mr. Giles said with a grimace. "She took a canvas. I think she intended to park the carriage somewhere and paint."

Fuck.

What a ludicrous idea.

It shouldn't surprise him, though. He already knew that Kate liked to retreat to her art when she was distressed. But why couldn't she have done so from within the safety of their home?

He looked out the window, and a chill swept through his insides. The clouds were shades of white and gray, the trees in the distance whipped back and forth in the wind, and snow was starting to cover the ground once again.

He couldn't help but remember the day he pleaded with his father not to go out into the storm. His father never came back. And as for taking a carriage…. If the roads were muddy, there was no guarantee she'd be safe even if she didn't intend to go far.

What the hell was she thinking?

"I'm going after her." He started toward the door, then paused and grabbed his coat and hat from the wardrobe. He didn't want to delay, but getting himself into trouble because he hadn't taken a few seconds to prepare wouldn't help anyone.

"Do you think you can catch her?" Nicholas asked, jogging to keep pace with Theo as he pushed out of the bedchamber and rushed along the corridor.

"If I go on horseback." It would be safer to travel on foot, but he had no chance of catching up to the carriage that way.

"Be careful." Nicholas grabbed his arm, forcing Theo to stop and face him. "I'm serious. Don't be reckless."

Theo tore out of Nicholas's grip and was about to lambaste him for slowing him down when he caught sight of his eyes and stopped. They were wide, the whites showing.

Nicholas was scared.

Not for himself, but for Theo. After all, they'd both lost their father in that storm. He probably feared losing his brother just as much as Theo feared losing his wife.

"I will," Theo promised.

"Good." Nicholas gave him a little push. "Go, then."

Theo bolted down the stairs and shoved the front door open, stumbling as he donned the hat and coat, realizing too late that he should have put them on before leaving the house.

He managed to work his arms into the sleeves as he headed for the stables, and by the time he got there, the front was fully buttoned up and he was ready to depart. He burst into the stables, startling the stable master, who was soothing one of the more finicky mares.

"My lord?" He straightened. "What is it?"

"I need to saddle Prince." Theo hurried to the stable that housed his favorite gelding, taking care to do what he could to regulate his breathing and release the strain from his muscles so he wouldn't frighten every horse here.

He opened Prince's stall door and led him out. The stable master grabbed his saddle, and together they strapped it onto the horse and made sure everything was in place. Theo sensed the stable master's curiosity, but the man didn't ask any questions.

Theo took Prince outside, mounted him, and steered him toward the road that led away from Blackwell Hall. He had no idea where Kate was going, but there was only one road leading to and from the estate, so if she had taken a carriage, that was the way she must have gone.

Snow stung his cheeks, and he used his left hand to dash it out of his eyes as he urged Prince faster. The horse knew the road well and dodged any holes and icy patches. It was fortunate they'd ridden this way so many times together because between the snow and the wind, Theo could hardly see more than a horse length in front of them.

He squinted into the distance, trying to make out the silhouette of a carriage. He saw nothing.

Prince rounded a corner, and there, up ahead, Theo finally spotted what he'd been looking for. He relaxed, grateful to have tracked Kate down without any harm coming to either of them.

But then, as he watched with his heart in his throat, the carriage began to turn. Its wheels slid on an ice slick and the carriage toppled.

A scream ripped from him, but he could hardly hear it above the roar of the wind, the clatter of wood, and the frantic cries of the horses.

The carriage tipped onto its side, and the driver was thrown from the front, hitting the dirt like a sack of potatoes and rolling once before coming to a stop. If Kate made any sound from within the carriage, Theo didn't hear her.

Prince was skittish, frightened to get close to the wreck, so as they drew near, Theo pulled him up short, slipped off the horse, and then raced on shaky legs to the carriage. It rose from the road like a nightmare of mist, blood, and memories.

He'd lived and relived this moment so many times in his dreams and the worst corners of his mind. He glanced between the carriage and the driver. He wanted to go to Kate, but it probably wouldn't take long to determine whether the man was all right, and then that would be at least one matter he needn't worry about further.

Making up his mind, he dropped to his knees beside the driver and turned him onto his back. The driver stared up at him, his eyes dazed but alert. Theo quickly checked his body, searching for any massive injuries. Not finding any, he hesitated for just one second more before assuring the man he'd be back quickly and rushing to the carriage.

The horses were struggling against their harnesses, and he feared they'd make things worse in their panic. He considered freeing them, but his hands were numb from the cold, and he feared it would prove challenging. He had no time to spare. He couldn't wait any longer to check on Kate. He'd return to release them as soon as he'd assured himself that she was safe.

The door lay flat against the road, so he had to enter by climbing over the carriage and lowering himself through the window. Kate lay sprawled on the other wall, unmoving. His breath caught.

No, she couldn't be dead. She couldn't be. He refused to accept it.

He wriggled through the window and fell awkwardly inside. There was a sharp twinge in his hip as he landed. He crawled to Kate and carefully pulled her into his arms. As he saw her face for the first time, he could hardly bring himself to look at her eyes, dreading the possibility that they'd stare blankly back at him.

He forced himself to check. They were closed. He exhaled

sharply and stared at her chest for several seconds until it rose and fell. A cry of relief passed between his lips.

She was alive.

Gently, he checked her for wounds. The side of her head was wet with blood, perhaps from where she'd hit it as the carriage rolled. Beyond that, nothing seemed amiss.

Thank God.

"Kate," he said, curving his hand around the side of her face. "Wake up, my love."

She didn't stir.

"Kate?" He jostled her shoulder but got no response.

Damn, he'd have to get her out of here on his own.

He grabbed her by the waist and, taking as much care as possible, maneuvered her up and through the window on the side of the carriage that now faced the sky. With a grunt of effort, he lifted her so that her torso rested against the exterior of the carriage.

"I've got her."

Theo's muscles went weak as he recognized Nicholas's voice. "Can you take her top end, and I'll lift out her bottom?"

"Absolutely."

Theo bent and wrapped his arms around Kate's thighs. His arms strained as he hoisted her out through the tight space, and he was relieved when the weight lessened as Nicholas took hold and she slid smoothly off the carriage.

"Do you need a hand?" Nicholas asked.

"No, just stand back."

Theo gripped the edge of the window and pulled himself through, the wood biting into his palms. As soon as he was outside, the snow chilled him anew. He dropped to the ground beside the carriage and knelt by Kate. Nicholas had set her on her back on the road.

"We need to get her back to Blackwell," he said, wondering how exactly they intended to do that. The carriage was likely damaged and not fit to travel. He could hardly take an unconscious woman on the back of Prince. She'd fall off.

"I brought one of our unmarked carriages," Nicholas said, squatting to study Kate's face. "The driver is already inside. He freed the horses and sent them back along the road. Once we return, he'll have a stable boy fetch them."

Theo closed his eyes. "You're brilliant."

If Nicholas hadn't had the foresight to bring a carriage, who knew how long it would have been before he'd managed to get Kate safely home and into bed? She was pregnant. They couldn't afford delays.

"Let's carry her together to the carriage." He moved around to slide one arm under her shoulders. He used the other to position her head against his abdomen so it wouldn't flop around and hurt her.

It would be better if he could avoid touching her head at all considering her injury, but the most important thing right now was getting her home and out of the storm quickly.

Nicholas scooped her legs up, and together they moved Kate's limp body to the carriage. The driver held the door open, and they placed her inside. Theo scrambled in with her while Nicholas went around the front of the carriage. He must have driven it himself. Theo supposed he shouldn't be surprised. Nicholas was an excellent rider, and he'd been known to race phaetons as well as on horseback.

Theo pulled Kate partway onto his lap to protect her from the bumps and jostling of the journey. He tried to examine her head wound more closely, but the angle was awkward. It worried him that she hadn't woken yet. Her breathing was steady, but perhaps the knock to her head had done more damage than he'd first thought.

His chest constricted. *Please be all right.*

As soon as the carriage stopped, he heard Nicholas shout for a footman and instruct the man to send for Dr. Hanson.

"Tell him to travel extremely carefully," Nicholas called, his voice growing louder as he neared the carriage door. "The roads are dangerous."

Nicholas and Theo carried Kate inside to where a worried Mrs. Tubbs waited with two maids on hand.

Mrs. Tubbs's mouth fell open as she caught sight of Kate, and she whimpered, all of the color leaching from her face. "Mary, light the fire in Lady Blackwell's room. Jane, turn down the bed and start filling a basin with warm water. We'll need to clean that head wound."

A footman stepped forward, reaching for Kate, but Theo shook his head. No one was carrying his wife except for him.

Well, him and his brother.

"Ensure Mr. Cartwright is taken care of," he said, referring to the driver. "He'll need a bath to warm up, and he may have some minor scrapes and bruises. He was in the accident too. When the doctor comes, he'll need to check over both the viscountess and Mr. Cartwright."

Mrs. Tubbs nodded. "I'll have Mr. Tubbs assist him."

"Thank you."

Theo and Nicholas continued up the stairs to the bedchamber that Kate was staying in. Jane, the maid, had already turned down the bed. They set Kate on the opposite side.

Theo huffed. "I'll have to undress her. I need Margaret to help."

"I can—"

He cut Nicholas off. "No." No one else would be seeing Kate in this vulnerable state. It was his job to care for her.

His brother acknowledged this with a tilt of his head and darted from the room. Less than a minute later, Margaret hurried in, her eyes wide and scared.

"I'm going to roll her onto her front," he told her as he

took hold of Kate's shoulder. "I need you to unlace her dress while I ensure she's able to breathe."

He shifted Kate without waiting for a response. Fortunately, Margaret responded promptly despite her obvious shock. The dress was difficult to undo because of the wet laces. As Mr. Giles had said earlier, Kate hadn't been dressed for the weather. She must have put on whatever was easiest before fleeing.

Why had she been so foolish?

Together, Margaret and Theo peeled the dress down, and then they worked on her undergarments, which were also wet, although, thankfully, less so. If she'd been soaked to the skin, the risk of catching a chill would have been higher.

When she was bare, Margaret went to get a towel. Theo dried her while Margaret carefully undid her hair so that the doctor would be able to see the head wound more easily. Finally, Theo dabbed at the wound with a clean cloth, ensuring it was free of debris and no longer bleeding before they wrapped her in the blankets.

Jane had pulled the curtains when she lit the fire, and the room was already beginning to heat. The fireplace was only small, but it would be enough to stave off the cold and damp.

As the maids cleared out, Nicholas knocked on the door before entering with a chair. He carried it over to Kate's bedside and then sat on the one in front of the writing desk. Theo sat on the chair that Nicholas had brought in and took Kate's hand.

His stomach was rock-hard, and his fingers were like ice as he stared at her beautiful face and waited for the doctor to arrive.

Please wake up, sweetheart. I need you.

CHAPTER 29

"...bed rest until..."

Kate struggled to make out fragments of a conversation through a blistering headache that fogged her thoughts and made it difficult to think of anything besides the pain.

"...the baby..."

That got her full attention.

She opened her eyes and blinked, grateful the room was only dimly lit as the throbbing in her temples worsened.

What had happened?

Where was she?

She racked her mind, trying to remember, but it hurt too much, and she gave up. A pair of brown eyes appeared above her, set in a harsh face with lines bracketing the mouth and deep grooves between the eyebrows.

"Theo," she whispered. "What...?"

"Oh, you're awake." A man hustled Theo aside and took his place.

She frowned, knowing she ought to recognize him, but she wasn't able to place him in the moment. He lifted a candle in front of her face, and she drew back, wincing as fire seared the side of her head. "Pupils are reactive. That's good."

"You were in an accident." Strong fingers wrapped around her own. Considering she could see the doctor's hands, she had to assume these ones belonged to Theo. "You were upset with me and left in a carriage."

A series of images flickered through her mind.

Theo in bed, his smile warm as he gazed down at her.

A man who looked so like Theo, yet had a freckle on his chin.

The truth she'd uncovered.

Her urgent need to paint as she worked through her conflicted feelings about Theo and the memory of that gnarled tree they'd passed. She'd recalled the tree only being a short distance from Blackwell Hall, and it hadn't seemed unreasonable to take a carriage there to paint it. She'd intended to return as soon as she'd gathered herself.

She closed her eyes. Her head felt like it was splitting in two.

"Look at me," Dr. Hanson ordered. "Now that you're awake, we need to keep you that way for a little while to make sure there's no underlying damage to your brain."

Somehow, lifting her eyelids took as much energy as climbing several staircases usually would. She longed to shut them again, but she'd already made enough foolish decisions today. No matter how upset she'd been, taking a carriage out while it was snowing *hadn't* been reasonable. She'd realized that before they'd gone far at all and had asked the driver to turn around. Unfortunately, the turn itself had caused the carriage to topple over.

"The driver," she rasped, wincing at how the words reverberated in her skull. "Is he all right?"

"Mostly," the doctor said. "He had a minor bump to the head and some bruising. I examined him after dressing your wound earlier."

Oh. So this must not be the first time he'd visited her room. If she was indeed in her room. She was too tired to look around and confirm.

"How do you feel?" Theo asked softly.

She tilted her face toward him and did her best not to grimace as her head pounded. "Sore."

Dr. Hanson tutted. "No doubt you will be for a while. The good news is that your body seems strong. I doubt there's much for us to do other than keep you warm and comfortable while you heal."

That was a relief. If she'd hurt the baby, she'd never forgive herself.

Oh no. The baby.

Her free hand flew to her stomach, clutching at it as if she'd be able to tell just from touching her belly whether the child inside was healthy.

Dr. Hanson's gaze softened. "There are no obvious signs of distress, but it will be a while before we can be certain whether they're unharmed."

Tears sprang to Kate's eyes, and the back of her throat thickened. What would she do if this stupid, impulsive decision made her lose the baby? Dear God, what would *Theo* do if that happened? He'd already been through so much.

"I'll give you two some time," Dr. Hanson said, glancing between them as if reading Kate's mind. He bowed and excused himself from the room.

Theo spoke before Kate had a chance to. "I'm sorry."

She froze with an apology on her own lips.

He squeezed her hand and shifted closer so she wouldn't have to strain so much to see him. "We shouldn't have continued the deception for so long. Nicholas told me it would be bad to keep it from you after we were married but I…." He shook his head. "To tell the truth, I worried you'd think less of me or perhaps feel you'd married the wrong brother. I care about you, and I didn't want to see you look at me with disdain or disappointment."

Kate tilted her head ever so slightly. "I am unhappy you deceived me, but I do care for you, too—I think that's what made it all the worse when I realized. I hindsight, I am… glad… to have married you and not Nicholas.""

"You are being more understanding than I deserve." He dipped his head and ghosted his lips over her brow. "I should have been forthright with you sooner. You deserved to know that it wasn't me on the balcony with you."

"I did," she agreed, because really, how fair was it that she hadn't even ended up married to the man who'd ruined her? Obviously it wasn't fair to him that he'd been forced into the situation, but it wasn't fair to her either. She'd had no idea what was happening in the background with his family drama.

He cleared his throat. "I don't regret marrying you, though. I never will."

She wet her lips, and her pulse ratcheted up. "You truly don't?"

She'd thought he'd been saddled with her as some kind of unwanted chattel. Someone he'd come to care for but never really wanted.

Theo scanned her face, his expression tender. "Not at all. It may not have been me on that balcony with you, and it's true that I didn't want a wife because of the suffering both Elizabeth and I experienced, but I'm so incredibly grateful to Nicholas for pushing the matter, because you make me happy, Kate."

Warmth suffused her, and the corners of her mouth lifted despite her wariness. She hadn't expected to hear that. He'd told her earlier that he cared for her, and he'd shown it in many ways these past weeks, but she had no baseline to compare him to. No way to know whether he was usually so considerate of others.

He dragged his teeth across his lower lip before releasing it. "I'm terrified of something happening to you. I'm sure you've realized that. But I also can't imagine being without you." His features tightened and became fierce. "I don't *want* to imagine being without you. When I saw that carriage tip over, I could scarcely breathe. Please don't ever do that to me again."

She lowered her gaze, ashamed of herself for being so thoughtless. "I won't. I never should have left. I'd already realized I was being foolish. We were preparing to return when… well, when something went wrong."

He blinked rapidly, and she realized that there were tears in his eyes.

"Don't cry," she murmured, sliding her palm against his. "I won't be such a ninny again. I'm sorry for how many unpleasant memories it must have stirred."

Now that her thoughts were clearing, she was so terribly disappointed in herself. She could hardly bring herself to look at him.

Not only had she made him relive Elizabeth's death, but she'd completely forgotten that his father had died during a storm. Considering the circumstances, it was amazing that he was so composed.

"You didn't mean to." His grip on her firmed. "Just don't do it again."

"I won't," she reiterated. "But I also want you to promise never to keep such a huge secret from me again. Can you do that?"

He nodded. "I give you my word, I have no other secrets from you. For the sake of full disclosure, I should tell you that I enjoy boxing and use it as an outlet. It's not a secret, but few people know."

"You box?" she asked, unsure why she found the idea so intriguing. Was that what the bag she'd found in that mystery room had been for? Boxing?

"Yes. While we're here, I either use a bag to practice or spar with Nicholas, but in London I occasionally enter matches at a gentlemen's club."

Heat blossomed low in her core as she imagined Theo in a loose white shirt, his fists wrapped, dripping with sweat as he exchanged blows with another man. His eyes would be dark and dangerous, his movements strong and lethal. She had no doubt he was capable of bringing down an opponent.

Drat, why was that so arousing?

She was injured. She wasn't supposed to be reacting to him this way. Especially not when she was still mad at him for deceiving her.

"Can I… watch sometime?" she asked hesitantly.

His eyes widened. "You'd actually want to see that?"

She narrowed her eyes at him. If he thought women were too delicate to see such things, he had another think coming.

But he nodded. "You're welcome to watch me as I practice. It will be more difficult to take you to a match, as women generally aren't permitted, but if you want to, we'll find a way."

"Good."

Perhaps, afterward, she could help him celebrate his win….

No naughty thoughts.

"There's nothing else." He bent and kissed her chastely. "I…. I want everything with you, Kate."

"I don't—"

He held up his hand. "I know it might take you some time to forgive me. I can live with that. But I do need to ask something of you."

She arched her eyebrow, then huffed when even that hurt. "What is it?"

He leaned forward until their faces were only a foot or two apart. "I need you to be more careful. I know I worry too much, and I fuss over you more than you'd like, but I've already lost one woman I loved. I can't do it again."

Kate sucked in a breath too quickly and hacked a cough as it hit the back of her throat. Her brain screamed, and she squeezed her eyes shut until the pain dissipated. "I beg your pardon?"

He frowned and cocked his head as if unsure what he'd said. When he caught on, his eyes widened. She waited, expecting him to beat a hasty retreat, but instead, his gaze steeled, and his eyebrows lowered determinedly.

"I do love you," he said, his jaw setting as if he thought she might protest. "I love you very much. I'm sorry I've been a frightened idiot, but that's behind us. I love you, and I'm not afraid to say it. Just… meet me halfway and take care of yourself, will you?"

"I will," she murmured, her lips curving up. Her heart felt too big for her chest, and she didn't even care. "I'll be more careful."

If he'd been brave enough to give her his heart, she needed to make sure he didn't regret entrusting her with it.

"Thank you." He lifted her hand and bussed a kiss over the back of it, intertwining his fingers with hers. "Do you feel up to speaking with Nicholas? He feels dreadful for his part in what happened."

"Yes." In all honesty, she didn't have much energy left, but she wanted to properly make the acquaintance of Theo's twin before she fell back asleep. Even though he hadn't said as much, she got the impression that the brothers were close, and if he was important to Theo, then he was important to her. Not to mention that they owed him their marriage, in a manner of speaking.

Instead of leaving her side, Theo called for a maid to bring Nicholas to the room. There was a firm knock before he entered, and he did so slowly, as if he feared what he might find.

Nicholas did, indeed, look like his brother. Their hair was a similar length, and their faces were, of course, the same except for that freckle. However, in contrast to Theo, Nicholas wore a gold brocade waistcoat and a stylish cravat. With the two of them in the same room, it was obvious who was whom.

Nicholas approached warily, his eyebrows knitted together as he noted the way they were sitting and the fact that Theo was holding her hand.

He bowed. "My apologies for the shock I gave you earlier, my lady. I hope you can forgive me."

She studied him with interest. "So, *you're* the one who compromised me."

Nicholas's gaze shot to Theo's as if searching for help. Theo just smirked.

Nicholas cleared his throat. "I'm sorry about that too."

She laughed softly. "I'm not. I'm still mad at both of you, but perhaps it was fate that the timing worked out so abominably for us because I doubt I could have respected or admired any of the other men of the *ton* as much as I do Theo. I'm fortunate to be able to call him my husband."

Nicholas's eyebrows flew up. "Theo, is it?"

"Indeed," she said primly. She wasn't giving him any more than that. Not yet anyway. "Sit and tell me about yourself, Nicholas."

Nicholas sat, and they chatted until her eyes were too heavy to remain open for any longer. She closed them and listened to the brothers talk as her consciousness faded out.

A while later, she opened her eyes. A large body was pressed along the length of hers, one arm slung over her waist. She snuggled closer to Theo, taking comfort from his nearness.

The fire had died, and the room was shrouded in shadow. She closed her eyes and breathed in his familiar minty scent.

"I love you," she whispered into the dark.

She'd been afraid to admit it earlier, too stunned by his revelation to reciprocate. Now, despite the lies and fears between them, she needed to say the words aloud.

She did love him. She'd probably fallen for him far earlier than was wise. She'd never expected to win his heart, since he'd made it clear that he'd loved Elizabeth, but the fact that he did—that he'd made space for her in his heart too—was more than she'd dreamed of.

She'd tell him so too. Just not when he might think it was a result of taking a solid knock to the head.

Perhaps tomorrow.

Or maybe she'd make him squirm for a little about his lies first.

CHAPTER 30

Oxfordshire
April 1823

THEO SLIPPED HIS HAND INTO KATE'S, NEEDING THE PHYSICAL connection between them as they waited for Dr. Hanson to arrive for the examination.

"Whatever happens, we'll be all right," Kate murmured, her clear gray eyes locking on his.

He swallowed past a lump in his throat. God, he hoped she was right. He supposed he'd just have to have faith that she was.

The past two months had been like a happy dream. Her belly had continued to grow and so had the bond between them. They'd spent hours together, getting to know each other better.

He'd started writing poetry again, although he'd forgotten how to structure poems well, so his progress was slow. She'd shown him some of the paintings she was most proud of, and they'd put one on the wall in the dining room and another on the wall in her bedchamber.

He glanced at that painting now, admiring the bright shades of the flowers along the side of a stream. Apparently, the spot was one of her favorites at the Longley estate in Suffolk.

"I'm sure you're right," he said, dragging his attention back to her.

He'd tried not to hover over her quite so much after she recovered from the carriage accident, but when his anxiety got too much for him and he couldn't resist fussing, she just smiled, amusement in her eyes, and let him do whatever he needed to reassure himself that she was whole, happy, and healthy.

Her good spirits never seemed to wane, and his fear that she would sink into melancholy as Elizabeth had was gradually fading.

They'd made it through the first few months of pregnancy without incident—or so it seemed. None of Elizabeth's pregnancies had progressed this far. According to Dr. Hanson, the risk of something going wrong diminished after the first three months. Every time he felt himself start to panic, he reminded himself of that.

"Are you… disappointed not to spend more time in your bedchamber?" he asked, looking around at the rose pink of the walls threaded through with the spidery lines of a dark blue and white pattern. The drapes were almost the same shade of blue as the accents in the wallpaper, and the bedspread was made from a similar fabric to the drapes.

Kate rested her head on his shoulder. They were propped up side by side against the headboard of her bed. "It's nice to have my own space, but I rather like spending my nights with you."

A knot in his gut loosened. She joined him in his bedchamber every night, only leaving if the baby made her too uncomfortable to sleep near him. He'd worried she might feel pressured to remain nearby because of his fears.

She rolled her eyes as if reading his thoughts. "You silly man. I adore cuddling with you."

He ignored the name-calling and dropped a kiss on her forehead. "I like having you close too."

There was a rap at the door, and Mr. Giles announced that the doctor had arrived. Kate lifted her head from Theo's shoulder, and he got off the bed and went to the door.

"Show him in, Giles."

While the butler went to fetch Dr. Hanson, Theo grabbed the chair from Kate's writing desk and carried it over so he could sit beside her.

Dr. Hanson sauntered in, windswept from the spring breeze. A friendly smile crossed his bluff features, and he dipped his head in greeting. "Good afternoon, Lord and Lady Blackwell."

Theo nodded politely. "Thank you for coming."

"It's no trouble at all." The doctor set his medical bag down and crossed the room to stand on the side of the bed opposite Theo. "How have you been feeling, Lady Blackwell?"

Kate tilted her head back to look up at him. "I've been better able to keep food down for the past two weeks. My back aches a little, and"—she colored—"my, er, hips do, too, but it's not constant."

He nodded. "That's likely from your body making room to accommodate the baby. The back pain could also be from carrying extra weight, although I doubt it's enough to cause too much discomfort at this point. Are you getting plenty of rest?"

Kate glanced at Theo and smirked. "Lord Blackwell has been ensuring I'm abed for at least nine hours. I don't always sleep well, but it's not from lack of opportunity."

Dr. Hanson knelt beside the bed. "Is it the back and hip pain keeping you awake?"

"Partially, but I've also been getting hungry at the strangest times."

And craving the oddest foods, Theo thought silently. Combinations that he'd never think to put together, such as sweet fruits paired with cheese or salt sprinkled on pudding.

"That's normal," Dr. Hanson assured her. "The baby may move around inside you, creating and relieving pressure on your stomach so that you think you're full when you're really not, and then, when it shifts, you suddenly realize how hungry you are. Just make sure you're eating plenty to keep your strength up."

"She is," Theo said.

He'd been unable to resist monitoring her eating patterns, just to make sure she was having enough. He needn't worry, though. She seemed to have matters well under control.

"Good." Dr. Hanson extended his hand toward Kate's rounded belly. "May I?"

She nodded.

He ran his palm over the bump. "Have you felt the baby move yet?"

"Yes," Kate said.

Theo caught her eyes and melted at the warmth he found there. It had been one of the most magical moments of his life when she'd burst excitedly into his office, hiked up her skirt, put his hand on the bare skin of her abdomen, and he'd felt the slightest nudge against his palm.

Proof that his baby lived.

Tears had sprung to his eyes, and he hadn't bothered to hide them as he'd kissed her belly. Kate knew how much it meant to him to feel evidence that all was well with their son or daughter.

Dr. Hanson opened his medical bag and pulled out a wooden tubelike tool. "This is a stethoscope," he said. "It's a reasonably recent invention. I only bought this one a month ago. I'll use it to listen to your heart and lungs and make sure everything is as it should be."

"It won't hurt her, will it?" Theo asked, starting to rise from his chair. No newfangled invention was worth hurting his wife, no matter what reassurance it might provide.

Dr. Hanson smiled kindly. "Not at all."

He pressed the one end of the tube to Kate's chest and seemed to listen through it, and then he got her to lean forward while he repeated the same procedure from the back. That done, he tucked the stethoscope back into his medical bag and zipped it shut.

He clasped his hands together and looked earnestly from Kate to Theo. "As far as I can tell, the pregnancy is progressing as it should be. You can have every expectation of delivering a healthy baby. Of course, I'll continue to monitor throughout the pregnancy, but if we were likely to have major issues, they'd usually have shown themselves by this point."

The tension fled from Theo's muscles, and he suddenly felt giddy.

The baby was fine.

Kate was healthy.

More than that, she was *happy*. And so was he.

Kate beamed back at him, obviously as relieved as he was. Excited too.

"We're having a baby," she whispered, her smile stretching from ear to ear.

"We are," he agreed.

"If we're done here, I'll be on my way," Dr. Hanson said. "I have another expectant mother to visit today."

Theo stood and shook his hand. "Thank you. We appreciate you coming here very much."

Dr. Hanson bowed. "My pleasure, my lord."

He excused himself from the room and closed the door behind him.

Theo offered Kate his hand, and when she took it, he pulled her off the bed and into his embrace. "I love you." He peppered her pretty face with kisses. "I can't wait to meet our son or daughter."

She hesitated for a moment, then asked, "You won't be disappointed if it's a daughter? Even though it means you still don't have an heir?"

He snorted. "Blast the need for an heir. Nicholas can do the job. Or one of our cousins. All I want from our child is for them to be born healthy and to never doubt our love for them."

The corners of her eyes crinkled as she gazed up into his. "And they will. I know it, and I think if anyone is qualified to speak on this, I am. You've shown me you love me in so many different ways that I can't possibly doubt it. I know you'll do the same for our baby."

He looped his arms around her waist and rested his hands on the small of her back. The swell of her belly was firm against his abdomen, and he loved feeling and seeing the evidence of their little one's existence.

"I do love you. Like I never thought I'd love anyone again. You mean the world to me, Kate."

He hoped she knew that. He was aware that he had pushed her away in the early days, afraid of making her miserable or, if he admitted the truth to himself, of falling for her and losing someone he loved all over again.

But loving her was worth the risk. She brought color and vibrance back to his life, and she might never know how much he adored her for that. No words would suffice.

"I love you too." She stretched up onto her toes and kissed him. "I love the way your smile always seems to surprise you. I love how you make me feel special. And I love your good, kind heart and your loyalty to the people you care about."

That heart she'd mentioned? It filled to the brim.

"Hello," a familiar male voice called. "May I come in?"

Theo reluctantly released Kate but kept one arm around her waist. "You may."

Nicholas swept into the room, grinning broadly, and offered Kate a wildflower. They had just begun to bloom in the fields around the estate, and Kate had spent more than one afternoon outside painting them.

"Congratulations," he exclaimed as Kate took the wildflower from him. "Dr. Hanson said that all is well."

"It seems so," she said, tucking herself under Theo's arm.

"Excellent." Nicholas put his hands behind his back and bounced on the balls of his feet. "I've received a letter from Mother. She's on her way here from London, and from what she said, I expect she'll be fussing over Kate a great deal."

Theo's hold on Kate tightened. He'd assumed their mother would make an appearance eventually, and he had mixed emotions about it. On one hand, she'd experienced pregnancy and childbirth, so having her on-call would be helpful. He also knew that she'd be thrilled about having a grandchild.

His reticence stemmed from her treatment of Elizabeth. She had never been cruel to her when her pregnancies failed, but she also hadn't provided the sympathetic womanly ear that his late wife may have needed, and she had made Elizabeth feel pressured to produce an heir. He couldn't help but hold that against her, although deep down, he hoped things would be different this time.

"I'll have Mrs. Tubbs prepare her room," Kate said. She turned to Theo. "I could use some fresh air. Will you walk in the garden with me?"

"Absolutely."

They made their way outside. Nicholas headed to the stables, while Kate and Theo wandered through the rose gardens. They weren't in full bloom yet, but the roses were starting to show signs of life.

When they reached the end of the garden, Kate stopped

and took Theo's hands. He gazed down at her, his head cocked to the side, waiting for whatever it was she wanted to say.

Kate glanced down, then straightened her back and raised her chin. "I would like to paint a portrait of you and Nicholas together."

He raised an eyebrow. Whatever he'd expected her to say, it certainly wasn't that. "What brought this on?"

"I think it's a shame that you don't have any paintings of the both of you together to display just because of your resemblance. I know you're reluctant to be seen together because of your mother's worries about being excluded from society if they discovered her lie, but wouldn't it be nice to have a likeness of you even if it's only kept privately within the family?"

Actually… it would be.

Theo had never much thought about the lack of any portraits of him and Nicholas together, but he supposed most families with children of their age would have at least one family portrait. They'd missed out on that. The dining hall featured a portrait of him, and there was one of Nicholas in the library—painted while his hair was longer and his face was bearded—but there were none of them standing side by side as brothers ought to.

Now that he considered it, he and Nicholas were close. They cared for each other deeply. The lack of a portrait of the two of them felt wrong.

"You're right," he said, bending to kiss the tip of her nose. "But please be careful not to overdo things while you're carrying our child."

The corners of her lips lifted. "I won't. Nothing is more important to me than her or him."

He knew she was telling the truth. While she had made a foolish decision that day she had found out about Nicholas and the role he'd played in their relationship, she'd taken care not to repeat her mistake.

That said, she'd told him in no uncertain terms that she wasn't spending the rest of her pregnancy cooped up in her bedchamber. She would be sensible, but didn't want to be treated as if she was fragile, and he respected that.

They wandered in the garden for a while longer, breathing in the scent of grass and country air.

An hour or so after they returned inside, Nicholas strode into the drawing room, where Theo was revising a verse about the way the gray of Kate's eyes changed from silver to slate to pale like fog depending on her mood. Meanwhile, Kate was making notes about how large the portrait of the brothers ought to be.

"Nicholas," Kate called, glancing up from her paper. "Would you be willing to sit for a portrait with Theo?"

Nicholas stopped in his tracks. His mouth fell open, and he snapped it closed. He stared at her for a long moment and then, to Theo's utter shock, his dark eyes gleamed with tears. All of a sudden, he became animated.

"I would be delighted to," he exclaimed. "What did you have in mind? Shall I strike a pose? When will we begin?"

Theo stared at his brother, caught off guard by his enthusiasm. It hadn't occurred to him exactly how much this acknowledgement of their relationship might mean to Nicholas. In her typical, perceptive way, Kate had noticed what he hadn't and had sought to rectify it.

While Nicholas started debating the merits of posing in different rooms of the house, apparently without the need for any input from either of them, Theo went over to Kate and cupped her face in his hands.

"You are wonderful," he told her, grazing her lips with his. "I'm so lucky to have you."

He hadn't even realized exactly how much was missing from his life until she showed him. Fortunately, he never planned to let her go again, so he would never have to return to his lonely, cold existence without her.

She gave a little shrug. "I'm the lucky one. If I hadn't seen you outside the tailor one autumn day, then I might not have spoken to Nicholas at the Wembley ball, and we might never have even met. I like to think everything worked out exactly as it was supposed to do."

He kissed her. "I love your romantic streak."

She crinkled her nose and kissed him back. "I just love you."

He grinned. Yes, he was a lucky man indeed.

EPILOGUE

Oxfordshire
August 1823

"Breathe through the pain," Theo urged, grabbing Kate's hand.

She squeezed his fingers, using the sensation of his palm on her as an anchor to distract herself from the throbbing pain between her legs and in her lower abdomen.

She dragged in air, trying to do so slowly as she had been taught. As she exhaled, another ripple of agony rolled through her, and she shrieked and arched off the bed.

Unfortunately, there was no way to escape the source of her pain when it was within her own body.

"The accoucheur and the nurse are on their way," Theo said, looking over his shoulder to where Nicholas hovered in the doorway, grimacing as though *he* were the one with a massive baby trying to tear through his flesh.

"They'd best get here soon, or they'll be too late," she gritted out from between clenched teeth.

Theo placed a soft, damp cloth on her forehead. "Breathe."

"*You* breathe," she snapped. "Where is my mother?"

As if saying her name had summoned her, Lady Drake appeared in the doorway with the accoucheur, Dr. Hanson, behind her and Nurse Wilkins at her side. Lady Drake rushed over to Kate and perched on the bed beside her, taking her other hand and squeezing it firmly as if knowing that was exactly what Kate needed.

"We need to get your skirt up so I can see what I'm dealing with," Dr. Hanson said briskly.

Another time, Kate might have been embarrassed or even horrified by this demand, but right now, she just wanted the baby out of her as soon as possible. She yanked her skirts up with the nurse's help, and Theo left his station by her side to maneuver off her undergarments.

The accoucheur examined her, and she tried to swallow a scream as her muscles contracted and…

Damn, that hurt.

As a lady, she'd never had much cause to swear, but she thought she could make an exception now.

"What's wrong?" Theo asked, trying to get between the accoucheur and Kate as if to protect her from whatever was causing her distress.

The accoucheur tutted. "Nothing is wrong. Childbirth is painful. I need you to step aside so I can do my job."

"But…." Theo trailed off. "Surely there's a way we can make it more comfortable for her?"

"There is," the accoucheur agreed. "But I prefer not to give her anything to deaden the pain unless it becomes unavoidable. There is a higher chance of something happening to the baby if we dose her."

Kate grimaced. She wished they'd stop discussing this and get on with it. Another contraction rolled through her, and she bit her lip so hard, she tasted blood.

Theo caught her gaze, and his eyes were frantic. He

spotted the blood, and his throat bobbed as he gulped. "What can I do?"

"You can sit down," Lady Drake said firmly. "Against the wall, where you won't get in the way of Dr. Hanson performing his duties."

Reluctantly, Theo did as he was told. Kate mouthed a silent "Thank you" to her mother. It was nice to have Theo's support, and she was glad he was in the room, but she was going through enough without dealing with his nerves too.

At least where he was now, he would distract her less.

The process of bringing her baby into the world seemed to go on forever. Waves of pain and discomfort rolled through her, each one building on the last in some kind of excruciating crescendo.

By the time the cry of an infant pierced the air, it was halfway through the night, and Kate was drenched with sweat that had started to cool on her skin. Her entire body ached, and there was absolutely no chance she wanted to answer the call of nature any time soon, but hearing her newborn wail somehow made it all worth it.

The accoucheur dealt with the afterbirth and the nurse cleaned the baby and wrapped them in a soft blanket. Theo, whose face was haggard, his chest rising and falling rapidly, dragged his chair over to her as Lady Drake approached with the bundle.

"You have a son," her mother said softly, offering the little boy to Theo first.

Kate didn't mind. She wasn't even sure she'd be able to hold him if she wanted to. Her arms were as weak as pansy stems.

"A son," she breathed, leaning over to see his little face.

Theo awkwardly took the infant from Lady Drake and cradled him against his chest, gazing down at him as if he was the most precious thing he'd ever seen. Kate couldn't take her eyes off the baby either. He had a few tufts of dark hair and red, squishy cheeks with a button nose.

"He's perfect." Theo raised his eyes to her. "You did it, Kate."

"We did it," she corrected because he'd been with her every step of the way.

He chuckled, the sound weary. "I'm quite certain that you did the hard part."

"Maybe so," she allowed. "But he was worth it. Look at him."

"Do you think he looks like an Oliver?" Theo asked.

"Ollie." Kate smiled. "Our little Ollie."

Dr. Hanson coughed to get their attention. "Congratulations, you have a healthy baby boy. I'll stay to keep an eye on Lady Blackwell and Oliver, as we discussed, but I'll leave you alone for now. Nurse Wilkins will be in the adjoining room should you need her."

He disappeared through the bedchamber door closely followed by Nurse Wilkins, and, with a wave and a longing look at her grandson, Lady Drake departed too.

Finally, Kate and Theo were alone with their baby.

"Are you all right?" Theo asked, his brows scrunched with concern.

She sighed. "I'm exhausted. Sore. But I'll be fine."

"Would you like to hold him?"

"I'm not sure I can," she admitted.

His expression softened. "Trust me."

Supporting Ollie's weight with one arm, he maneuvered himself onto the bed and lay alongside her body. He slid his free arm behind her back and, with the other, guided Ollie onto her chest and helped her wrap her arms around him.

The baby was warm and squirmy. She closed her eyes and breathed him in.

"We're a family now," she murmured, nuzzling his fuzzy little head.

"We always have been," he said. "Now, we just have one more member. Hopefully not the last?"

Kate gave him a look. "The first is only just born, and you're already planning a second?"

Secretly, she was glad. She'd always wanted more than one child.

He kissed her forehead. "I don't care if we only ever have one or if we have a whole passel of them. I love you, and I love our family. We're going to be very happy together, I'll make sure of it."

Her heart fizzed. She didn't doubt him for a moment. She had gotten what she wanted, after all.

Love. Family. Happiness.

A future.

THE END

ABOUT THE AUTHOR

Jayne Rivers adores regency romance books, especially those by Sarah MacLean and Julia Quinn. She writes feel-good stories with heroines she'd love to befriend and heroes she'd love to sweep her off her feet—if she wasn't married, of course.